THE ART OF
THE ASSASSIN

THE ART OF
THE ASSASSIN

KEVIN SULLIVAN

Allison & Busby Limited
11 Wardour Mews
London W1F 8AN
allisonandbusby.com

First published in Great Britain by Allison & Busby in 2021.
This paperback edition published by Allison & Busby in 2021.

A CIP catalogue record for this book is available from
the British Library.

10 9 8 7 6 5 4 3 2 1

ISBN 978-0-7490-2666-0

Typeset in 11.25/16.25 pt Adobe Garamond Pro by
Allison & Busby Ltd.

The paper used for this Allison & Busby publication
has been produced from trees that have been legally sourced
from well-managed and credibly certified forests.

Printed and bound by
CPI Group (UK) Ltd, Croydon, CR0 4YY

For Marija and Katarina
with all my love

Clyde Yards Compete for Orders from Black Sea

. . . The tense state of relations among the principalities on the Black Sea coast has produced considerable disquiet in Constantinople and Saint Petersburg. The Sultan is determined to prevent further erosion of influence in parts of Rumelia, while the Tsar and the more energetic of his ministers have cultivated a restive spirit among radical factions in the Wallachian gentry. Prince Danilo's acquisition of a torpedo boat (financed indirectly by Vienna, if the reports are true) has added fuel to the Balkan furnace. The Russians and Turks are as one in believing that violence must be their exclusive prerogative, undisturbed by the ambitions of Teutonic incomers.

It has been noted that Archibald Auchinleck, whose yard at Anderston is among the most profitable as well as the most aggressive on Clydeside, has obliged Prince Danilo with the manufacture of his warship in record time. More orders will come if the Black Sea arms race proceeds at a clip.

The Prince will be feted during his two days in the city. Following the launch of *The Sceptre*, he will attend a gala performance at the Theatre Royal. The Balkan visitors are to be guests at Auchinleck House in Milngavie. They will travel to Balmoral by special train on Friday 1st September and continue thereafter by Royal Navy frigate from Leith to the continent.

From the *Glasgow Herald*, 25th August 1899

CHAPTER ONE

Tristan MacKenzie was taller than I had expected, and thinner too. I had imagined he would be short and round and elderly, like Señor da Costa, my lawyer in Santiago. The Glasgow solicitor was in his early forties; his build was athletic, and he had the sort of face that can only be rendered less intimidating if its owner allows it to break into a smile, which MacKenzie did not deign to do during our interview.

'This could have been settled while I was away, Mr Cameron.' MacKenzie made no effort to pronounce 'Camarón' in the Spanish way. As he spoke, he looked down at the document in front of him. When he had finished speaking, he looked up and across the table. He waited for me to explain.

'I was told by your office that it must wait until your return.'

His expression changed microscopically – a slight narrowing of the eyes that stretched the pale skin over his cheekbones even more tightly. 'It is a simple transaction.'

'I had no idea that my father owned property in Scotland,' I said. 'No idea, at least until I discovered these documents.'

This observation was too inconsequential, in delivery and substance, to be of interest to MacKenzie, who was conspicuously disinclined to engage in small talk. I added quickly, 'I would like to see the property and then I would like to sell it.'

He shook his head. It was not immediately clear to me whether he intended by this to indicate that I could not proceed in the manner I had described, or that what I had said was so obviously my intention that it hardly needed to be stated.

After my father was killed in the American siege of Santiago de Cuba, I found among his papers the deed to a property on the Isle of Bute on the west coast of Scotland. My mother was Scottish. I spent time there when I was very small – so small that I can remember almost nothing about it. I do not remember my mother at all.

'All that you have to do is to sign this Deed of Succession, which we will countersign and notarise. This, together with your mother's death certificate, will be sufficient for you to come into your property, Mr Cameron. After that you may live in it or sell it . . . or demolish it if you like. That is not a matter for this firm.'

His indifference was exasperating, but exasperation was not uppermost in my mind. I had a more practical preoccupation.

'I don't have my mother's death certificate,' I said. 'I have had no connection with my mother since I was a child.'

'No connection?' He spoke as if I had acknowledged some sort of inexcusable dereliction of duty.

'That is why your clerk advised me to wait for your return.' I had waited more than two months for MacKenzie to conclude a visit to his family in Cape Town.

He was unwilling to concede that his initial remark – to the effect that the business could have been dispatched easily without his involvement – was misplaced. 'Well, it's only a matter of finding a record of your mother's death,' he said.

'I don't know if she's dead.'

His expression was transformed by a curling of the thin lips. 'You don't know if she's dead?'

I shook my head.

'Then she may be entitled to a third of this estate.'

'Which is why I was advised to wait until your return.' I cannot say I invested this statement with the sort of sonority that indicates the conclusive settlement of an argument. All I had done was transfer an important piece of information – with difficulty – to the mind of an indifferent and rather rude solicitor.

'You will have to establish whether or not your mother is dead,' he said.

'I had hoped that you would be able to do that on my behalf. I have only been in this country for a short period. I am not a citizen. I do not have any legal standing—'

He waved his hand. 'Yes, yes, we can do this, but it may take time.'

The delay, it seemed to me, could only be viewed as an irritant from the point of view of the heir to the property, yet MacKenzie spoke as though this additional imposition were a personal affront.

'I do not intend to live in the property,' I said. 'I will sell it.'

He stared at me. I paused before I obliged him by explaining why I repeated my intention to put the house on the market. He was the sort of individual, I had gathered by now, who strives to maintain a certain advantage by requiring others to assume a position of harassed defence.

'It is not clear to me how much it may be worth.' I said. 'If my mother is alive, I have no objection to her receiving whatever she is entitled to.'

'These things are a matter of law,' he said, as though I had suggested otherwise.

I waited for him to continue.

He chose not to.

'How much is the property worth?' I asked.

He shrugged. 'You cannot know that until you sell it.' He glanced down at one of the documents in front of him. 'A modern villa built on the waterfront near the new pier at Rothesay, eight rooms, extensive grounds . . . an orchard . . . outbuildings.' He looked up at me. 'Assuming it's in good repair, and there is nothing here to indicate that it isn't, you would stand to make a tidy sum, Mr Cameron.'

As I walked away from MacKenzie's office I experienced a succession of emotions. The lawyer had offered no apology, not even the formulaic one that would have been a matter of courtesy on the part of one professional gentleman whose prolonged absence had caused inconvenience to another professional gentleman. On the contrary, he had spoken to me as though the complications in the case of my inheritance were in some way my own fault and represented an onerous and unwelcome obstacle to the speedy completion of a transaction in which he had not even the remotest interest.

I crossed the river and moved through an area of tenements beside the new railway line. In a bar there, I ordered a whisky, lit a pipe and considered the indignity of my interview with MacKenzie. He had spoken to me with an indifference that bordered on insolence. As I sipped, I looked around in the gloom and picked out shadows; noses and lips and eyes were configured and reconfigured; patterns shifted so that a variety of disparate emotions were conveyed; however, the dominant emotion in this room, I thought, was a kind of watchful resignation. There was a murmur that sometimes rose, when the punchline of a story was reached or when a statement was contradicted, but these were no more than undulations in a sea of stoicism.

The lawyer's deportment had not *bordered* on insolence. It had *been* insolent. The speed with which I slipped from speculation into certainty should not have surprised me. Nor should it have surprised me that from the conviction that an offence had been committed against my dignity I began to develop a corresponding conviction that an offence was being planned against my interest. This man, who had shown no inclination to indulge me as a client and a gentleman, was now entrusted with establishing whether or not my mother was dead. I should have taken my business elsewhere. I should not have been so acquiescent. I should have been forthright in terminating my association with him. He had been cagey about the value of the property. That was, no doubt, because he had already begun to think of ways in which he could swindle me out of it.

How quickly arbitrary images and sequences of thought can be transmuted into nightmares. Released from the strictures of reality, the mind creates patterns that mirror truth but magnify it so that it assumes preposterous and frightening forms. I should not have been surprised at the way my thoughts about MacKenzie unfolded, but I should have been astonished by the fact that when I left the public bar I saw this same MacKenzie walking on the other side of the road, from the river towards the south side of the city. I should have been surprised too that I chose, without giving this a moment's thought, to follow him.

Coal dust from a million fires and factory furnaces had formed that acidic mist that turns to fog in wintertime. MacKenzie made an even more imposing figure now, his long raincoat picked out by lamplight. His black bowler cut into the white cloud. He walked with the swagger of a man accustomed to dominate, accustomed to intimidate others with a manner that is hectoring and abrupt. Our steps were muffled by the mist. Muffled too were the sounds of horses' hooves and steel wheels on cobblestones. A tram passed; its klaxon sounded as though it were three blocks away and then in a moment it clattered next to us, as if emerging from a curtain of fog, like one of those heavy curtains in the theatre designed to contain everything combustible within the confines of the stage. I hurried to keep up with MacKenzie and felt the mist on my cheeks.

We passed a public house and then the figure in front of me entered an opening in the tenement that was broad enough to accommodate a carriage. I darted forward so as not to lose sight of him, and I entered the passageway. For a moment I saw nothing, not the raincoat, not the bowler, so dark was the carriage entrance. Then I made out his silhouette at the end of the passage. In the distance there was a dim gas jet and MacKenzie's form was picked out and transformed by its light.

We were in a back court laid out in a rectangle and enclosed by four tenement terraces. The oblong was criss-crossed by washing lines, some of them sagging beneath the weight of laundry. Shirts and sheets floated in the breeze like phantoms. Radiating from brick sheds that housed dustbins were low iron fences separating the areas allocated to each of the tenement entrances. MacKenzie walked beside one of the sheds towards a wall that led along the middle of the quadrangle. Another wall, which had once been the side of a shed but now stood bereft of any obvious purpose, created a kind of cul-de-sac, a small area obscured from the view of the surrounding windows. This was where MacKenzie stopped and turned.

It was dark, so dark, the darkness of death. It was the darkness that descended on Santiago when the Americans bombarded the city and at night not a candle or a lamp was lit. I heard the scuttle and scratch of rats and the sound of an argument in one of the tenement flats. In Santiago, the night was punctured by the screams of those who were wounded and those who were afraid.

When you have witnessed the aftermath of a murderous assault your thoughts move in particular ways. My thoughts moved towards horror.

Limbs that have been amputated with clinical precision leave a wound that is quite distinct from wounds created by demented fury. Great quantities of blood, of course, but the nature of the injury differs according to the mind that caused it. I have seen the cleanly chopped spaghetti of severed veins and ligaments when the work was done carefully. I have seen the gruesome mélange that is the legacy of a maniacal attack.

The maniacal attack is caused by a misalignment, a miscalculation as old as humanity itself. It is caused by the futile attempt to assuage the pain and imperfection of our mortality through violence. The greater the imperfection, the greater the violence. Whatever the momentary release, the consequence must ever be the same – a new and wretched addition to the sum of human misery.

The man who seeks to right a wrong, to respond to injustice, perceived or real, through violence does not think in a measured way, however. He acts on impulse. He responds to his elemental dissatisfaction by raising a hand to strike at the source of his injury.

When my eyes became accustomed to the darkness, I could see MacKenzie's raincoat. It was splayed out on either side of his body like a blanket in the mud and ash between the shed and the two walls, and his bowler hat lay a little way away. Great quantities of blood. He had been felled not by one blow but by twenty, the rhythmic, vicious, bone-shattering application of a blade to his neck, his shoulders, his torso, even his arms and legs once he lay on the ground.

The results of this animal violence jolted me as though I had been in a trance, as though I were waking from a dream so vivid as to be confused with reality. This dream was woven into my reality. I could not dismiss it, as though my thoughts, my impulses, were unaffected by the violence I had witnessed since the shelling of Santiago.

CHAPTER TWO

The nature of the sound that wakens a person is defined by the dominant feelings when the brain drifted into sleep. A clear knock on the bedroom door might be taken as a bright invitation to begin the day, if the feelings on going to sleep were bright. The same sound might be abrasive and unwelcome, if those feelings were infected by anger or by fear.

Confused by the transition from sleep, I could not at first define the meaning of the sound – a knock that was clear and consistent. As I pulled the covers back and swung my legs over the side of the bed, I detected a note of authority and a note of detachment, too. It is quite absurd to suggest that I could derive such a detailed impression from an everyday sound, but I did. Even before I opened the door, I knew that the person on the other side was not an acquaintance or an employee of the hotel.

I looked at the man who had wakened me. I looked *up*: he was very tall. He was well dressed, in a grey, three-piece suit, and he was perhaps a decade older than me. When I glanced down, I saw that his brown shoes were polished to a military sheen. He was clean-shaven, with a broad chin and his cropped hair was beginning to thin at the front. The expression in his pale blue eyes put me on my guard.

As I considered all these things, I considered, too, that I did not know what time it was; I was standing in my pyjamas; I was not yet fully conscious; I was being addressed by name.

'Señor Camarón?'

'*Soy* Camarón,' I said, and then, as the stranger, even though he pronounced my name in the Spanish way had indicated with a slight mis-inflection that he was not a native speaker, I added, 'I am Juan Camarón.'

'My name is Smith,' he said. 'You have been referred to me by the City of Glasgow police.'

I noted the absence of any apology for waking me. The man watched me with disagreeable frankness, as though he were making an assessment and didn't care if I noticed or not.

He presented his card. In addition to his name, it bore the designation *Captain, Special Branch*, and a London address. In one corner was a neat circular stamp with the words 'Metropolitan Police'.

I looked up from the card. 'What is it you wish to speak to me about?'

'I need you to come with me.'

'You need me to come with you?' His peremptory manner had a certain absurdity to it.

'You recently assisted the police,' he said, 'in a murder investigation.'

This was true, and rather well known. My assistance had been crucial in identifying the killer.

'There has been another murder,' he said. He waited for a moment – to assess my reaction, I thought – and then he added, 'There is a view that your *particular* photographs may be of use.'

It was shortly after eight o'clock when Captain Smith and I stepped down from the brougham outside a tenement south of the river.

A police constable stood at the entrance to the close. He was an imposing figure: middle-aged, with a thick black moustache, the tip of his helmet obscuring a large part of his pock-marked face, shoulders back, chest bulging over the top of his belt. The sight of him depressed me. I had not wanted to be here, but Smith had overcome my objections. He was the sort of man who gets his way. Apparently, I was the sort of man who gives in.

It wasn't my intention to continue with serial photography the technique I had invented to identify patterns of activity in a particular space – a street or a square, for example – by making photographs from the same vantage point at fixed intervals throughout the day. I didn't see it as the panacea that Smith had been told about. It had worked, quite inadvertently, the first time I used it, and a killer was caught. But I didn't believe it could be relied upon to work again and in any case, I was without the necessary equipment: the timing device on which the method depended had been sent away for repair.

Yet, I was here, and I was holding my camera. Smith was an overbearing sort of fellow and I had already formed a profound dislike for him, but beyond his importunate insistence, I was obliged to acknowledge that I *wanted* to see what that scene looked like. I wanted to see if it was familiar, if it prompted some sort of recognition.

Experience of evil can cast a long shadow and there are people who return again and again to that violence that wounds the soul.

I looked at the constable as I waited for Smith to pay the driver. I was impatient to know what lay beyond the entrance to the tenement.

Although it was early, a small posse of bystanders had gathered. There was no physical barrier, yet the men and women and children who looked on as Smith and I entered the building were careful not to cross an invisible line that had been marked by the constable, first through a spoken instruction and thereafter by a glance here and a cautionary growl there. We were in a district where a man in uniform exercised authority: it might be resented and surreptitiously flouted, but it would not be openly challenged.

The constable saluted and escorted us into the darkness. The close smelled of tobacco and cabbage and damp. The darkness deepened at first, and then we were able to see a little better in the weak but serviceable light from a cupola, high above, at the top of the central stairs. There were doors to the ground-floor apartments on either side of the first flight of stairs. The corridor continued after this, becoming brighter as we moved along it because the rough wooden door that led onto the back court had been left open.

It is absurd to speak of 'a premonition' of evil. Memory is misleading and it is impossible to *dis*remember things that we later learn about an event but did not know at the time. Knowledge of evil consequences, for example, will permeate the memory so that these consequences appear always to have been in view. The mind stores random details that can bring us instantly to a place of long-ago terror.

As I followed Smith through the close to the back court and the shape of the buildings came into view, I was gripped by a feeling of the deepest unease. My skin crawled. I gripped the camera and the tripod tightly, as though they might be wrested from me by an invisible hand. When we emerged into the back court, I stumbled, as though I were drunk. Another policeman was guarding the entrance here. I felt his hand reach out to steady me.

'Shall I take that?' Smith asked, turning to see me being momentarily propped up by the policeman. He indicated the wooden camera case.

I regained my balance and shook my head.

The back court was the size of a football field, and the same shape. In front of us stood a line of four-storey tenements. At this hour, with the sun yet to rise high enough to shine directly into the closed quadrangle, the lines of windows appeared silver and black. If there were onlookers behind the glass – as surely there were – they were invisible. Many of the windows had been drawn up, however, and at these people looked out in the uninhibited way that comes from knowing you are perfectly at liberty to watch whatever you choose. Children peered down, their hands on the windowsills to steady themselves. There were men in shirtsleeves: some stood with their hands spread out in front of them like shopkeepers or barmen waiting for custom. Women, in various states of indoor dress, leaned on the sills with their elbows. One woman had placed a pillow under her arms so as to lean more comfortably.

To our right, the tenements were the same as those in the main block, but there were fewer entrances. A carriageway provided a direct exit from the back court to the street. The building on the fourth side of the rectangle was not a tenement. It had a grey, plaster facade.

Smith saw me looking. 'It's a brewery,' he said.

A faint aroma of rotten eggs – fermenting hops – had descended on us when we entered the back court. There were no windows on the brewery facade, but a row of small vents along the top.

I had brought the Eastman camera and the Kessler tripod. Although there was no question of serial photography as such, because of the absence of the timer, I proposed to photograph the murder scene and then analyse the images in the detailed and systematic way that I had developed for that system. The camera sees more than the naked eye: it records *everything*. The camera does not distinguish; it does not judge; it does not jump to conclusions. Details missed by the brain are preserved by the machine and studied carefully, these details can be used to assemble a new understanding of events.

I had explained my method to Smith when we travelled here in the brougham, and I had explained my reservations. He did nothing to indicate that he did not share these reservations. I sensed that he had been instructed to enlist my help and was doing so only with reluctance.

'What's that?' I asked, pointing to the right, where a low annexe protruded from the tenement facade. It had windows looking onto the back court and a wooden door. The gingham curtains were closed.

'Shirt makers,' Smith said. 'Working men's club.'

As if he felt that the narrow confines of my role as a photographer did not merit further discussion, he increased his pace and led the way to the place we had come to see. It wasn't difficult to identify the precise location. Along the middle of the back court there were sheds. From the malodorous emanation, I gathered that the privies for perhaps a hundred households were in some of these sheds. Between the privies there were larger structures with tin chimneys above them. Milling around one of these, near the middle of the back court were at least ten constables. They stood in the way that policemen do when their very presence, rather than any useful activity, is their principal function.

A sergeant was stationed near the door of the shed, speaking to three constables. When he saw Smith, he stepped away from them and advanced towards us. He tipped his helmet in a manner that I sensed was slightly reluctant and I wondered if Smith had been foisted on the sergeant in the same way I had been foisted on Smith.

'This is Mr Cameron,' Smith said, pronouncing my name in the Scottish way. 'He's here for the pictures.'

The sergeant gave me a frank, almost contemptuous look.

'We huvnae taken the boady tae the mortuary till ye came fur the phoaties,' he said.

Smith stared at the man with an expression of exasperation. In that moment, I realised something that might have been glaringly obvious to me if I had not been preoccupied by my growing dislike for Smith. Like me, he was an alien here. I should have noted his accent – English, possibly from the very south. He did not fully understand what the sergeant had said.

I had spent several months in Glasgow. I was practically fluent.

'I won't take very long,' I said, ignoring Smith's temporary embarrassment. 'I'm sorry I've held up the proceedings.'

The sergeant softened. 'Aye,' he said. 'Dinnae worry aboot that. Thon body'll keep.'

Death announces itself in different ways. Its smell is among the less tolerable. It is an unholy combination of excreta and boiled vegetables, together with something faintly chemical. This was, no doubt, why the constables had elected to remain outside. Apart from the sergeant, none of them followed us into the shed. Smith put a hand over his nose. The sergeant, who had been at the scene for several hours, had a handkerchief ready. He watched me over the top of his makeshift mask.

I stepped forward into the dingy room and my gaze moved instinctively to the far corner, in the direction of something that was not at first very noteworthy. It was a collection of clothing that had been bundled on the floor at the foot of an iron bed.

But it wasn't just a bundle. There was a body inside it.

It seemed that the corpse called out to us. I did not have to check where Smith and the sergeant were looking. They were looking in the same direction as me.

I took another step forward. If they did the same, I didn't notice. I thought only about the bundle in the corner.

Death announces itself with a bad smell and then it breaks cover in other ways. It isn't a purely physical phenomenon. It cannot be. Life in its essence is not physical. The body is animated by an invisible force, and when this force departs, there is a space. I stared into this space.

The dead man's eyes were still open. His expression was one of surprise. He was middle-aged, with a black moustache and pronounced cheekbones that made him look tubercular. Protruding cheekbones, of course, are common in the dead, if – as this man was – they are facing upward. Gravity draws the skin towards the floor, giving the cadaver an emaciated appearance. The skin was white – not pale, but white, as though it had been bleached. And in a certain sense, it had: the colour had been removed by a chemical process that occurs when blood is entirely drained from the body.

This man's blood lay all about him. Someone might have spilled a tureen of it onto the floor. And the unevenness of the surface had caused the liquid to collect in a pool, so that the body seemed to be floating.

I looked down, and the dead man looked up. The eyes of the corpse were in a position corresponding to my chin, and its chin was in a position corresponding to my eyes. The body stretched away from me towards the wall. In order to step round and view it from a more satisfactory angle I would have to stand in the blood. I did not wish to do this. I say the body 'stretched', but this is not quite the right word. It was spread-eagled, on its back. One leg extended towards the wall; the other leg, the left one, was bent; the knee had come up and then fallen over the thigh of the right leg. The left arm stretched away from the body, but not completely; its trajectory had been arrested by the frame of the bed, the elbow resting on the bloody floor and the hand raised languidly as though holding an invisible cigarette. The right arm had fallen over the stomach.

It was from the chest that the great fountain of blood had come. And the cause of that fountain, the implement of violent carnage, remained in situ. A kitchen knife had been inserted, to the handle, between the victim's ribs. Between the third and fourth rib, I guessed, straight through the heart.

27

'Can you photograph this?'

I became aware that Smith was speaking to me.

I turned, but only partially. I did not want to draw myself entirely away from the corpse almost as if, in the normal manner of conversation, it would be impolite to turn one's back on one of the participants.

Smith seemed to me to be less assured now, less certain of his own position in the scheme of things.

'Of course,' I said.

He still had his hand over his nose and the sergeant still had his handkerchief deployed.

'How long will ye be?' the sergeant asked.

I glanced around the room – a view from four directions, a view at floor level. I looked into the corner behind me, where there was a sideboard on which I guessed I would be able to stand, giving me a view from above.

'Half an hour,' I said. 'Maybe forty minutes.'

The sergeant walked quickly out of the room. We heard him issuing instructions. The mortuary van was to be sent for. He also directed that the sheets hanging on the washing lines should be gathered and made into a kind of screen to prevent the gawkers at the tenement windows from viewing the corpse when it was removed.

I stood with my back to the open door. The thin mattress on the iron bed was covered with a threadbare sheet and there was a blanket, carelessly folded, beside the striped pillow. The calendar above the bed was for last year. Above the bedhead, the plaster was discoloured where a picture had once been hung. The nail was still fixed in the wall. Three of the walls had been papered with an oriental bamboo motif. To my right, the paper was peeling badly at the top where dampness had come in through the roof. On my left, next to the bed, there was a steel stove. There was a circular vent in the stovepipe close to the roof; a wire clothes line stretched from the wall a little below the vent all the way across the room to the opposite wall.

'How will you set up your camera?'

It was as though there were some sort of delay in my thoughts. I realised that I was looking at Smith only after I had absorbed what he had said. I realised, too, that he was asking for the second time. I had not responded the first time round.

'Set up?'

'You need to photograph the body from above.'

I considered this for several moments. Then I said, 'Why?' He was right. I intended to make an image from an elevated position in the room, but – and this may have come, I am obliged to acknowledge, from a certain pettiness – I did not want to give Smith the satisfaction of directing me.

He seemed irritated. 'That's how these photographs are taken, isn't it?'

'What photographs?'

'*These* photographs. Photographs of murder scenes.'

I shrugged. 'I have my own method.'

'You need to photograph the body from above,' he repeated.

'Captain Smith, if you will allow me, I know my business.' I noticed that he was no longer holding his hand to his nose.

I put the camera case on the chipped linoleum that partially covered the floor. The strips were curling up at the edges, and the case wobbled on the uneven surface. I assembled the tripod and placed it at the entrance, then stood behind it and crouched down a little, framing the room with my hands. Smith stepped out of my way – as though my hands were going to take the photograph. I walked round the tripod and picked up the case. The Eastman, with its refined lens, has the advantage of picking out detail in a landscape image. It is not ideal for portrait photography. I was glad I had brought it instead of the Eclipse. I cannot say that this was a consequence of foresight: I had been reluctant to come in the first place, and I had only selected the Eastman because it was lighter and easier to carry.

I placed the camera on the tripod and tightened the screw. Then I took the magnesium strip from my satchel and attached it to the elevation rod.

'Captain Smith,' I said, 'I'd be grateful if you would step outside. You can observe the process from behind me if you like.'

He looked for a moment as though he might not oblige me – he disliked being directed, I could see. At last, he nodded and moved out of the room and stood behind me.

I looked through the viewfinder and adjusted the lens. Fifteen or twenty seconds elapsed before I was sure that the view was as broad as possible and that each object was in focus. When I was satisfied, I removed a safety match from my pocket and struck it. The flame flickered in the putrid air and when the strip ignited, I pressed the shutter button.

The picture was made.

I carefully removed the plate and placed it in the satchel. I took another plate, inserted it in the camera and stepped into the room.

I heard Smith and some of the constables coughing. Smith was waving his hand in front of his face to disperse the cloud of incinerated magnesium. These were the same men who had been standing for some time in the infinitely more toxic miasma emanating from the cadaver.

I carried the tripod across the room and stood with my back to the wall between the sideboard and the stove. From here I repeated the process. I framed the end of the bed, the upper torso and head of the corpse, the kitchen table, which had an armchair in front of it, the bare wall and a portion of the ceiling where the wallpaper was peeling, and the empty corner next to the door. I struck another match, lit the magnesium strip, waited for the flash and pressed the shutter button.

Taking the tripod and camera to the other corner I stood with the body to my right and the door to my left. I had a view of the bedhead and the discoloured section of paper with the nail still in the wall where the picture had been, the stove, the sideboard, the corner next to the door and part of the door, where Smith stood watching me. I might have advised him to step back so as not to be in the picture of a murder scene as some people are superstitious about such things. I did not imagine, though, that Smith was the superstitious sort. And in any case, it might offer a useful perspective when I came to examine the images to have a living human figure in at least one of the compositions. It might represent the departed soul – or the killer. Smith's silhouette cast a faint shadow into the room.

When I had taken the photograph, I moved to the middle of the floor, careful not to step on the blood.

'I'm going to stand on the bed,' I said.

'What?'

Smith came back into the room. His sense of smell had adjusted to the air outside, even when it was clouded with magnesium. His hand moved instinctively to cover his nostrils.

'I'm going to stand on the bed,' I repeated.

He seemed to consider this for a moment and then he shrugged. I placed the camera next to the bed and then, inspecting the soles of my shoes in case they had mud or blood on them – decorum is oddly persistent even in macabre of circumstances – I climbed onto the iron frame first and then, more gingerly, onto the mattress.

There is something altogether unnatural about standing on a bed with your shoes on. This was compounded by the fact that a blood-soaked corpse lay partially in view. I lifted the tripod and camera and placed them in front of me.

When I looked through the viewfinder, any reservations I may have had about the propriety of standing on the bed were dispelled. The higher angle offered clarity. The body, on my left, and the stove, on my right, were not in the frame but everything else was.

'You may wish to stand off-camera,' I said. Smith's

silhouette had little utility from this angle. He stepped quickly outside and out of view. The constable who had been loitering a little way beyond Smith followed the captain's example and moved out of sight. In front of me, through the door and across the courtyard I could see the kitchen window of the nearest apartment. The window was open and the two brass taps above the sink were visible. A woman stood in the kitchen watching me, an infant wrapped in a shawl around her neck.

I struck a match, lit the strip and let the shutter fall.

I jumped down from the bed, crossed the room and climbed onto the sideboard. It was a solid piece of furniture, like the iron bed. But while the bed looked entirely at one with its surroundings, the sideboard was out of place. It was rather ornate, and it may have been recently varnished. At twice the elevation afforded by the bed, it offered a panoramic view. I lit the strip and pressed the shutter, lowered the camera and tripod, and jumped down onto the floor.

The linoleum caused me to misjudge the height of the sideboard and the proximity of the floor: my left foot hit the surface with greater velocity than I had anticipated, and in order to break my fall I allowed myself to tumble forward. I had, I suppose, intended to steady my forward progress by bringing up my right foot, but the tip of my shoe caught one of the upturned edges of linoleum. I careered towards the opposite wall, landing on my stomach. From here, I had the disconcerting experience of seeing the room from the vantage point of the corpse.

I felt myself being lifted – with more ease than suited my sense of dignity. Smith returned me to a standing position as if I were a rather unwieldy rag doll. But indignity wasn't uppermost in my mind.

'There's something under the bed,' I said.

He knelt down and inclined his head sideways to see beneath the iron frame. Smith got up on one leg and moved forward, kneeling again and reaching beneath the bed. He pulled out an envelope. Without comment he folded it and put it in the pocket of his jacket.

'I'm going to make another picture,' I said, 'from this height.' I indicated the level of the floor. 'It would be consistent with my method if everything is where it was, as much as possible . . .'

'I will remember where *this* was,' he said, tapping the envelope in his pocket.

'You are in the way,' I said.

I separated the camera from the tripod and placed it on the linoleum. Then I lay down behind it and framed the picture. Smith walked round me and took up a position at the doorway. I adjusted the viewfinder.

The smell in the room was marginally less unpleasant at floor level. Cool air circulated. There was an odour principally from the dusty linoleum and the distant scent of hops. Through the viewfinder I could see the legs of the two chairs, the bed, the table, the black belly of the stove and the handle of the kitchen knife where it protruded from the dead man's chest. The thinning hair of the victim revealed the beginning of a bald patch, a little oval of pale skin that winked at me now as though the deceased had a third eye on the top of his lifeless head.

I lit the strip and when the magnesium flashed, I dropped the shutter.

Just as Smith had surprised me by pocketing the envelope without comment, there was, I thought, something surreptitious that jarred with his otherwise officious manner. He surprised me again by not returning to the subject of a photograph of the cadaver from above. I had not wanted to make a picture from this angle because the Eastman would not deliver an entirely satisfactory one; the Eclipse would have been more appropriate. But there was more than this. I would study the *patterns* in the room. In some respects, the body wasn't the principal object of interest – rather, it was the things *around* the body.

And I disliked being told what to do.

As we left the shed, two men from the mortuary van walked towards us carrying a folded canvas stretcher. The constables had draped sheets strategically over the washing lines, as instructed, creating a makeshift screen.

'How long will it take you to make the photographs?' Smith asked as we entered the close.

'This afternoon,' I said. 'I will be able to develop them then.'

'I will come and look at them around six.'

'No!' I was suddenly exasperated. 'The pictures will serve no purpose until I have examined them.'

'*I* will examine them.'

'No!' My voice reverberated along the plaster walls of the corridor. I sounded petulant, but I spoke in this way because Smith, like so many others, misunderstood the process. The pictures had to be studied in a disciplined way. 'I must apply my own method,' I said. 'It requires detailed inspection, quadrant by quadrant, image by image, otherwise the photographs will reveal very little.'

He glanced over his shoulder. 'Is this what you did in Crown Street?'

In the case of Crown Street, I had taken serial photographs for three days. A systematic comparison of these images revealed a figure who – through timing and proximity – could be tied to the murders committed in the area.

'It is similar. I don't have the mechanism for serial photography. In Crown Street I made a very large number of photographs and it took many hours to compare them. I will try to do something similar with the images I have just made, but I will need two or three hours.' He was about to speak so I added quickly, 'I have engagements throughout the day. I will endeavour to have the pictures and notes ready for you in the morning.'

We emerged onto the street, where the sergeant was speaking to the constable on guard. The crowd had grown larger; the arrival of the mortuary van had revived interest.

'I will come to your hotel in the morning,' Smith said. He nodded in the direction of the sergeant. 'Now, I must attend to things here.'

I disliked being dismissed in this perfunctory way, and

I resented the fact that Smith had not taken me into his confidence in regard to the likely contents of the envelope that I had drawn attention to under the bed. I said, 'May I ask if you know the identity of the victim?'

He looked at me as though the question were somehow impertinent, but then he said sourly, 'Yes, we know who he was. He was a policeman, an associate of mine.'

He began to move away. 'Until tomorrow then.'

CHAPTER THREE

I took the camera and tripod back to the hotel and then caught a cab to the office of the Raeburn steamship company, located by the wharves on the Govan side of the river. The cab dropped me at Finnieston and I crossed on the ferry. I had ordered the new Lumière Cinematographe from Paris, but when I provided my details to the woman in the Raeburn office, she was solicitous. 'It hasn't arrived yet, Mr Cameron. Trouble in the Channel. A storm has prevented all movement out of Le Havre.'

The Raeburn office faced the Simpson-Burley paint factory on the other side of the river. A sleek and unusual vessel was moored at the wharf near the factory. It was less than eighty feet long, with a recessed prow; the deck had not yet been fitted out with the usual accoutrements and there was a single funnel. Vessels in various states of construction lined both banks, so the unfinished deck was common, but in this case the grey hull was armour plated and that was why it was low in the water. There were no portholes. I guessed that the expanse in front of the funnel would be fitted with a gun, and there would be mechanisms to lower torpedoes into the water. I had seen American ships like this were anchored in Santiago after the siege.

The sounds that emanated from the torpedo boat were no more bellicose or strident than anywhere else by the waterside, where sailors and workers exchanged greetings and instructions. Crewmen moved to and fro on the unfinished deck. Stray voices floated in the early morning. I heard a language I didn't recognise, Russian, perhaps. Small vessels moved back and forth between the gunboat and me.

I left the Raeburn office and stepped onto the ferry just as it was about to depart. As soon as I was seated, I savoured the familiar tang of tar, oil, sea salt and decay that rose up from the choppy black surface of the river.

My father was shot outside the cathedral in Santiago on the 27th June 1898. He died at the very moment he completed his pictorial record of Spanish architecture in Cuba. The work had been commissioned by William Collins, Sons & Co of Glasgow, London, Bombay and Toronto. It was now to be published in a splendid edition that would be my father's testament.

My father was a fine photographer. He made images with skill and with insight, and they were all the more important because the country he photographed had changed utterly. My father's pictures were an intimate and accurate record of a vanished world.

These things could not begin to compensate for the injustice of his death at the hands of a marksman who picked him out and shot him when he was in the very act of making his final photograph. Yet I had come to understand a little about life and death. We are an idea, an essence; we are reflected in what we do and in what we have done.

As the last person who had boarded the little ferry, I was the last person to disembark. I climbed carefully the four slippery black steps that led to the high-tide mark, after which the granite slabs were a lighter colour. At the top of the stairway I stepped onto the long, busy thoroughfare of the Broomielaw. I waited for three heavily laden carts carrying barrels of Jamaican syrup to pass before I could cross to a narrow street that led first between the gable ends of two warehouse sheds and then between black tenements and finally to the main road.

I was on my way now to William Collins, for a meeting with Benjamin Jackson, the editor of my father's book. With the steady rhythm of my footsteps in the sunlit street, I began to consider my encounter with Captain Smith – and with the murder victim – more carefully. The mind sometimes moves of its own accord. I had hurried away from the scene of the crime and then I had hurried to the offices of the steamship company and now I hurried to my next appointment, as though hurrying would prevent more sombre thoughts from settling.

I slowed my pace and looked up at the canvas awnings and into shops where the first customers had begun to disturb the stillness of the morning. Trams trundled by; women in straw hats and brightly coloured scarves looked out at me, men in caps and bowler hats peered at the street. I walked through a gallery of colour and shape and expectation. The sunlight enlivened everything. This was just a few miles from that dingy room where the policeman had been butchered, but it seemed to me like a different planet. The murder had taken place on the moon. I walked through the morning as though with each step I placed a distance between myself and the ugliness I had seen.

At the entrance to the publisher's office, a young woman escorted me to a conference room on the ground floor. This was unexpected. I had visited William Collins on two previous occasions, the first soon after I arrived in the city, when I was assured that my father's portfolio and the accompanying commentary not only met but greatly exceeded the publisher's expectations, and the second, more recently, when issues related to the size and tint of some of the pictures were discussed. Both of these meetings had taken place in Benjamin Jackson's office, a spacious room on the second floor with a bay window that admitted light.

After I was shown into the rather gloomy conference room, I had to wait fifteen minutes for Jackson to arrive. This, too, might have alerted me to the fact that something was wrong.

When we first met, I had formed the opinion that Jackson was something of a secular monk. A monk because he was skeletal, and his narrow face, high forehead and thinning hair – he was perhaps in his late forties or early fifties – gave him an ascetic appearance; and secular because his view of my father's pictures was devoid of sentiment or any of the spiritual aspects of appreciation.

My father's portraits of people were at once sensitive and celebratory. He understood that the family photographs we were commissioned to make on First Communion days in Granada would stay for lifetimes at the centre of collective memory; perhaps they would act as a residual cord of affection and solidarity in lives torn by emigration and disappointment and betrayal. 'You must photograph the *soul*, Juan,' my father said. He photographed buildings in the same way, identifying the elements that were distinguished, and identifying, too, the elements that were intended to be distinguished but hadn't quite managed to fulfil this intention – some of the buildings he photographed looked better in the image he created than they did in real life.

Benjamin Jackson, in contrast, was preoccupied by form. Everything he said about the pictures was intelligible and much was shrewd, but he seemed to me to be entirely adrift from my father's way of seeing the world. Perhaps it was a measure of my father's art that it could be understood and appreciated in different, even opposing, ways.

Jackson's handshake was as neutral as the expression on his face. He walked to the other side of the large mahogany table that filled the room and sat down. As he did so, he placed two pieces of paper in front of him.

'Señor Camarón, may I ask if you are acquainted with a Señora LaGuardia?' Jackson began. 'Señora Mona LaGuardia.'

'No,' I said. 'Why?'

'We have received a letter from Señora LaGuardia. In it she informs us of extremely disturbing circumstances in which the pictures which you say were taken by your father came into your possession.'

That qualification, 'which you say', was shocking and offensive.

'What do you mean?' I heard the tone of my own voice as though the words had been uttered by a third party. I was appalled when I sensed that my indignation was infused with fear.

'Señora LaGuardia has written to tell us that the portfolio which you have presented here as the work of your late father, was in fact made by her husband, and she has furnished us with photographic plates which, as she has reasonably pointed out, could not otherwise be in her possession if her claim were untrue.'

'But the plates were lost,' I said, understanding in the same instant that this did not constitute a compelling rebuttal. 'In the bombardment; there was a fire and I had to collect as much as I could. I rescued the photographs, but I could not rescue the plates.'

The very incoherence with which I recounted a series of events that were themselves characterised by disorder seemed to undermine my argument further.

'Señora LaGuardia says that you stole what belonged to her.'

'This is preposterous!'

I could not have spoken more emphatically, and yet I could not have spoken to less effect. The allegation made by this Señora LaGuardia and repeated to me now by Benjamin Jackson was certainly preposterous. Yet, it sprang from those murderous mornings, from those mornings that can never be conveyed in a photograph or a painting or a poem or a book; those mornings when a man is in one breath whole and normal and alive and the next breath is mangled and dying. It came from Santiago, a burning city in the summer of 1898, when my father's chest was turned to a bloody morass and my father's relatives were killed at the height of the American attack.

'Señora LaGuardia has informed us that she will take action against us if we proceed with publication,' Jackson continued. He spoke like a judge handing down a particularly heavy sentence, perhaps even a sentence of death. But he was not a judge; he was an editor at a publishing company. In the seconds during which I absorbed his measured, stern delivery, and the careful formula of words that he had, it seemed clear to me, prepared in advance, I conceived a dislike for the man that was almost visceral. He addressed his remarks largely to the table, but also, from time to time, to the wall behind me. It was only with the final sentence – *We do not, therefore, propose to continue* – that he looked at me.

Jackson stared, and I felt obliged to respond. 'But this is preposterous!' I said again.

He glanced down at the paper in front of him and then he began speaking to the wall again. 'Señora LaGuardia has also made charges against *you*,' he said. 'I will not repeat these charges. They may be . . . libellous.' He looked at me as he pronounced the last word. Then he looked at the wall again.

I sensed that Jackson was the emissary of a committee, and the knowledge that my father and I had been discussed by others prompted a renewed surge of indignation. 'But this . . .' I began, further disconcerted by the high pitch of my voice, '. . . cannot be.'

It was a statement so general as to be meaningless, delivered with so little authority as to lack any value as an argument.

Jackson stood up.

I remained seated. I found myself contemplating the cream-coloured plaster of the opposite wall. I looked down and in front of me was an expanse of polished mahogany.

'Señor Camarón,' Jackson said. The tone of his voice was that of a schoolmaster addressing a recalcitrant pupil who has chosen the wrong topic on which to be obstinate.

I got to my feet, but instead of beginning to walk towards the door I remained where I was. 'I would like to know where this Señora LaGuardia may be contacted.'

Jackson held out the second of the two pieces of paper he had brought into the room. I took it from him. As I touched the rough surface, I felt a sudden resistance, as though the paper itself were impregnated with toxin, with hatred.

'The address of her solicitor in Edinburgh,' Jackson said.

'Edinburgh!'

Jackson appeared to soften for a moment. 'I believe I may be permitted to tell you that Señora LaGuardia is temporarily resident in Leith. She is breaking her journey there, as I understand it, en route from Cuba to Spain.'

On the pavement outside I watched the traffic. I looked stupidly at omnibuses and coal lorries and phaetons and a troop of mounted police. I did not know which way to go. People had to walk around me. A woman clicked her tongue against the roof her mouth as she changed course. I began to walk south towards the river. I did not look at the shop windows. I did not look at the people hurrying past. I did not listen to the noise of carriages on cobblestones. I walked in a daze, only faintly conscious of the pale blue sky. Inhaling the scent of coal dust and manure and human sweat, I tried to breathe more steadily.

Libellous. It could not be.

The day after my father was murdered, I confronted his cousin, Paco, and Paco's wife, Eleanora. My father had come to Santiago to claim an inheritance they believed was rightly theirs. Eleanora was a woman of such selfishness that even my father – always courteous and sympathetic to the needs of others – had shown a certain coolness towards her. I challenged them as they were trying to escape from Santiago. The shelling had reached a new intensity by then.

I found them in the stables. They were frantic; they wanted to harness their horses and get away. I tried to speak to them. But they simply swotted me to one side, as though I were an insect. I remember Eleanora's pistol. She had put it to one side as she tried to get the horse to be still. The beast was wild because of the explosions. I remember the screaming and the crash and snap of shells and shots. I remember the dust and the smell of cordite and plaster. Paco lay on the ground. Eleanora's clothes were disordered and covered in dirt. I ran into the house and rescued my father's papers and his photographs.

His papers showed my father to be the rightful heir to the plantation near Santiago that Eleanora and Paco claimed was theirs. And he had other property – property in Scotland he had never spoken of. I collected what I could and left the building before it burned to the ground. I could not carry the photographic plates. I was sure that Paco and Eleanora were dead. I was sure of it.

Señora LaGuardia from Cuba; allegations best not repeated because they were libellous – I felt a great wave crash down upon me.

The pictures from Cuba were my father's work. There was no question. I was his assistant in the making of every one of the one hundred and twenty-four photographs in the collection. We made the pictures over a period of twenty months; we travelled right across Cuba from Havana to Santiago visiting towns and hamlets where there were examples of the distinctive architecture that melds the Spanish baroque with the materials and climate of the Caribbean. We had come to know the country better than many of its inhabitants.

This collection was my father's masterwork. I would not allow it to be stolen.

The masts of vessels moored on either side of the river came into view. I struck out again into the traffic of the Broomielaw, which was dense here as two large ships downstream were being unloaded. I could see the hemp winches. Three carts laden with molasses passed in front of me and I darted to the other side of the road.

I walked along the embankment to the suspension bridge and began to cross. With each step, the sounds of the city diminished. When I reached the middle of the bridge, there was almost quiet, the stillness of the morning interrupted by the sounds of men speaking to one another on the little skiffs that criss-crossed the river below.

I leaned against the wrought iron guardrail and looked downstream towards the ships and shipyards that stretched for miles. There is a calm at the centre of every storm. If you can find that calm and occupy it, you may survive the fiercest crisis.

From here the world looked different. I began to consider what might be done. I had the address of the woman's lawyer. I would make contact. A steady nerve would be required.

In Cardenas, shortly before we descended to Santiago from the sierra, we stayed with two Presbyterian missionaries. Robert and Effie McClellan were interesting and lively. When we sat at dinner with them, my father surprised me with a reminiscence. 'In Glasgow, you liked to go down by the river, Juan. You loved to sit and watch the little ships go by.'

CHAPTER FOUR

In Glasgow, Robert and Effie's niece, Jane, took me under her wing. She was the same age as me, and clever, confident and so full of life, so passionately engaged with everything and everyone in the world around her that I came to worship the ground she walked upon.

Love blossomed in circumstances that were fraught – my serial photographs were instrumental in solving a crime, but not before Jane made a bold intervention in a moment of the greatest danger. Our engagement followed. Love finds a way past even the most profound evil.

I had arranged to join Jane for lunch. Her uncle Alan and I had something important in common: we were both photographers. He had made his name a generation earlier with a ground-breaking portfolio of portraits of city characters, from barefoot hawkers to the pillars of the Corporation in all their pomp. Alan's images of the poorest districts had pricked the municipal conscience and prompted a succession of improvement schemes. After that, he stopped taking those kinds of photographs – he was disillusioned, Jane said, by how little the bleak reality of some city lives changed. He also mismanaged his finances. His gallery was a monument to good taste, but it made little money. In the past year, he had mortgaged his wife's West End villa.

'Jane's gone down to Central Station to meet Doctor Breitling,' Alan told me when I arrived at the gallery. He shrugged. 'I would have gone too, but I didn't want to shut up shop. Anyway, I speak poor German and Doctor Breitling knows no English apparently.'

Alan's customary attire tended towards floppy hats, colourful cravats and light-coloured suits. Today, the suit and tie were black, the shirt white and the collar starched. I gathered that he wanted to impress his visitor with the business rather than the bohemian side of his character.

He wasn't satisfied with his own explanation. 'I suppose, if I'm honest, I was a little too grand to go and meet him.' He pushed a hand through his longish grey hair and favoured me with a look of manifestly inauthentic penitence. 'Inexcusably vain?'

'Not at all,' I said, in a voice that may have lacked conviction.

Just then, the door to the gallery opened. At first, we could see only Jane; Doctor Breitling was behind her.

In any configuration, though, I would have seen only Jane. In a room of a thousand people, I would have seen only her.

When we first met, Jane was all in black. Her parents had died the year before, killed when their horse bolted and the buggy they were travelling in overturned. In the time since we had promised to marry, she had, unobtrusively at first but then more conspicuously, begun to wear more colourful clothes. Today, she wore a dark blue velvet jacket and a light blue skirt. She had a little pillbox hat, too. It was black, with a yellow and red line running through it and it sat on her head at a jaunty angle. I thought it the most beautiful hat in the world. It conveyed a natural, infectious *joie de vivre*.

When Doctor Breitling came into view, he did this not by stepping to one side so that he could advance towards us beside Jane, but rather by leaning the top half of his body sideways and peeking at us still from behind her, almost like a child playing hide-and-seek. Jane made way for the doctor, and the four of us stood for several seconds on opposite sides of the room, like people playing tennis doubles.

Breitling was physically imposing and dressed in a casual style that bordered on exuberance. He wore a grey three-piece suit and a white shirt with a soft, wide collar that was fastened with a silk tie bearing the bright motif of some sort of flower. I concluded that Alan may have misjudged the sartorial terms of this encounter.

When the doctor removed his grey fedora, the dome of a

large skull was revealed. He had a round, genial face across the top of which sat a pair of horn-rimmed glasses, the rims thick and circular and the lenses not so thick as to obscure a pair of restive brown eyes.

After the initial introductions had been made, Jane turned to me and, *sotto voce*, said, 'I'm sorry I wasn't here when you arrived.'

In the manner that I suspect must be common for couples who have newly established their affection, I reached down discreetly and for just one blissful second took Jane's hand. Then I stood at a decorous distance, while Alan asked if the doctor had had a comfortable journey from Vienna to Glasgow. Jane translated.

It is extraordinary how people change when they are speaking another language. It was as though I watched a second Jane. She was focused, of course, as an interpreter must be. She had an easy way of conveying what was said, but she was not merely a cypher. When the doctor related a mishap on the journey – his suitcase had been placed on the wrong train in Paris as a result of which it had not appeared on the platform in London, though it was delivered to his hotel the following day – Jane's tone was serious and sympathetic.

When we began to move towards the studio, I allowed my hand once again to hover in the vicinity of Jane's hand and was rewarded by a second fleeting engagement. Her fingers grasped mine, but then, as Jane had to step forward to interpret a remark made by the doctor when we passed through the anteroom, they parted again.

As suddenly as a magnesium strip lights up a room, my thoughts flitted from the joy of being close to Jane and returned to a less agreeable place.

Who was Señora LaGuardia? The only person in the world who might have borne a grudge against me was dead. I was sure of it. I was there when she died. Eleanora would have killed me if she'd been able; she was behind my father's murder. Of this I was certain. The only other person was Paco himself, and he too was surely dead. I had seen him lying on the floor of the stable, a deep gash on the side of his head and blood flowing from a shrapnel wound in his leg. Paco did not share his wife's singleness of purpose. His character was yielding, perhaps even gentle. Yet, he had been there when my father was killed; he had spoken to the men who killed him. I had seen the incontrovertible truth, because the three pictures my father made in the moments before he was shot showed his killer and they showed Paco, too – just before the assault – speaking to that same killer. But Paco was dead. I had checked his pulse after the violence that descended on the stable and swept two living souls into eternity. I saw everything. How could I have been deceived? No one else knew what happened in that house in Santiago during the American siege. No one else knew the looks and words and arguments that were exchanged. No one else had any claim to my inheritance or an intimate knowledge of my father's work.

And yet, the original plates had been left in the house. I had not rescued them from the fire.

'Juan!' Jane was looking up at me. She was smiling. 'You were far away.'

The others were looking at me too.

'Alan and Doctor Breitling will join us for lunch,' Jane said.

Before we left the gallery, Doctor Breitling showed us some of the work he had brought from Vienna. His pictures were striking. They bore a significant resemblance to the work Alan had done in Glasgow, documenting the city's poorest districts. Breitling had developed a visual style in which both the people and the places could be viewed as one subject. The finish, I noticed, was exceptionally fine.

'Peroxide emulsion?' I asked.

Jane translated.

'Not peroxide. I tried that in the beginning, but I have found sodium oxide is easier to handle,' Breitling said.

The resemblance between the Vienna images and the Glasgow ones lay in their sympathy for the subject. I saw echoes of my father's work. The lines etched in aged faces, the expressions of children – smiling, staring glumly at the camera, looking away at something beyond the photographer's frame: these were portraits of individual souls – not 'the poor' but people who were poor.

'The subjects are willing to be photographed?' Alan asked.

'Often they would request a little time to make themselves presentable,' Breitling said. 'Few have clothes beyond the ones they're wearing. Making themselves presentable likely means little more than wiping a child's face or putting a lock of hair in place.'

Jane's delivery was crisp. I wondered if she made the doctor more succinct in English than he was in German.

'And the authorities?' I asked.

'*Und die Stadtverwaltung?*'

I think what I enjoyed most was that, when she interpreted my questions, Jane shared my thoughts. The business of translation seemed to me to serve as a magical expression of love.

'The authorities never object. People think that governments wish to hide the ills that afflict society, but this is not true. They do not wish to hide the ills; they simply wish not to be *blamed* for them. To avoid blame, they will publicise whatever they are doing or trying to do, including ...he smallest things. Looking busy is an indispensable skill, even among the indolent.'

I was sure my fiancée had a hand in the elegance of the doctor's construction.

'But I will show you more of Vienna,' he said. 'I have spent a great deal of time among the workers, in hard places like Ottakring and Neulerchenfeld, but I have my own vices too.' At this he made a face, like a schoolboy who simply cannot stop himself from being naughty. 'My particular weakness is the music of the theatre.'

Breitling opened a second folder and began to leaf through portraits of people and places. There were interiors and exteriors, most of them noticeably better appointed than the images that had been taken in Vienna's poorest districts. I could not at first see the common theme running through the views of writing desks and bedrooms and balconies and salons and garden nooks, until Breitling said, 'They are places where music has been made, by which I mean where music has been conceived, where it has been written.'

One of the photographs showed a man with a prodigious white beard, and white hair swept back over a high forehead. His moustache was stained with tobacco and he held a cigar in his raised left hand, his right hand pushed deep into the pocket of his trousers. The man was unsmiling, and he peered at the camera somewhat pugnaciously. Behind him, his study included a writing desk strewn with manuscript paper; there was a rocking chair with cushions, and a rug and a large table covered in a brocade cloth on which lay more musical scores and writing implements, and on the wall was a bust, the unmistakable likeness of the composer Beethoven.

'Mr Brahms,' Breitling said. 'The picture was made at his residence in Karlsgasse.' He turned to the next image, of Brahms and another man, standing on the veranda of a house. Behind the balustrade was an effulgence of greenery. Brahms stared at the camera now with a more benign expression. He looked older and his clothes were more rumpled. The man beside him was more dapper. 'Mr Strauss,' Breitling said.

'Johann Strauss!' Alan was more impressed by Strauss than by Brahms.

I did not know either of these men.

'The waltz king,' Jane told me. I wondered if she could read my thoughts.

Strauss was dressed smartly. He wore a light-coloured shirt and trousers, and a silk tie. His shoes were polished, and his jacket and waistcoat were elegantly tailored. The most striking things about him were his thick black moustache and his longish wavy hair, and the fact that he was smiling.

'But is it possible to convey some sense of music without sound?'

The question was put by Jane, and for a second I wondered how the doctor had been able to formulate the interrogative without using any words. Then I realised that Jane was speaking on her own behalf. After asking in English she asked in German.

I began to respond before the doctor could. I surprised myself by how quickly and emphatically I entered the conversation. I knew little about the subject. 'The trees behind them,' I said.

Jane translated and then all three of them looked at me. I gathered that I must elaborate. 'They exist in their world,' I said. I looked at the picture of the two men on the veranda and then, nodding to the doctor in a way that sought permission to turn back to the previous portrait, I lifted the thick tissue paper and the cardboard to which the image was fixed and exposed it again. 'There is a bust of Beethoven, of course, but I believe this could be a novelist's study, or the office of a businessman, for that matter.' I placed the picture again facing down and covered it with the tissue paper that separated it from the next picture. We turned our attention again to the two men on the veranda. 'They are in their world,' I repeated. 'We think of creative artists as observing life from a privileged vantage point, and perhaps they do have insights on how the world works, but they produce ideas, they produce music and literature and art, even when they are embroiled in the day-to-day considerations that preoccupy every human being, from the rich to the poor, from the powerful to the weak.

'When I look at this photograph of the two musicians I'm struck by the fact that they are on the veranda on a summer's day and the lush vegetation behind them seems to me to show very powerfully how life presses in on all of us. I ask myself how they arrived on this veranda and where they will go after they have left it. Have they eaten? Will they eat? Did they take a tram from the city, or will they return to the city in a phaeton? I cannot say that I would have recognised that they are musicians, but now that you have told me they are, then I truly believe I might understand their music a little better, because from this photograph I believe I understand *them* a little better.'

I had said more than I had intended to say. Jane completed the translation and then – to me – she added, 'You have never spoken like this before.'

'You are right,' I said with some contentment. 'I have not.' We were at that stage where everything we learn about the object of our love seems wondrous and good.

'Last year,' Breitling said, 'I visited London. It was in the late spring and I stayed with my good friend Mr Hubert Parry. We enjoyed making music together, and Mr Parry was gracious enough to conduct me around the places in the capital that have been blessed by the presence of musicians, including the house in Belgravia where our Mozart spent one whole summer when he was just a little boy, and Handel too – we visited his rooms in Brook Street.'

'Handel?' I asked.

'The "Hallelujah Chorus",' Alan said.

I may have looked blank. 'It's a popular piece of music,' Jane explained. 'We have a Handel concert every Christmas at the City Halls.' Then she added, 'I'll take you there.'

'And there are places in Glasgow I would like to visit, places I would like to photograph,' Breitling continued.

'Oh?' Alan said.

'Yes!' Breitling was excited in the way that people with a particular enthusiasm sometimes warm to their theme when a conversation has necessarily attended to things of interest to the rest of the participants but has finally arrived at the thing of interest to them. 'There is the place where Friedrich Chopin' – he pronounced the name in the German way and in the English version Jane did the same – 'performed during his tour of Scotland, the Business Hall.'

'The Business Hall?' I asked.

'That would be the Merchants' Hall,' Alan said.

Jane appeared uncertain.

'It's the Sheriff Court now,' Alan explained.

'That was a concert hall?' Jane was surprised.

'They used to entertain the defendants,' Alan said.

Jane hadn't translated the last few sentences. She turned and spoke to Breitling in an apologetic tone, and then to Alan she said, 'I'm just letting the good doctor know that you are sometimes inclined to be flippant.'

Breitling smiled, but it seemed to me that while he grasped the literal meaning, he missed what was communicated above and below the words.

'And when Arthur Sullivan was in Glasgow—' Breitling began.

'Arthur Sullivan was in Glasgow?' Jane asked Alan, after translating.

Alan shrugged and indicated with a hopeful expression that she should put the question to Breitling, who seemed to know a great deal about the city's musical antecedents. She did so.

'Yes!' she translated, speaking in a lively way that reflected some of Breitling's own excitement. 'He was the leader of a choir here, twenty years ago or so. He stayed in a villa by the loch.'

'A villa by the loch?' Perhaps I simply wanted to be part of the conversation.

Breitling produced a small black notebook from his inside pocket and leafed through it, glancing at each of us in turn as he did so, an expression on his face that seemed to indicate he might have been able to find the sought-after information more quickly but was mischievously keeping us all on tenterhooks. When he found what he was looking for he pronounced very carefully, 'Mil–in–ga–vee.'

Jane stood alongside the doctor and, glancing up to secure his permission and then glancing down again, she perused the notebook. I could see from where I stood that there was a good deal of neat but very small script on the rice-paper page. Jane studied this for several seconds before she announced,

'*Mull Guy*,' and then to me, 'It's pronounced differently from the way it's spelled.'

'Sir Arthur Sullivan lived in Milngavie?' Alan asked.

'Apparently,' Jane said.

'I should like very much to visit the house where the composer lived,' Breitling concluded. 'We believe it is the house where he created the aria that Little Buttercup sings.'

'Oh!' Alan said. 'Bravo! That's a favourite of mine!' He said this with uncharacteristic enthusiasm. Perhaps that was my first intimation that something was amiss.

CHAPTER FIVE

For lunch, Alan had chosen a restaurant in Buchanan Street. There was a steady hum of voices, and a pall of smoke had gathered between the tables and the high ceiling. Light flowed in from a stained-glass cupola.

Alan sat to my right and Breitling to my left, while Jane completed the square, sitting on the opposite side of the table from me. Although I was further away from Jane than I wished to be, I could gaze from a distance.

When Breitling spoke about his work, the bumbling geniality with which he had first greeted us gave way to something shrewder and less accommodating. There was, I thought, a certain hardness at this man's core. Watching him articulate his well-reasoned analysis of events in Austria, and watching Jane turn his soft German into her musical and magical Scottish brogue, it occurred to me that creating art of any value requires moral purpose.

I dwelt on the loveliness of the interpreter more than the points being made by the man whose words she was interpreting. However, there was a juncture where I began to pay attention. This was when Breitling said, 'We are making remarkable progress in mending poverty, but the city's soul cannot be so easily fixed.' He appeared to be surprised by his own observation. He considered for a moment, as though absorbing a new idea. 'The buildings west of the Landstrasse were . . .' He stopped and his left hand circled up from the tablecloth as he searched for the right word. 'The *consequence* of vice . . . a consequence of the unjust way in which we organise our cities, the rich in one part and the poor in another, but in order to *marshal the forces of change*' – I had a sense that he was quoting from a political tract – 'our city fathers have pitted one group against another, the liberals against the monarchists, the Catholics against the liberals, everyone against the Jews.'

'I don't follow,' Alan said.

Neither did I.

'Our mayor is a splendid fellow,' Breitling said, 'and popular too. He understands that we want change and he is making that change. Every year, our city becomes better and our slums become fewer.'

'Sounds commendable,' Alan said.

'But to be popular, a leader must cater to the darkness just

63

as he caters to the light.' I thought Breitling was going to ignore Alan's comment; he was already speaking when Jane translated it, but he stopped and nodded to Alan. 'It *is* commendable. The change is happening, and it is positive change, but the fuel, the motive force is a kind of resentment.' He stopped again and then his eyebrows rose. 'Resentment is combustible. When you use it, even to make positive change . . . well . . . it's like putting kindling under a new house so when the dry weather comes and the wind blows, the house will burn!' Breitling chuckled. 'I am boring you . . .'

All three of us rushed to assure Breitling that we wished to hear more.

'When I travelled in the train from London, I had with me a recent copy of the *Free Press*, which I had borrowed from a very charming lady whose husband is a functionary at the Creditanstalt in Piccadilly . . .'

I found myself wondering if the word 'functionary' sounds as bad in German as it does in English, and if there was a Mrs Breitling.

'. . . I chanced upon a particularly interesting piece about the Balkans and it was all the more interesting because it made reference to your city.'

This was mystifying. 'A reference to Glasgow?' Alan asked.

Breitling nodded. 'One of the princelings that we export from northern Europe to southern Europe from time to time is here at this very moment. He is to view a new and wonderful gunboat, recently acquired by his new and still rather modest navy. It is, so the *Free Press* believes, to change the balance of forces in the Black Sea.'

'Oh!' I said, 'I've seen it! Down by the Broomielaw!'

'You've seen it?' Jane asked.

'The gunboat,' I said. 'This morning.'

Jane translated for Breitling, who said, 'This Prince Danilo is not very different from our mayor of Vienna.'

'I'm sure the mayor doesn't have any gunboats,' Alan said.

'He does not have gunboats, but he shares a passion for neatness.'

'Neatness?' Jane asked.

'He believes the Germans should be in one place, the Ruthenians in another; the Jews here and the Christians there. And the Prince who is collecting his gunboat believes that all the Bulgarians should live in one country and all the Romanians in another. The Turks, of course, he would chase away to Anatolia!'

'And this,' Alan said carefully, 'strikes you as being . . . wrong?'

Breitling shrugged and then, as if he had only just remembered his soup, he took three spoonfuls before wiping his lips and continuing. 'I am from another age. Perhaps the past, perhaps the future,' he said. 'We are separated by many things.' He put his spoon down and made an arc round the table with his open right hand, indicating each of us in succession, 'We are separated by language, by allegiance, perhaps by custom and religion, but we are photographers.'

'You can't build a nation out of photographers.' I was sceptical about efforts to understand how the world works; I had seen the world not working. I remembered how people in Cuba imagined that everything would be better when the Spanish left and even Spanish people sometimes thought that. I remembered the optimism that was felt at the prospect of doing things in a different way, the American way.

Breitling chuckled again. 'I know!' he said. 'And I believe this is a great pity. But at the same time, I believe you cannot build a nation out of Germans, or Russians, or . . . if I may say so . . . Spaniards. I believe in the' – he used a word here that caused Jane to hesitate before finding the matching English word – 'higgledy-piggledy way, where we are all thrown in together and we make do. Now, if we go along that route, we won't need so many gunboats.'

I could not grasp his point in its totality.

Nor could Alan, apparently. 'Gunboats?' he said.

'Doctor Breitling means, I think, that it requires force to build nations on the basis of language or culture or religion. Better a continent where the communities intermingle, where we have a jumble of languages and cultures and we make common cause on the basis of our common interest . . . like photographers. He believes cities should be likewise higgledy-piggledy. It is the natural order of things.'

Breitling nodded enthusiastically to indicate that this was exactly what he had meant. So, I gathered, he knew rather more English than he had let on.

Breitling was to deliver a lecture on 'Photography and the Coming Crisis'. Alan had arranged a venue, the public rooms on the second floor of the building adjoining the Hays Gallery in Sauchiehall Street. Jane was to act as interpreter, a demanding prospect which, I sensed, she looked forward to with considerable relish. The talk was almost fully subscribed. If there had been any reservations about Breitling's capacity to hold an audience, his observations on gunboats and the social order must surely have dispelled these.

Alan asked Breitling about his talk.

'Empress Sissi,' Breitling said. His conversational style was becoming familiar: he moved from key point to key point as a man might jump on stepping stones to cross a stream.

'Yes?' Alan asked, in the manner of a man more accustomed to using a footbridge.

'The fellow who murdered her . . .'

Here, Breitling spoke in an aside to Jane and she answered in an aside before turning to us and saying, 'Doctor Breitling has apologised for the infelicity of his subject. I have assured him I am not a delicate flower.'

'Oh!' I said, wishing to assure Jane that, as far as I was concerned, she was a very delicate flower indeed. But I did not elaborate, as this would have undermined the position she had taken up on her own behalf.

'The photograph of her killer, the anarchist Lucheni, appeared in newspapers all around the world. It has even been reproduced on souvenir postcards! The man has a broad smile on his face. It is my contention that this smile is important in a new kind of politics – a kind of politics that may overthrow our system of justice, even our system of morality. It is the triumph . . . of violence.'

All four of us, of course, had seen the image of Luigi

Lucheni walking between two gendarmes, his hat at a jaunty angle, his arms swinging. The policemen were taller than the assassin but looked somehow detached, somehow ineffectual. The killer was the centre of attention, and he was smiling precisely because he was the centre of attention.

'But this photograph,' I said, 'reflects what *is* rather than what we would like there to be.'

'You are right, but it is not sufficient to say that the photograph simply reflects reality. It is an instrument that shapes reality. Lucheni is a principled man and I truly wish the world were free of principled men as they bring chaos.'

For the briefest moment, Jane looked puzzled. The words made sense, but they were shocking. I was captivated by the way in which she transferred meaning between languages and at the same time assessed the concepts that were being conveyed. I could have sat opposite Jane for a hundred years and I would not have begun to exhaust the wisdom and sympathy that lay beneath her dazzling beauty.

'Because he is a principled man,' Breitling continued, 'and because he has acted in accordance with his principles, he is content. His contentment is evident in the photograph. The photograph doesn't lie but rather it records the truth and it does this absolutely. However, the photograph has been printed millions of times and it has been seen by people in every part of the world. There is no one in this restaurant who has not seen Lucheni walking towards the camera and grinning.'

I thought about Michele Angiolillo, the man who shot Prime Minister Cánovas. That was at the height of the war in Cuba – Cánovas was a great exponent of the iron hand, whether in Cuba or in Spain. Angiolillo, like Lucheni, was Italian. Briefly, I found myself wondering what it is about Italians that makes them go around killing other people's dignitaries. Angiolillo said he murdered the prime minister because Cánovas was guilty of making war on his own people.

Breitling continued to look fixedly across the table, his hands on the tablecloth on either side of the empty soup plate.

'In this way,' he said, 'the photograph becomes more than a means of documenting an event. The image of a short Italian man walking to the courthouse in Geneva becomes *a weapon*, a weapon of enormous force. I believe that other principled men who wish to improve society by means of violence – I believe they will not only allow themselves to be photographed, they will *seek out* the photographer. The image that accompanies their crime will be an important part of the crime because it will assert a claim to moral rectitude. It will testify to their satisfaction with what they propose to do, with what they have done. And this is just one aspect of the crisis – the crisis that is unfolding around us because of a technology that is simple enough and easily mass produced but the tremendous effects of which have not been yet been understood. Because surely if we had seen the moment when the Empress was stabbed, surely if that horrible image had appeared in millions of newspapers, the impact of Lucheni's principled act would have been even greater.'

He sat back.

'I photographed a corpse this morning,' I said.

Jane looked at me with an expression of the utmost astonishment and said, 'What?'

'I was wakened very early,' I said. 'A policeman – he came to the hotel and insisted I accompany him to a place on the other side of the river. There had been a murder . . .'

'But why?'

I may have looked confused.

'But why did he ask you to accompany him?'

'He had heard about my method. He believed I might be able to assist in the investigation.'

'But isn't your timer . . . isn't it being repaired?' Jane said.

Alan turned to Breitling. 'Juan has developed a remarkable photographic technique. He and Jane had quite an adventure this summer. They caught a murderer!'

Jane's earlier poise appeared to have deserted her. She translated what Alan had said and then, I surmised, what I had said.

'I told him I could not do what they thought I could do,' I said, 'but the officer insisted . . . so I went along anyway.'

'He had no right to insist.'

I was stung by the sharpness of Jane's tone and by what I took to be the implied criticism that I should not have given in.

'They will pay you, Juan. It's very unwise to turn down an invitation if it involves payment.' Alan said this in a way that was intended to be jocular. Yet it sounded rather crass.

Jane had stopped interpreting.

'In any case,' Alan continued after an awkward pause, turning to Breitling, 'I wondered if we might discuss the other proposal that I wrote to you about?'

Jane translated.

Breitling's expression became suddenly and quite explicitly remote. 'I would rather not speak about this now,' he said.

I remembered the way Benjamin Jackson had looked at me when it had become clear that I could expect no further cooperation from him or his firm. That was the way Breitling looked at Alan now.

The atmosphere around the table cooled.

Later, when I had a moment alone with Jane as we left the restaurant, I said, 'What on earth happened? Breitling cut your uncle.'

She looked at me unhappily. 'I don't know. My uncle's affairs are somewhat complicated.'

I left the three of them outside the restaurant. I had to develop the photographs I had taken in the morning. Jane still seemed irritated by that.

CHAPTER SIX

If you stay in a hotel long enough, there is a point where members of staff begin to treat you as a colleague rather than a customer. I had taken a room at the end of June and it was now the end of August. For three weeks or so I had been on good terms with two of the reception staff. Archie was generally there in the afternoons, and Bessie sometimes worked just for the afternoon and sometimes for the whole day. It was because I had become friendly with them that I had a key to a room, hardly bigger than a cupboard, at the end of a corridor leading from behind the reception desk. It was an ideal space in which to develop photographs. There was a sink and even an air vent that drew off some of the fumes that can make working in a darkroom unpleasant. As the arrangement was informal, I was obliged to bring my equipment down from my room, along with some of the necessary fluids, though I did store two large ewers of potassium and sodium under the table next to the sink, along with two developing basins. And as I had not officially rented the space, I might be disturbed at any moment and obliged to explain myself.

Long ago, in a Madrid apartment that was sparsely furnished and often rather cold, my father first showed me how places and people could be made to appear, as if by magic, on a piece of paper placed in developing fluid. Since that first time, I have always watched this process as though watching the creation of a world. This is what I did as I developed the images from the murder scene.

I worked in the same order in which I had taken them. The first showed the room from the doorway. I had been concerned that the natural light, that was just at that point beginning to establish itself in the back court, would disturb the settled dimness of the interior, which was illuminated but not distorted by the magnesium flash. This had not happened, at least not to a great extent. There was at the very edges, the top corners, a slightly excessive brightness, which made the furthest points, where the wallpaper touched the ceiling in the two faraway corners of the room, fractionally opaque. This was the only blemish in an otherwise complete record of the forms and figures in the room. In keeping with the nature of photography – at least *this* kind of photography – the most prominent figure in the image was not the dead body at the end of the bed; from here it was not entirely visible, just the head and shoulders and part of the chest, with a portion of the handle of the kitchen knife. The bed itself was the main figure. It was as though everything else in the room was oriented towards it. And this struck me as natural. The image showed a dwelling of the most primitive kind, a one-room shed situated among a jumble of huts used for the most prosaic of daily activities, including laundry and refuse disposal and the bodily functions of a hundred families. It had been turned into a place of shelter, and the stove and the bed and the table reflected the primitive nature of this space. I noticed that the wallpaper behind the stove was not peeling as the heat from the pipe must have created an area free of damp.

The second photograph showed the side of the room with the table, and the third showed the side with the stove. When I looked at the third picture, emerging in the tin tray, shade by shade beneath the surface of the developing fluid, it wasn't the stove that attracted my attention but the sideboard between it and the door. Again it struck me as being conspicuously out of place in this miserable shelter. It was elegant as well as substantial, with a grand, curvilinear backboard that rose behind the main piece and above the flat surface where I had stood with my camera and tripod. The sideboard made the wall behind it appear even more desolate and dirty. I wondered what the police might have found inside it.

From the top of the sideboard, the bed looked lower and shorter, and the cadaver in this image was a more natural centre of attention. It was possible to see the startled look on the murdered policeman's face, and the knife, of course. The light from the door had caused the buttons on the waistcoat to gleam, and at the very furthest point of the camera's reach, there was a gleam too on the tip of the dead man's right shoe.

The perspective from the bed was less precipitate but every bit as odd. There was a mat at the doorway, extending unevenly across the edges where the linoleum curled up to trip the unwary. Above the door, the mirror, which was fixed at an angle, with the top part several inches out from the wall, appeared smaller. The sideboard, however, remained distinct and at odds with the rest of the room. There were four doors in the bottom part, below three drawers. One of the doors was open.

The floor-level photograph, the last in the sequence, was the most disturbing. Nothing was as it would have appeared from a more conventional angle, and this applied first and foremost to the cadaver. The startled policeman was going bald. From ground level, his emerging tonsure could be clearly seen. He had a paunch. Despite the blood loss and the general subsidence of tissue that occurs before the onset of rigor mortis, the handle of the kitchen knife was set against the curve of his stomach. The polished shoe on the left foot was visible in this picture, though the shoe on the right foot was obscured by the right knee.

I wondered again what was in the envelope that Smith had pocketed after I spotted it under the bed, just as I wondered what might have been found in the out-of-place sideboard.

Using the adjustable steel clips I had brought with me for this purpose, I hung the pictures on a metal wire over the sink that connected two wooden frames designed to hold dishes. Then I rinsed the developing trays, extinguished the blue light and opened the door.

To my considerable surprise, a man was standing in the corridor facing me, his fist raised.

I took a step back and nearly fell over. I grabbed hold of the sink. I was in darkness; the man was in daylight. As he lowered his fist, I recognised him.

'Mr Cameron,' he said, 'I was about to knock but' – he chuckled – 'you beat me to it.'

I gathered that his fist had not been raised with violent intent.

His name was Bannerman and he was the manager of the hotel.

'I have just been informed that you are using these premises . . . for your business,' he said. 'I cannot have that, Mr Cameron.'

I stepped into the corridor. Bannerman was the same height as me, middle-aged, trim, moustachioed, with rather long, thick black hair that was brushed back and kept in place with pomade. He wore a slightly threadbare three-piece suit.

'I have only developed a handful of photographs,' I said. 'The room, the cupboard is ideal as it has a sink and it's dark and it didn't seem to be used for anything else . . .'

I added a number of other details with the object of minimising the extent of my use of the room. I was keen to ensure that Bessie and Archie didn't get into trouble on my account. As I spoke, I grasped from Bannerman's expression that there might be a commercial route to resolving the issue. He was willing to be as accommodating as his employees, but a certain amount of cash would have to be exchanged. As soon as he had assured me that no one would be disciplined for allowing my irregular use of the hotel's facilities, I handed over a pound.

The pictures had time to dry during this exchange, so when Bannerman returned to the front of the hotel I went back inside, took them down from the wire and carried them upstairs.

I did not have time to study them with the rigorous application of a grid analysis and written notes. I intended to do that when I returned from the theatre.

CHAPTER SEVEN

I think the theatres I remember in Granada when I was five or six years old were not quite theatres; they were cafes where performances by singers and actors brought in a crowd. I remember the reds and blues and yellows and golds. I remember how satin and crepe de chine look under a flickering taper light and how the painted backdrop of a castle perched on a promontory by a woodland lake can seem utterly real when the actors standing in front of it begin to lure the audience into a long-ago tale.

When the lights dimmed in the Theatre Royal, I was taken back into my childhood. Jane and I sat behind Breitling, Alan and Mary – Alan's wife – in a box in the dress circle.

The evening began with an overture and moved on to a series of recitations, some comic, some tragic. The second half comprised an operetta about a jilted bride who sues the groom for breach of promise and falls in love with the judge.

As the orchestra struck up the first bars of the overture I looked down at the fingers of my gloves and it occurred to me that the white fabric, almost luminous in the near pitch-dark had a ghostly appearance. I raised my hands from my lap, palms down and it was as though two spectres climbed through the darkness. I felt Jane's elbow on mine, and I allowed the two spectres to settle on my lap again. The overture began with a dramatic motif in the Japanese style before moving on to something effortlessly lyrical and lovely. It was the loveliness, I have no doubt, that caused me to raise my hands again and, immediately, as I had anticipated, Jane's elbow made contact with mine in a gesture of restraint, but this time, I allowed one of the spectres to drop by my side and hover towards what I felt sure would be a hand waiting in a spirit of affection rather than restraint, and I was not disappointed.

I felt Jane's fingers grasp mine, our skin separated by the twin membranes of opera gloves just as we were separated by inches of darkness. Our hands clasped as the music meandered up from the orchestra pit and across the stalls beneath the great chandelier, settling on the balustrade before tumbling in among us.

The moment lasted no more than a second or two, yet it was like a star in the night sky, bright, immutable and seared into my thoughts in a way that I believed must surely be for ever.

It was shattered by Breitling, who turned and whispered in German. Jane leaned forward and let go of my hand. After a few seconds she translated for Alan's benefit. I did not hear what it was that Breitling had suddenly had to communicate but the intrusion was absolute, and it was repeated several times during the first and second parts of the evening's performance, ensuring that the moment of intimacy we had enjoyed was not repeated.

The music moved by turns from lyrical to comical to sentimental before reverting to the full-throated grandiosity of the oriental opening. My thoughts, too, meandered. I remembered my father's body on the cobblestones, the blood on his shirt.

The overtures were followed by a series of ensemble recitations that covered the whole gamut, from nonsense rhymes to epic verse. In one – a long and lively piece about a house party at which an expensive necklace goes missing and turns up variously in the possession of each of the five principals – the actors appeared in different parts of the theatre among the audience. The woman who played the dowager matron of the country house exited the stage and after just a few seconds burst in upon the box next to ours, garnering a wave of delighted applause from the audience.

'How did she do that?' Jane whispered. I remember the sensation of her breath on my ear. I wanted to kiss her.

During the break, Alan took Jane and Breitling off to meet Mr Cavendish, the manager of the Hays Gallery, where Breitling's talk was to be given.

Alan was not on form. I had the impression that Breitling

was turning out to be a somewhat onerous guest – or perhaps Alan was turning out to be an erratic host.

I watched them walk away. Jane wore a turquoise evening gown with a high collar. The dress was a kind of brocade, and there were sequins above the waist and on the shoulders. Her hair had been raised to the top of her head to make a sort of exuberant bouquet, with wisps coming down on all sides. And she wore diamond earrings that sparkled in the soft lobby light. For one moment, I thought this beauty might prove to be beyond me, to be elusive.

'You are very glum, Juan,' Mary said.

I liked Mary Fletcher. I admired her fortitude. I was surprised that she spoke so directly: she was usually reticent, perhaps as a shield against her husband's irresponsibility. Alan was charming, but I couldn't imagine him as anything other than a terrible mate, and that was before taking into consideration what I knew of his marital and financial improprieties.

'The music,' I said. 'It was very lovely, very thought-provoking.'

She looked at me with a sceptical expression. Her eyebrows rose. 'Alan told me that you were asked to take more photographs for the police. Is that what's bothering you?'

'Yes,' I said, perhaps a little too emphatically, 'that has been preying on my mind.'

I wasn't inclined to speak to Mary about William Collins and the new difficulties regarding my father's photographs. It was a complicated subject that touched upon my innermost thoughts.

Mary, however, appeared to have reached her own rather misplaced conclusion. 'Oh, Juan!' she said. 'I hope you are not a flighty sort of young man. Jane is dear to me. I would not have her heart broken.'

I opened my mouth to reply, though I do not know what I would have said. However, I had no opportunity to find out, because Mary smiled, looking over my shoulder, and said, 'Look, they're back again!'

All three were rather earnest. Jane was speaking to Breitling; Alan walked behind them, deep in thought apparently, gazing down at the plush red carpet.

'How was Mr Cavendish?' Mary asked.

'Very well,' Jane said brightly. She sat beside me, and Alan and Breitling resumed their seats on either side of Mary. 'We met his brother-in-law, Mr McElroy,' Jane added. 'He's at Simpson-Burley . . . the paint maker.'

Jane, I gathered, was substituting for Alan, who wasn't inclined to speak. He stared at his programme as though it were suddenly very interesting. The lights went down.

During the second part of the performance, the operetta about a girl who is jilted by her feckless lover, Jane and I did not hold hands. Whatever had transpired in the interval had punctured the mood. After the final curtain had come down, we stayed a little way behind as Mary, Alan and Breitling moved to the top of the stairs.

'What happened?' I asked. 'Alan is out of sorts.'

She shook her head. 'Oh, I expect he's tired. We have been chasing around all day, introducing Doctor Breitling.'

'Is everything all right?'

Jane hesitated. When she spoke, I knew that she had chosen not to take me into her confidence.

'But you look a little worried too,' she said, ignoring my question.

I resolved to be candid. 'I had some news today. William Collins have received a letter from a woman I do not know, claiming that my father's book is not his own work, claiming that it is the work of someone else – this woman's late husband.'

Jane waited.

'The woman lives in Leith. Jackson – the editor – told me that much. The letter came from her solicitor in Edinburgh. I have the address. I have written to the lawyer. I will travel through to Edinburgh and endeavour to clear the matter up.'

'A woman who lives in Leith?'

'Well, Leith by way of Cuba. She is travelling to Spain.'

'You knew her in Cuba? Your father knew her?'

'No! I have never met this person! I know nothing of her!' I may have asserted this lack of connection with almost too much emphasis. 'Collins have withdrawn their offer to publish the book,' I said, more calmly.

The magnitude of this could not be disguised. Collins would surely not have made such a decision if there had not been something plausible in Señora LaGuardia's allegation.

'What will you do?'

'I will investigate. I will do everything in my power to clear the matter up.'

Alan reappeared at the top of the stairs and called over.

'Jane, are you coming?'

I had never seen him behave so brusquely.

'I have to go,' Jane said. She looked at me with sudden tenderness and I was filled with a desire to hold her in my arms and reassure her that, whatever difficulties we might face, we would surely overcome them together.

But she had already started to move away.

A sergeant, his helmet held like a football under one arm, stood at the bottom of the stairs to the upper circle. I had noticed two constables in the main foyer, and there were several on the steps at the front of the theatre.

'They are preparing for Friday evening,' Jane said.

'Friday evening?'

'A gala for the Prince, the one who's here to see his gunboat.'

CHAPTER EIGHT

'*Buenas tardes*, Señor Camarón,' Archie said as he handed me my key. '*¿Qué tal?*'

'*Muy bien, gracias.*'

'*¿Y el espectáculo?*'

Archie enjoyed dabbling in Spanish. I gathered a dictionary had been consulted.

'*Era maravillosa,*' I said. '*Y has estado estudiando, evidentemente.*'

He gave me a look of disappointed blankness. 'I just got as far as the word for "concert",' he said.

'You pronounced it perfectly.'

'*Usted es amablemente.*'

'I hope there was no trouble today, after I spoke to Mr Bannerman . . .'

'None at all.' Archie looked quickly from side to side and then whispered, 'You spoke a language that Mr Bannerman understands.' He rubbed his index and middle finger against his thumb to indicate money. Then he handed me my key.

'*Hasta mañana.*'

In my room, I laid the photographs I had taken that morning on the desk by the window beside my notebook. Then I opened a cardboard folder in which I kept papers the size of photographic plates, with windows cut out in different sections of each paper. When the paper was placed over a photograph, the exposed area could be analysed and annotated, without distraction from the bigger picture. This was a technique I had developed for serial photography, to study and compare multiple photographs of the same scene taken at forty-five-minute intervals over nine or ten hours. The present case was different. I had six photographs of the same scene, all taken at about the same time but from a different angle. I proposed to study each section of each photograph in minute detail. Nothing in any of the images would be left unrecorded.

This work is painstaking, although it is anything but tedious. Through close analysis, all manner of things come to light. The photographs reveal themselves in their almost infinite complexity. There really is much more to an image than initially meets the eye.

It was just after ten when I began work, and well after midnight when I finished. Two things floated to the surface from the great mass of information in the photographs, two things that might have been missed in a routine inspection of the room but which were revealed in the systematic scrutiny that close analysis of a fixed image makes possible.

When I worked my way across the six discrete sections of the photograph taken from the bed, looking towards the door from an elevated position, my attention was drawn to the mirror. It was fixed at an angle, so that someone standing in the middle of the room could look up and see their own reflection, the sort of mirror that is found sometimes above a bar, allowing the barman to have a view of the whole room. In fact, the mirror in the murder room may have begun life in a bar, because it bore the name and the familiar lettering of a French brandy. Perhaps a mirror lower down on the wall would have been more functional, but in a room filled with second-hand furniture, the mirror above the door was not entirely surprising. I noted the elements of the room that were captured in the mirror's reflection; the floor as far as the bed, part of the sideboard and the stove and, opposite them, the table. If I had not been standing on the bed when I took the photograph, the mirror would have reflected more. I wondered what could be seen in the mirror from the corner of the room, where the body was found.

The other thing that came to the surface appeared not just in one picture but in three. In the lower right sixth of the picture taken from the doorway, I made a note of the configuration created by the end of the bed and the corner of the room. In the picture taken opposite the stove and the sideboard, I made a note of the angle at which the chair was placed between these two pieces of furniture. It did not quite fit the space. Because of this, one corner of the chair jutted out into the corner of the room. The back of the chair was wedged against the side of the stove. And in the picture taken from the bed, the back of the door was visible. I noted that there was no clothes hook, not even a nail.

These things tugged at my thoughts after I had finally put down my pen, dimmed the lamp, undressed and got into bed.

Smith arrived at the hotel at eight o'clock the next morning. I was already in the dining room. When he was shown in, I asked if he would care to have tea. He declined.

I had just finished breakfast. I passed an envelope over the top of the teapot. 'The photographs,' I said, 'and my notes.'

He emptied the contents of the envelope onto the tablecloth and glanced at the notes. 'What have you found?'

'Sometimes, it's not easy to say what has been found. Even when it has been found it may not be apparent.'

He gave me an irritated look.

I indicated the notes. 'Several things are listed there. I have highlighted two.'

He continued to look at me, ignoring the notes. My dislike for the man grew with each minute I was obliged to be in his company. I resolved to get this interview over quickly.

'The body was found with the head facing upward and pointing towards the door,' I said. He nodded. 'This would suggest that the victim was facing away from the door when he was killed. He was stabbed, he fell backward; his head was facing up and the body was pointing towards the door. That indicates that his killer had his back to the wall, standing in the space at the end of the bed.'

'Yes?'

'Do you carry a knife?'

Smith looked at me with a combination of distaste and incredulity. 'That's none of your—'

I raised a hand and said, 'A knife can be carried in different ways and the key issue in some cases – I am guessing this – is to have it in a place from which it can be taken quickly and easily. I suppose there are several options. I imagine in the belt of your trousers, perhaps a trouser pocket at the back.' I reached behind my back as though for an imaginary knife.

'What on earth has this to do with—?'

'It may have no bearing at all on what happened, but if the killer was facing his victim and was able to look up and see what was reflected in the mirror, and if his victim had reached, for example, behind his back then the killer would have been able to see—'

'What mirror?'

'The mirror above the door. It reflects the whole room.'

Smith simply stared at me. Then he said, 'What's the other thing – you said there were two things.'

'Look at this picture.' I reached around the teapot and lifted the image of the sideboard and the stove and laid it on the top of the other pictures. 'Look at the chair.'

He looked quite carefully at the picture.

'Do you see anything unusual?'

He continued to study the picture.

'It doesn't fit,' I said.

He looked up. His expression of irritation was mixed with something else now. Curiosity perhaps.

'The chair doesn't fit,' I said, 'and the back of the chair is wedged against the stove.'

'Mr Cameron, if you have a point, you would oblige me by getting to it.'

I noticed an odd thing: as he became more officious, Smith became more English.

'It's wedged against the stove, which means that if I were staying in this room and I wanted to undress and put my clothes on the chair, I would not be able to hang my jacket over the back, which would be the natural place to put a jacket in a room like this.'

'The back of the door?'

I shook my head. 'There's no hook. I quickly showed him the photograph of the door and then I showed him the picture taken *from* the door.

'The chair doesn't fit next to the stove, but it would fit very neatly in the space at the end of the bed. The way the room is laid out now is not right.'

He shook his head and looked at me as though he was now quite certain that enlisting my assistance – no doubt done with reluctance – had been a waste of time.

He stood up and put the photographs and the notes into the envelope.

'May I keep these?'

I shrugged.

'Then, I would like to thank you, Señor Camarón, for your cooperation . . . and I will wish you good morning.'

I began to get up. I had intended to shake hands. To my astonishment, and considerable indignation, Smith turned and walked away before I could do so.

I sank back into my seat and looked down at the crumbs on my empty plate. My fists were clenched. I very much wanted to use them – and with force.

It was a short walk from the hotel to the tobacconist. After I had bought a shilling's worth of Farmer's, I decided to continue walking. I was angry over Smith's behaviour, and angry with my supine response. I tried not to think about him, but his image recurred. I saw him at the breakfast table insolently quizzing me.

I was standing at a junction waiting to cross when a cab moved slowly towards me. Even before I had decided what I was going to do, my arm rose, as if of its own accord, and I waved to the driver. I gave the address that Smith had given when he took me to the murder scene.

I knew there was a deeper cause to my agitation. I was angry at Smith because I was angry at Benjamin Jackson, and perhaps I was angry at Jackson because he was the latest connection to a place and a time from which, it seemed, I could never escape. Perhaps it wasn't anger. Perhaps it was fear. In order to resolve the matter of my father's book, I was seeking an interview with a woman who had libelled me.

The cab stopped. I climbed down.

There was no policeman at the close, no crowd of curious onlookers. I moved quickly to the back court. The gate had been closed. When I opened it, stepped through and closed it again, the wood shuddered and screeched as it scraped the ground.

I wanted to see inside the shed again. I had given the matter no more thought than this. I was curious about the mirror. I was curious, too, about the chair, and about what might have been inside the sideboard.

The door was closed. I knocked and the sound carried across the morning. I looked up and around. I felt quite certain I was being watched. A man had been murdered here.

I knocked again, then I reached down and turned the handle. The door opened. When I looked inside, I was taken by surprise: the shed had been almost emptied.

Without a bed or a table or a sideboard, it looked twice as large. The only deviation from the regular line of brick and plaster was the stove pipe. I walked over to the corner where the body had been. The blood on the floor had been washed away, though there was a discoloration on the curled linoleum, a brownish tint on the dull surface.

I stood in the corner and looked up at the mirror.

It was possible to see the whole room. If someone had been standing facing me, I could have seen him from behind.

I turned round and faced the wall, imagining that I was the victim, facing my assailant. Perhaps I was angry. Perhaps I was afraid. What happened then? Why did my assailant suddenly plunge a kitchen knife into my chest?

My thoughts were interrupted.

'What are you doing?'

I spun round.

The man in the doorway wore a white shirt of indeterminate cleanliness, a black waistcoat and black trousers that were caked in dust. His shoes were muddy and his moustache was stained with tobacco. He looked at me with an expression of incipient disapproval, but I sensed that he would prefer to be reassured rather than challenged.

'I was here yesterday,' I said.

This really conveyed nothing that would explain my presence today. In fact, it might have placed me at the scene during the crime. The man, however, seemed to relax.

'I took photographs,' I said.

He nodded. 'You're police.'

'I was with the police, but I'm not a policeman.'

He jerked his head to indicate the whole room, 'What is it you want?'

'I left something here, but I think it's gone.'

'They took everything away,' the man said. 'They'll be getting a new tenant. I expect he'll bring his own things.'

'But who took everything? Who cleared the place?'

'The shirt makers.' He jerked his head towards the corner of the back court where the union premises were. 'You'd best ask them.'

'I'll do that,' I said. I began to walk back towards the door, while the man, apparently satisfied, crossed the courtyard to an entrance next to the one I had used.

Outside the shed, I picked up a tin pail next to a mop that was drying against the wall. There were still suds at the bottom, clearly the pail had been used very recently, perhaps to clean the blood from the linoleum. I glanced around and went quickly back into the room.

I had my own theory about why the chair had been next to the stove instead of in the space at the bottom of the bed. I placed the pail upside down and stood on top of it and reached up so that my fingers touched the rim of the bracket holding the vent towards the top of the stovepipe. The rim was convex, about three inches broad. I had to stand on tiptoe in order to run my fingers around the inside. When I did so, I touched a piece of paper. I had to stretch even more to get my index finger under the edge of the paper to prise it out of the rim. Instead of moving up and out, however, the paper simply adhered to the inside, and because of the angle of my outstretched hand, all I was able to do was press it against the surface of the rim.

I heard footsteps.

I tried to scoop up the paper again, but it was firmly stuck. I couldn't stretch any further, so, instead of trying to lift it, I wagged my finger to create a little breath of air. Rather to my surprise, this worked. The paper detached itself from the surface. I tapped the edge and it moved along the side until the corner peeped over the rim and I caught it between my fingers, and lifted it down.

I put it in my pocket and stepped onto the floor as a woman outside screamed.

'Who's ran aff wae ma pail?'

I carried the pail outside. The girl was no more than fifteen or sixteen. When she saw the pail, she stepped back uncertainly, snatching up her mop and holding it, I thought, like a soldier might hold his rifle when the bayonet is fixed.

'My apologies,' I said.

I put the pail down beside the wall of the shed and quickly withdrew.

The main door of the Amalgamated Shirt Makers Friendly Society resembled that of a saloon bar. There were cursive brass handles in front of frosted glass, with the name of the association written in ornate lettering across the glass. I pushed one of the doors open and stepped into a large public room. On one side was a reading frame where a few men were perusing the day's newspapers; more men sat around a large table on the other side, the surface of the table cluttered with books and paper.

One of the men stood up from the table and came towards me. He wore a grey suit and a shirt with a starched collar and a dark tie. He was short and thin and the silver of his watch fob, stretching across his waistcoat, gleamed in the way that watch fobs do when they are the subject of habitual, absent-minded polishing.

'Can I help you?'

'I am a photographer,' I said.

He looked at me with an expression that was well-disposed and apprehensive at the same time.

'I came yesterday to make pictures of the . . . scene . . .' I pointed in the general direction of the back court. Some of the men were looking up. '. . . where the man was killed.'

'Yes?' I noticed that his beard, which covered his face right up to his cheekbones, was grey in the lower part but darkish red above the line of the mouth. The overall effect was that of a mask.

'I understand the furniture has been removed by this association?'

'What is this to you?' Polite but pointed.

To my own surprise, I sighed. Perhaps because I did not know the answer to his question.

'I took pictures,' I said at last, 'and afterwards I studied them, and I noticed that one of the pieces of furniture rather stood out—'

I stopped speaking because a man who had been standing with his back to us reading a newspaper now approached and said, 'You are the one who took the photographs in Crown Street.'

I acknowledged that I was.

He spoke to the man with the beard. 'He helped to catch that . . . that lost soul . . .'

There was a pause, and then the man with the beard said, 'You had better come through.'

I followed him across the room and along a corridor to a

small office at the back of the building.

He took his seat on the other side of an empty desk. 'It was a terrible thing,' he said, pointing to a chair opposite.

It was the same chair that I had seen in the shed the previous day, wedged up against the stove.

'Tell me, how is it that your photographs solve crimes?'

I raised my hands to indicate bafflement. 'I do not honestly know. And in this case, the images I made were different from my serial photographs.' I wondered whether it was indiscreet to speak freely, but I saw nothing to be gained from circumspection. 'In Crown Street, I photographed the street many times, always from the same position. I looked for patterns – the same people, the same situations, the same traffic and so on. One figure stood out.'

'I see,' he said.

I didn't see how he could see, but we had established a rapport of sorts, so I said, 'The sideboard that was in the shed . . . when I studied the photographs it occurred to me that this was a rather fine piece of furniture. I wondered how it had come to be in this rudimentary dwelling. The man who was in the courtyard just now – perhaps he is the caretaker? – he said that you had taken away all the furniture . . . or rather' – I waved my hand to indicate the office we were in – 'the shirt makers took away the furniture.'

'But you're not a policeman. Why are you making these enquiries?'

'I'm not a policeman,' I admitted. 'But I'm curious. After I studied the photographs I came back to have a second look at the room.' I took my name card from the inside pocket of my jacket and presented it to him.

'Mr Ca . . . marón . . .' he said.

'I am from Spain, by way of Cuba.'

His eyebrows rose.

'And you are?'

'My name is Knox, Arthur Knox. I am the convener of our West of Scotland chapter.'

He looked at my card again and then placed it on the desk in front of him.

'It was terrible, what happened over there.' He nodded towards the shed.

The curtains in the little office had been opened, and from where I sat, I could see the chimney on the roof of the shed.

'We had rented the premises,' he said. 'It's part of our lease. It was sublet and I expect we will sublet it again. We had the furniture removed because . . . well . . . I suppose there's a sense . . . a need to make a clean break.'

This seemed sensible to me.

'But why are you so interested in the sideboard?' he asked.

'Because . . . in a sense . . . it disturbed the pattern of the room. It has been my experience that when a pattern is disturbed, there may be reason to take a closer look.'

'But why?'

I could not answer this easily, so I said, 'I have no idea.' Then continued, 'The man who was murdered was a policeman.'

Knox sat forward in his chair; his eyebrows rose and some of the colour drained from his face. 'Mr Cama . . . arón' – even in the midst of what appeared to me to be genuine dismay, he made a courteous effort to pronounce my name in the Spanish way – 'I did not know that.'

'But you leased the room. What has happened to the tenant?'

He sat back in his chair and thought for a moment before speaking. 'He has been travelling,' he said. 'We believe the place . . . Well, it has grim associations so he will not wish to return to it.'

'Then why were the men in his lodgings, I mean the policeman and the man who killed him?'

Knox shook his head, and then, looking through the window, he said, 'Is that the man who told you to enquire here?'

I looked out and saw the man who had spoken to me in the shed. I nodded.

Knox got up quickly and rapped his knuckles on the window. Then he opened the door and stepped out and said, 'Charlie, where did we sell the furniture?'

I couldn't hear the reply so I followed Knox out into the back court.

'Some of it has gone,' Knox told me. 'Some of it is waiting to be taken away.' He pointed to the carriage entrance.

I could see the edge of the sideboard.

He hesitated and then he said, 'Mr Camarón, our members come and go. If you wish to know more about our work, our evening meetings are from seven until ten.'

I followed Charlie across the back court. He was pushing a

wheelbarrow. When we were almost at the carriage entrance, he turned off the slated path and moved forward quickly so that he had enough momentum to push the barrow up a wooden plank and tip its contents into a container that protruded from a brick shed. There was a cloud of debris and the smell of refuse wafted through the air.

I carried on towards the carriage entrance. Just as it had looked out of place in the shed, the sideboard looked out of place now. It sat next to the door of an apartment. Opposite the apartment was a double door. One of the doors was open and I saw a flight of stairs inside.

I placed my hand on the sideboard and felt the polished mahogany. I opened the drawers one after the other. Empty, of course. I put my hand inside and felt towards the back. No false bottoms, no hidden compartments. I bent down and opened the first set of doors and peered inside. Two shelves, entirely bare. I opened the second set of doors and repeated the inspection. There were three shelves here, likewise empty. I looked on the insides of the doors to see if a packet or an envelope could have been secreted in some way, but the wood was clean. I stood up and stepped back. In the photograph, the door at the end on the left had been ajar.

I was quite suddenly assailed by a sense of hopelessness. I had stumbled on the notion that photographs can offer a new path to knowledge. But it was only a notion. I had been lucky with serial photography. Now I was rooting about in an amateurish manner. To imagine that the half-open door of a sideboard might have some significance was surely a very desperate way of endeavouring to understand the world.

I strolled back into the courtyard and watched Charlie reverse his wheelbarrow down the plank. He did this with remarkable skill. We imagine that surgeons are skilful, and musicians who have mastered their instruments, and artists too, but we don't accord much notice to the skill of working men. Perhaps I considered this because I had just come from the premises of the shirt makers. The atmosphere there reminded me of something, and I realised now what it was. At the university in Granada there was an association of students dedicated to the proposition that in order to change Spain, the peasants must liberate themselves. They could not be set free by others, because then they would be dependent on their liberators just as now they were dependent on the landowners. It was a rather circular argument, but I thought now of the study room at the shirt makers'; working men reading and writing, taking control of their world.

Perhaps I entered this reverie because I did not know what I was doing in this courtyard. I had come here for no more reason than indignation. I was angry with Captain Smith for treating me with insufficient respect.

I had wandered towards Knox's office. I turned to go back, and as I did so, I heard the sound of one of the sideboard doors being opened. When I reached the entrance to the carriageway, I caught a man doing exactly what I had been doing just a few seconds earlier, examining the sideboard to see if anything was still inside.

He had a round face, with eyes that may have been bloodshot, and his chin had not been shaved for several days. His body, like his face, was large – very large. When he stood up he assumed the posture and demeanour of one of those beasts described by explorers in the heart of Africa: a gorilla. He wore a black suit and a bowler hat.

I cannot say that the man was startled. He looked up at me and his expression was one of irritation, or perhaps disdain. He turned on his heel and walked through the double doors that led to the stairs.

When I stepped after him, I saw a pair of scuffed black shoes halfway up the first flight.

'Wait!' I shouted.

My voice echoed in the stairway, along with the sound of the gorilla moving quickly up the stone steps. I began to give chase. I did not consider the wisdom or the usefulness of this. I was driven by little more than a kind of primeval instinct.

As we climbed, the stairs became easier to see – the light from the cupola became stronger as we moved closer to it. The gorilla was fit, a decade older than me, but perhaps he was accustomed to flight. I was winded when I reached the top landing. He had climbed onto a coalbunker between two apartment entrances and pulled himself through an opening in the roof. I caught my breath, then I jumped onto the bunker and reached up to get a purchase so that I could pull myself through the opening. As I did this, I realised that the man I was chasing could stamp on my fingers or bring the trapdoor down. I imagined fingers amputated cleanly by a heavy metal frame.

But he was still in full flight. And for my part, the very fact that he had fled made me the more determined to speak to him.

I made a supreme effort and got myself onto the roof, covering my waistcoat and the lapels of my jacket in green slime from the moss that had congealed on the slate around the opening.

Once on my feet, I had the satisfaction of seeing the bowler hat fly off as the man raced away from me. When he reached the edge, he stopped and turned, and, almost as though he were doing this in the exaggerated manner of a villain on a music-hall stage, he drew a knife.

I remembered the corpse.

I remembered the blade, through the waistcoat between the third and fourth rib. Three storeys below and just a few yards away.

I marvelled at my recklessness and my stupidity.

I hadn't followed him here. He had lured me.

I stopped and stood still. He took a step towards me, holding the knife, it seemed to me, with the familiarity of a man accustomed to using it as a weapon.

I do not know why, but I glanced across the skyline, and in a moment of bizarre joy I absorbed the beauty of red and green and grey tiles reflecting sunlight, row upon row.

And having done this, I continued on a course that was

impulsive and unreasonable. I charged at the man with the knife.

When I was studying in Granada, I learned from a venerable old Jesuit some elements of the oriental art of judo. The first and most important rule is to make use of the opponent's weight and momentum – to his disadvantage.

In my furious dash towards the knife-wielding gorilla, I dispensed with this first rule.

My opponent displayed no such lapse. At the final moment, as I endeavoured to fell him with a body blow, circumventing the hand that held the knife, he stood to one side and pushed me on the same trajectory I had foolishly begun. I moved forward with a momentum beyond my own control, past my assailant and over the edge of the roof.

I saw the whole of the back court. I heard a woman scream. My senses jostled one another as though I were in the midst of a seizure. I felt the cool air and I felt my muscles contract as they sought to arrest my forward, and downward, motion. I saw the blue sky, and the rooftops again, but now from a different angle. I felt the very force of gravity, and in a peculiar and entirely unfamiliar way I found myself preparing to encounter the earth at an unnatural velocity. And finally, I felt a sharp pain in my palms and fingers. I felt this pain before I understood it. My body acted to protect itself before my brain had settled on a means of doing so.

I caught hold of the gutter that ran along the roof. It was a physical manoeuvre that I could not have executed if I had thought about it. But once I was holding onto the gutter, I knew not to let go. I held on for a full minute. In the first thirty seconds, I heard my assailant running away. In the next thirty seconds, I heard someone coming in the opposite direction.

'What in the devil's name are you doing!' It was an exclamation, not a question.

I was unable to look up, but I recognised the voice. I felt a hand take hold of the lapels of my jacket.

Just as I would not have had the presence of mind to catch hold of the gutter, so I did not have the mental acuity to assist in my own rescue, other than to allow my rescuer to seize my jacket and manhandle me onto the roof. I rolled over on my back and looked up.

Captain Smith was looking down at me.

I felt my blood boil. I would not have chosen him as my saviour.

'There was a man,' I said, 'with a bowler hat.'

I lifted my shoulders and glanced across the roof. 'He must have passed you on the stairs.'

'What on earth were you doing?'

'I was following him. He was tampering with the furniture in the carriageway.' Even as I uttered these words, I grasped that they were wholly inadequate.

I got up on one knee and felt Smith lift me to my feet.

'I came here,' I said, 'because there were details in the photographs, which I drew to your attention this morning, that intrigued me. I was curious.'

'But this is a police investigation!' he said. 'You're not

authorised to——'

I waved my hand. 'I understand the nature of an investigation.'

'I'm not sure that you do.'

Downstairs the sideboard and the remaining furniture had been taken away. I proposed that we go together and speak to Mr Knox at the shirt makers' union. He might know who my assailant was.

Smith reminded me that I was not a policeman. In his insufferably patronising way he insisted that I return to my hotel and recover from my 'excitement'. He flagged down a cab and ushered me into it. Then he called up the address to the driver and stood by the side of the road as I was taken away. My humiliation was acute.

After a few moments, as I recovered a measure of calm, I reached into the pocket of my jacket and took out the paper that had been hidden in the stovepipe. As I did this, the cab swayed abruptly and I was pushed up against the door. Perhaps I was still in the throes of my 'excitement' as my muscles tensed, and my arm shot out to the side of the cab. When I opened my palm to place it flatly against the fabric on the inside of the door and steady myself, the paper dropped to the floor.

It didn't stay there. The cab righted itself and the paper floated away from me. I lunged forward to catch it, but there was a breath of air – we had picked up speed and the window was open. The paper slipped from beneath my fingertips. I reached out with my other hand, and, just as the paper rose and moved towards the open window, I stopped it in its path.

I closed my fingers over it as if it were a butterfly, ready to escape if given another chance. When I was sufficiently composed, I read what was written: *Lawrence Stoltz, The Friends, Melville Lane, Edinburgh.*

CHAPTER NINE

For the duration of Doctor Breitling's stay, he was to be the focus of Jane's time and attention. I understood that she must oblige Alan, who clearly had an interest in the success of this visit, but I disliked being deprived of her company. This is why when Jane arranged for Breitling to visit Sir Arthur's villa in Milngavie and photograph the rooms where the composer had penned his Buttercup aria, I had offered my services as assistant and general factotum. After I returned to the hotel and changed out of my moss-covered suit, I went out again to meet Jane and Breitling. My excitement of earlier in the day seemed far removed from a jaunt to the composer's house, and I resolved to keep it that way. I did not tell Jane about my rather inglorious rooftop encounter.

Larch View was about five miles from the centre of the city. Part of the house was rented, but Jane had obtained permission for Breitling to photograph the rooms on the ground floor, the rooms that had been occupied by Sir Arthur twenty years earlier. The housekeeper, Mrs Anderson, was expecting us.

The house was a sandstone villa standing on the edge of a picturesque body of water that was larger than a pond but not quite large enough to qualify as a proper loch. There was an extensive garden and a multitude of larches and beech trees. It wasn't difficult to imagine how a composer might have found inspiration in these surroundings.

At the front door, Jane raised the heavy brass knocker and brought it down three times creating a noise that must have been loud enough to be heard throughout the house. I disliked the fact that Jane did this and not Breitling. Of course, I could have stepped forward myself and knocked on the door. Yet, I felt Breitling was too comfortable in the role of *seigneur*. Perhaps I was already resentful because I disliked my role as assistant, even though it was the very role I had chosen for myself. Breitling had carried his camera from the phaeton and had allowed me to carry the tripod, which was heavier.

The door was opened by Mrs Anderson, a stout woman in a thick black dress over which was a yellow pinny. Her grey hair was tied up in a bun from which wisps flew out at odd angles, giving the top of her head the appearance of a windswept haystack.

'We are the photographers,' I said.

She nodded. 'Doctor Ratković is out on the water. You've to do your photographs downstairs.'

I confirmed that this was our understanding. Doctor Ratković was the tenant who had leased the top part of the house.

'And you won't be more than an hour?'

'That's what we agreed,' I said.

As Mrs Anderson and I reviewed the terms of our visit, Jane whispered in Breitling's ear.

Mrs Anderson was keen that Doctor Ratković should not be inconvenienced, and I was keen to assure her that she must not worry on this account. I was accustomed to putting people at their ease: it is part of the photographer's bag of tricks.

'He does not want his things to be disturbed,' Mrs Anderson said.

'His things will not be disturbed,' I assured her.

As we moved from the lobby to the sitting room, Jane said, loud enough for me to hear but out of Breitling's earshot, 'I can speak for myself, Juan.'

I didn't grasp her meaning.

'You announced us and explained who we were.'

I still did not understand.

'That was for *me* to do. *I* made the arrangements. I do not need you to speak for me, Juan. I can speak for myself.'

'But I thought—'

'You thought you would take charge.'

I wondered if she was teasing me, but she carried on walking across the lobby.

In the sitting room, Breitling began speaking and Jane translated. As she was doing this for my benefit, I listened attentively but I was stung by the rebuke I had received moments earlier.

'I have the details from Mr Parry, and he has it from Sir Arthur himself,' Breitling said. 'The composer slept in the large room facing the loch on the ground floor.'

All three of us looked first to one side of the sitting room and then to the other. There were double doors at either end. I walked to the nearest set of doors and tried the handle. One of them opened. Jane and Breitling came forward and we peered into the room. It was empty but for a large leather sofa against the wall facing the window, stretching from there was a mass of polished parquet but not another stick of furniture.

'That room isn't used,' Mrs Anderson said. She was standing at the door of the sitting room.

'Was it once used as a bedroom?' Jane asked.

Mrs Anderson looked surprised. 'Aye.'

'Were you here when Sir Arthur stayed?'

Her face lit up, and her manner became more affable. 'I was! Are you friends of Sir Arthur?'

'Doctor Breitling is a friend of Mr Parry, the composer, and Mr Parry is a friend of Sir Arthur,' Jane said.

'Oh, sir!' Mrs Anderson said. 'You will know that Sir Arthur has been poorly. Is there any report of his recovery?'

Jane translated. Breitling communicated his sympathy by raising his eyebrows and pursing his lips. 'I'm afraid I have no news, but surely we may hope for the best. Sir Arthur is still a young man.'

'You're very kind,' Mrs Anderson said.

I was still smarting from Jane's reprimand and from having to act as Breitling's junior. I didn't see what was kind about the doctor's rather unenlightening response.

Mrs Anderson crossed the large expanse of empty parquet and stood beside us. 'I think Sir Arthur liked it because that tree there' – she pointed to an oak a few yards away from the window on one side, framing the view of the water – 'had a pair of birds the year he was with us. I don't know what sort of birds they were, but Sir Arthur insisted they were gifted – he said their song was *particularly* melodious.'

'And this was the sitting room at that time?' I asked, indicating the larger room.

Jane translated for Breitling's benefit, so I gathered that she didn't object to my taking part in the conversation.

'It was,' Mrs Anderson said, 'and yonder was the place where Sir Arthur worked.'

No one spoke, but we all moved at the same time, away from the bedroom and back across the sitting room to the doorway on the opposite side.

Like the former bedroom, the former composing room was empty but for one piece of furniture, a huge desk that almost filled the wall adjacent to the window overlooking the loch.

'He would have had a piano here?' Jane asked. As soon

as she had spoken, she repeated the question in German. Breitling nodded.

'He had the harmonium,' Mrs Anderson said.

'He has just the use of the floor above,' Mrs Anderson said.

The desk was a remarkable piece of work. There were perhaps a dozen drawers: within some of which there would be more drawers, no doubt. I remembered the desk in the photograph that Breitling had taken, of Johannes Brahms in his study in Vienna.

As we stepped back into the sitting room, Jane dropped behind Breitling and Mrs Anderson, and for one bright moment, she held my hand.

I felt as though I had been granted absolution for a multitude of sins.

We started in the working room. I set up the tripod and Breitling measured the distances before, together, we placed the tripod about halfway between the desk and the garden and about halfway between the side window and the double doors. We worked steadily for forty minutes, first in the study, then in the sitting room and finally in the bedroom. In the bedroom, Breitling peered out and said, 'We must have the tree.' Jane reminded him that we had agreed to photograph only inside the house. 'It can be done from here,' he said, and he approached the glass doors that looked onto the back garden and tried to open them. 'Locked,' he said, as though this surprised him.

Mrs Anderson had gone to another part of the house. I examined the door: no bolt or lock was visible though it was securely closed. On the wall to the right, just above the skirting board, was a mechanism of a type I had seen once before, in Madrid in the house of an English architect. The device operated by means of a spring that released the bolt if pressed firmly a certain number of times. The spring was pressed through a tube, and the end of the tube was a bevelled wooden handle the same colour as the parquet. I pressed the handle once and nothing happened; twice, no change; and so on, until on the sixth attempt, I heard the mechanism click and there was a soft crack at the centre of the door and the bolt slid back.

'That was very clever, Señor Camarón!' Jane said.

We opened the doors and Breitling established an image that included the interior of the room, the open French window, the tree where the gifted birds had sung and the loch. The contours and texture of the loch were very clear in the afternoon light. The sunshine was refracted through the treetops on the other side of the water, and the image of the loch and its surroundings was well defined.

Breitling fussed with the camera and then, when I asked him what was wrong, he said, 'The branch.'

I looked through the viewfinder. One branch intruded on the image, like a stray wisp of hair in an otherwise flawless portrait. I considered the practicality of climbing the tree and pulling the branch upward. I therefore felt a little sheepish when Breitling came up with an easier solution. He adjusted the tripod so that the camera was lowered six inches. Peering through the viewfinder again, he said, '*Perfekt!*'

After the picture was taken and I had dismantled the tripod, I stepped out to close the double doors. On the far side of the loch, a man was climbing into a rowing boat. I had a clear view of him: tall, well-built. He moved quickly, sitting down on the middle bench and manipulating the oars to push the boat from the bank and set it on a course towards Larch View. He began to row.

I turned to close the double doors and as I did so I noticed a little wooden bulb, painted black and partially hidden by a row of large plant pots. Its function would not have been guessed by anyone who was not familiar with the bulb on the other side of the wall that operated the lock. I stepped inside and closed the doors.

'Will you wait for Doctor Ratković?' Mrs Anderson asked.

'We won't stay,' Jane said, translating for Breitling. 'Please convey our respects.'

In the phaeton, Jane said, 'We'll drop you off at your hotel, Juan.'

I believe I may have glowered. I had imagined we would spend the rest of the afternoon together.

'Alan has arranged for Doctor Breitling to meet some of his friends from the Corporation,' Jane added quickly. 'They are interested in the city improvements that have been introduced in Vienna.'

CHAPTER TEN

At my hotel, I was handed a letter from the solicitors A. W. Croft & Croft, inviting me to an appointment at a quarter past eleven the following day at the company's offices in Edinburgh's Old Town. I carried the letter up to my room, holding it as though it were a key or a sorcerer's wand. It pointed to a rearrangement of the heavy elements that had settled in my path. Communication with the lawyers representing this Señora LaGuardia meant that I could take the initiative.

I set out paper, pen and ink on the desk and sat down to write. The desk faced a wall on one side of a large window that looked out onto the street. There were just a few loiterers by now and the occasional sound of footsteps. The window was open an inch or two and I heard voices rising. I could see at the end of the street one corner of the main square: two statues were visible, both of them long-departed dignitaries riding long-departed horses: these two were the advanced guard of a troop of stone horsemen facing the City Chambers, the railway station, the Corn Exchange and the grand hotel recently built beside the station. My account of my father's life was like that – a glimpse, a tiny fragment of something infinitely greater. I spent the next hour writing the things that I should have explained with more fluency and grace when I sat opposite Benjamin Jackson.

I was born in Scotland and I lived there until I was a little over four years old. I learned to speak English, but Spanish is my first language. I do not remember my mother, but I remember playing with a little wooden horse, and that someone played with me and she had a word for horse that was different from the word my father used.

My father loved buildings. He would stop abruptly when we were walking along a thoroughfare, and he would begin to examine a facade or a roof or a balcony. Sometimes he would even stop in the middle of the road, heedless of carts and carriages coming towards us, and he would crouch down and point out to me the thing that had caught his attention. 'See that pillar, Juan! Without it, the geometry would be spoiled. It's there to balance the picture. See how it does that.' I remember the contentment I felt when my father crouched beside me and his hand rested gently on my shoulder. It was as though we stood together on a high peak and looked out across all the beauty of the world.

When I was still too young to know the difference, we moved from Glasgow, first to Madrid and then to Granada and, much later, to Cuba. My father arranged for me to be educated at the Jesuit gymnasium in Granada, and then, briefly, at the faculty of fine art.

My father's contract to produce a portfolio of architectural portraits that would capture the majesty of colonial Cuba was already in discussion with William Collins, Sons & Co before we sailed from Spain. The contract was signed and notarised soon after we arrived in Havana. My father's association with the company was, therefore, one of long standing and was based on this central undertaking, which he had fulfilled – at the cost of his life. The malicious and utterly unfounded allegation that my father had stolen someone else's work was contrary to his character, contrary to his documented way of conducting himself as a photographer and contrary to common sense.

I rescued my father's portfolio and other documents from the house where we were staying in Santiago before it burned to the ground. Later, I returned to the ruins, but I was unable to retrieve the plates. I believed that it was these stolen plates that were now being used by this Señora LaGuardia as the basis for her fraudulent claim.

These were the points that I outlined in my letter to Benjamin Jackson. I concluded by explaining that I now proposed to investigate the source of the present difficulty and establish the truth. I was confident that when the truth was known, William Collins would proceed with publication.

I posted the letter after breakfast the following morning on my way to the station to catch the Edinburgh train.

Henry Farquhar, the solicitor at A. W. Croft & Croft who had been assigned to deal with me, was brusque and, as far as I could see, entirely indifferent to the details, merits or possible outcome of the business at hand. Señora LaGuardia, I gathered, was not a long-standing client, and her business meant little to the company, or so it could be presumed from the somewhat dismissive way in which Farquhar spoke about it. This, I concluded, could make things easier.

'William Collins have informed you of Señora LaGuardia's letter?' he asked when I was seated on the other side of his desk on the second floor of Croft & Croft's offices behind the Cowgate.

I said that they had.

'Is this something you propose to take issue with?'

'It is something I know nothing about.'

He waited for me to continue. I guessed that if I did not speak, he would fill what he perceived to be a vacuum.

And so he did. 'You know nothing of the theft of these pictures?'

'I know that the plates were stolen.'

Farquhar looked at the open file in front of him. The page at the top of a slim pile, which I guessed consisted of correspondence between Señora LaGuardia and the solicitors, had half a dozen lines, each beginning with an asterisk. I could not read what was written.

'The plates were stolen by your father . . . according to Señora LaGuardia.'

'Who is Señora LaGuardia?'

'My client.'

'But who is she? Where does she come from? What is she to me?'

'I'm not sure I can help you with any of that.'

'Then why did you invite me to come here?'

He seemed briefly at a loss, but then he said, changing his tone to one of weary common sense, 'Look, I don't want to spend a great deal of time on this, Mr Camarón, and I believe it's a matter that my client would like to see resolved. Is there anything you can tell me that will make it easier for us to arrive at a solution?'

I raised my hands and said, 'Mr Farquhar, William Collins have received a letter from your office containing baseless allegations against my father and against me. I think *you* should do *me* the courtesy of explaining the origin of these allegations.'

'No, no, Mr Camarón, that is not how the legal process works. I have the brief from my client—'

I interrupted. 'I would like to speak to your client. I am absolutely certain that this matter can be concluded to everyone's satisfaction. I don't know if you are familiar with the role I played in helping the police in Glasgow to solve the case of the Crown Street murders, but I cannot imagine that the facility with which you and your firm help me to resolve this issue will have anything but a positive bearing on your company's business and reputation.'

I hadn't intended to say any of this. The words surprised me as they came out of my mouth.

Farquhar became suddenly animated and leaned forward. 'What was your role . . . with those murders?'

'I was the photographer.'

'The man who photographed the killer . . . that was you?'

'That was me.'

He looked at me with an expression that was suddenly collegial. I continued speaking, keen not to lose a momentary advantage.

'I won't take up more of your time, Mr Farquhar. I believe this can all be sorted out quickly. If you would provide me with Señora LaGuardia's address—'

'I can't give you her address.' His tone was resolute and apologetic at the same time.

'Would you write to her and request a meeting, here at your offices or anywhere of her choosing? I would prefer to return to Glasgow tomorrow, but I can wait a day or two.'

A note arrived at my hotel in the afternoon, indicating that I could call at the Marchmont Boarding House in Leith the following afternoon at half past four, 'where a meeting with Señora LaGuardia might be arranged'.

CHAPTER ELEVEN

I ate dinner at a club recommended by Alan. I sat alone in the corner of a well-appointed dining room, where I was served Scotch Broth, baked turbot with mushrooms and pureed potatoes, followed by apple crumble with clotted cream. This was accompanied by a carafe of wine which was represented to me as having come from Navarre, though it had the slight, and not unpleasant, sourness of a vintage from the other side of the Pyrenees. As it was very good, and as I had finished the first carafe before the arrival of dessert, I ordered a second.

I should not have done this. I was drunk when I returned to my hotel.

'There's another letter for you, Mr Cameron,' the clerk said.

I absorbed the meaning of his words and noted the various ways in which the expression on his face seemed to change, before I grasped that he was actually proffering the letter. I reached out to take hold of it but then I realised that since my key was in my hand. I could not take the letter from him. After some thought, I put the key on the counter and accepted the letter, but then I was faced with the same difficulty, because I now held the letter and could not therefore pick up the key. I looked closely again at the clerk to see if he had noticed any lack of sobriety on my part.

'When did this arrive?' I asked, holding up the letter.

I wanted to show that I was perfectly capable of carrying on a conversation.

'This evening, sir. It was posted in Glasgow this afternoon.'

I nodded in order to indicate that I was now apprised of the necessary information. Then I had an inspired idea: I picked up the room key with my left hand.

I began to make my way along the corridor towards the stairs.

'It's that way, sir.'

I turned to focus on the clerk again.

'It's that way,' he repeated. He pointed to the stairs.

I looked back. I disliked being corrected, but there was no escaping the fact that there were no stairs there.

The letter in my hand seemed to exert a calming influence, as though Jane were beside me addressing me by name. 'The man is quite right, Juan. Take the stairs, *these* stairs.'

'Shall I walk up with you?' the clerk asked.

This was surprising not simply because he asked in a rather emollient tone, but also because he was standing beside me. He had come round from the other side of the desk. As we climbed the stairs, I looked at the letter and concentrated on how, once inside my room, I would sit by the little desk facing the window, and I would open the letter and savour every word of it.

At the back of my mind was an inchoate feeling that something was missing. I realised what it was when we reached the end of the short corridor where my room was located. A narrow but thick carpet ran the length of the corridor, which meant that we moved silently, myself in front and the clerk behind. He had taken my elbow once or twice as we climbed the stairs. I was aware of this. I thought it entirely unnecessary. Now we walked silently along the corridor like two ghosts. At the door, I reached out to put the key in the lock. But, of course, there was no key.

'I have it, sir,' said the clerk.

I heard the sound of the bolt being drawn back. The door swung open and, to my surprise, the clerk stepped in.

'Would you like me to light the lamp, sir?'

As he moved to the window, I noticed for the first time that he was not wearing a jacket. His white shirt seemed to me to correspond exactly to the image that had flitted across my mind moments before, of phantoms walking in the night. He lit the lamp on the desk and opened the window a fraction so that the gas would dissipate if the lamp were left on.

'I thought you might wish to read, sir,' he said, coming

back to where I stood. He stopped in front of me and I wondered why, until I realised that in his outstretched hand he was holding the key. I took it.

'Please lock the door, sir.'

He stepped out. I listened for the sound of his footsteps walking back along the corridor, but, of course, he made no sound at all. I closed the door and locked it, feeling the bolt settle firmly in the hasp.

Then I sat down at the desk and tore open the letter.

My dearest Juan,

It is lunchtime. I decided not to go out today as I am alone in the shop. I will tell you more about that shortly, but first I will tell you about much, much more pleasant things.

I think of you. I think of you all the time. I wonder where you are eating lunch, if you have found somewhere agreeable. I remember the first time you came to my aunt and uncle's house. We drank lemonade. I think I knew then that I loved you.

I love you for so many reasons. One is the way in which everything in the world seems new to you; it seems fresh. You have this great capacity to look at things in an original way. Maybe it is because you have occupied so many worlds. You see things as an outsider might see them, as someone who is learning about the customs of a country for the first time. You are good at learning. You have had such experiences, so much more varied than anything that I have seen. You have memories of Scotland and you have those wonderful stories of Madrid and Andalucía, and the great trek that you and your father completed on the island of Cuba. It is a mystery to me, but one that I contemplate with bliss, that after all of your adventures you would find me interesting. I have spent my entire life here in Scotland and have been content until now to hear the adventures of others. How I long to discover the world in your company. I will feel safe and protected, and I will look after you and together we will have our own adventures. How I long to see Paris. And Madrid. And Granada. I can imagine the two of us at the Alhambra. Juan, I will wear one of those dresses that the Spanish ladies wear. I will have a mantilla and a fan – can you imagine? A girl like me from Glasgow. Do you think I will be able to pretend that I am from the mountains of Andalucía?

Do you know what I began to do this morning?

I began to learn Spanish. I have a book from a friend of my uncle. He was in the wine trade and spent time in Gibraltar and Jerez. I have been studying since nine o'clock. Estoy estudiando.

I have thought about the matter that preoccupied you when you left. I am sorry that at the theatre and afterwards we could not discuss this properly. I know that you were even more concerned than you admitted to me. The attitude of the publisher leaves a great deal to be desired, and you are right to speak directly to the woman's solicitors. It is very possible that when the misunderstanding, as surely it is a misunderstanding rather than anything more sinister, when it is resolved it will be seen in its proper light, as no more than a bump in the road.

I am filled with admiration, Juan, for the dedication you have shown to your father and to his work. When you speak of him, you change. You become somehow older and gentler. When I see this, I long to know you, to know you more and more. I have only glimpsed the things that lie beneath the surface. Yet I believe, with a certainty that makes me joyful, that these are wonderful things. One of my uncle's friends teaches philosophy at the university. At dinner last winter he spoke of a new branch of learning that is exploring the mechanics of thought. He explained a theory about something called the 'personality'. The personality is our way of thinking. Everyone has a different way of thinking – but not only this. Everyone has different levels of thinking. Sometimes we think on one level and sometimes on another. This is why the same person will behave very differently at different times and in different circumstances – all of us do this! After I learned about this theory, I tested myself and I was able to determine different ways in which I think about things, depending on my situation. Of course, all of us change as we grow older, but what is less well known is that we change in distinctive ways in the space of a single day in that we have more than one 'personality', or rather, we have 'layers' of personality and we dip in and out of these layers.

I want to know all the layers of your personality, Juan, and I want you to know all the layers of mine. I want us to be of one mind.

And now I must tell you of a matter that has begun to concern me, and I am sorry to draw your attention to it when you are rightly occupied in sorting out the difficulty that has arisen regarding your father's book. But even though we are not yet married, I turn to you as my support and my guide.

You met Doctor Breitling and you will have formed an opinion of him. My uncle had hoped to gain a great deal from this visit. He imagines Breitling can open up commercial possibilities for him in Vienna and elsewhere. But I suspect that he has been disappointed. There is something amiss.

Last night, when we returned from the meeting at the City Chambers, there was a note from Doctor Ratković. It was addressed to my uncle. This Ratković sought a meeting this morning with both my uncle and Breitling. He wanted them to bring the photographs that were taken when we visited the villa. They have not yet returned from this rendezvous. I had expected them before now.

By the time you receive this, the matter will undoubtedly have been resolved. I will have been exposed as a flighty young woman, a flibbertigibbet – but perhaps my girlish fancy will amuse you, perhaps it will arouse in you the tenderest feelings of concern.

I hope you will return tomorrow, because I wish to be with you and this wish is not predicated on my present anxiety but on the disposition of my heart.

Yet, I am a little anxious and I hope you will not stay away for a moment longer than you must, Juan.

Your love,

Jane

I looked up and pondered the leafy, lamp-lit street. The cobblestones, glimpsed beyond a delicate tracery of branches that stretched from the street to the edge of my window, glistened dimly. There was no sound; the brougham that had deposited me outside the hotel was the last vehicle to disturb the silence outside.

A cool jet of air streamed in through the window. The fog of nonsense that had befuddled my brain just ten minutes earlier began to lift. I started to make sense to myself. This was accompanied by some embarrassment. I remembered climbing down from the cab and seeking to resolve the disparity that had arisen between the driver's calculation of the fare and my own. And I remembered the business of losing my key and having to be helped upstairs to my room.

I stood up and walked to the sideboard, where there was a pitcher of water and a glass. I poured myself a drink. Then I poured a second glass and brought it back to the desk. I filled a pipe and lit it, sat down and read Jane's letter twice more.

When I had finished reading, I took a sheet of notepaper

from the desk, dipped my pen in the small glass bowl of ink next to the blotter and began to write.

> *My love,*
> *Your letter is wonderful and troubling at the same*
> *time – wonderful because you have expressed about*
> *me an emotion that fills me with joy. It is an emotion*
> *that I wish you to know is the very same as the one I*
> *feel for you.*

This was clumsy. I sucked on my pipe and blew a cloud of smoke towards the window. I resolved to press on, putting down my thoughts as they came to me. In the morning, I could adjust the text so that it communicated more completely what I felt.

> *Troubling because you have expressed concern*
> *about Breitling and your uncle, and the possibility of*
> *their involvement in a scheme of some sort.*

I felt I was entering territory where I might blunder into some unintended offence. This thought for several moments derailed any effort to continue. I was distracted by a consideration of just how little I knew about Jane and her family. Our actual knowledge of people, even those close to us, covers only the tiniest fraction of their lives, that fraction which they are content to share with us. The rest is a mystery, and its occasional illumination must be cause for surprise, quite often cause for disappointment.

However, I returned to my earlier resolution. Puffing evenly on the pipe so that the very repetitiveness of this action and the steady stream of small circular clouds that attended it lulled me again into a satisfactory state of concentration.

I cannot say that I noticed anything particularly unusual in Breitling's inclination to leave the villa before Ratković's return. Our business was with the building rather than with its tenant. Nor can I think of any subterfuge that would be attendant on making pictures in the place where a famous composer created a famous piece of music.

I wondered if this was a little pompous and perhaps also too blunt, but it did seem to me to be a necessary corrective to Jane's somewhat fanciful concerns.

It is in the nature of business that certain things are sometimes understood rather than said and this may result in evasiveness or obscurity. Clearly, your uncle would like Breitling to open the way for exhibitions in Austria. Can you imagine that, Jane? You would surely go as your uncle's interpreter, and I would accompany you as your assistant and bodyguard – and your husband too.

There are so many reasons why Ratković might have wanted to see the pictures that were taken. Perhaps he wants to commission more for his own purposes. It is surely not unusual that your uncle and Breitling have not yet returned. They may have gone on to conduct some additional business somewhere in the city.

I felt that much of this had the correct calming tone, and I continued with renewed anticipation.

I have received an invitation to be in Leith tomorrow afternoon at half past four, with a view to meeting Señora LaGuardia. I will return to Glasgow as soon as this meeting has been concluded. I hope to be with you, my love, less than a full day from now. By then your anxiety will have passed, or if indeed there is a reason for you to be anxious, we will act together to restore things to the way they ought to be.

Everything I do, I will do for you.

Your love,

Juan

When I awoke the following morning, I moved through a series of memories that began with the moment I finished my letter to Jane and then moved backwards, through reflections that included my exchange with the clerk at reception, my exchange with the cab driver and the exchanges I now recollected with various people at the club where I had taken dinner. These memories involved a great deal of banter; I hoped, with the uncertainty that comes from a memory of drunkenness, that the banter had been jovial on all sides and that I had not been ushered from the club as a garrulous and unwelcome guest.

But when I reread the letter I had drafted, I felt that it said quite well what I wanted it to say. I changed the order of words here and there and made a fair copy.

Downstairs, I was relieved to see that the night clerk had gone. The woman who accepted my letter undertook to have it sent without delay.

CHAPTER TWELVE

After breakfast I walked west from Elm Row, first along Albany Street and then by way of Abercromby Place. I did not know why, after the near-disastrous rooftop debacle that followed my interference at the crime scene, I elected to interfere again, yet I had a curious conviction that if I did not investigate, I would suffer consequences. I had been threatened with violence and this drew me on rather than scaring me away.

In the fresh sunlight there was a great miasma of scent – rhododendrons and azaleas; crocuses and dahlias and hydrangea in the park to my left. There were effusions of pink and blue among the trees. The occasional cart or carriage passed, the horses moving without complaint on the well-paved street. From the park came the sound of children playing. The houses were grey granite; the huge windows conveyed confidence and ease; the streets were clean. I was inclined to think indulgently of the lives that might be lived in homes as pretty and prosperous as these, though the scent of summer and the sight of comfort didn't quite lull me into a sense of well-being. Misery thrives in comfort as well as want.

I thought about Cuba. I looked at the houses in Moray Place and Ainslie Place, and it occurred to me that a key to understanding violence may lie not in wealth that is created and stolen but rather in what is done with it. I could imagine the ruthlessness that placed these sparkling facades in the middle of Scotland. Yet they were elegant rather than ostentatious; the streets were quiet; the people who came and went were sober and serious in the Presbyterian way. I thought about Jane and her family, and I wondered what drama might lie beneath a 'respectable' veneer.

When I reached the little lane behind Melville Street, my thoughts became more focused and, in an odd but not inconsistent way, my course of action became more tentative. I did not have a house number. I walked slowly, looking at the entrances on either side. Halfway along, on the left-hand side, there was a two-storey building so low that if I had raised my hand, I could have touched the eaves where they descended on one side below a gable wall. The facade was painted yellow and beside the door was a small, rectangular tin plaque with the painted legend, 'Friends of the African Slave'.

I lifted the brass knocker and rapped twice.

The door was opened by a middle-aged man with a kindly, clean-shaven face and a hairline that receded like the letter 'U'. He wore a grey suit with a black shirt and a clerical collar.

'My name is Juan Camarón,' I said. 'I am a photographer. I would like to speak to Lawrence Stolz.'

'Lawrence?' he asked. 'Do you mean *Lorr-ong-ss*?'

He used the French pronunciation.

My only response was an expression of bafflement.

'You had better come in,' he said.

A cramped lobby opened onto a long, old-fashioned, wood-panelled room. On one side there was a sideboard, sufficiently similar in design and quality for me to make at once a comparison with the sideboard that had been removed from the shed in Glasgow. Opposite the sideboard was a long table cluttered with books and papers, prompting another comparison, with the study table in the reading room of the shirt makers' union.

The man walked to the end of the room, where two doors stood open, revealing a small hall with chairs arranged in front of a dais.

'Lawrence,' he called into the hall, 'you have a visitor.'

He walked back to where I was standing.

'Lorr-ong-ss?' I repeated.

'Our new helper,' he said, 'from Belgium.' Then he extended his hand. 'I am Alexander Napier. Please sit down.'

There was a leather sofa of the sort that is customary in waiting rooms and there were two, similarly functional but equally unhomely, armchairs. I sat on one of them and looked around the room. On the wall above the table there was a framed photograph of a dozen African men dressed in little more than loin cloths, with their hands bound and their feet manacled. At one end of the line, a man – also an African – in white suit and pith helmet, stood facing the camera. He was holding a Bible, the gold cross on the dark leather cover was visible. At the other end, a man in tribal dress was bending down at the feet of the first prisoner.

'Our brothers in the Congo,' Napier said.

'The Congo?'

'Our society works all across the continent, but many of our brothers are today in the Congo.'

'You are missionaries?'

He shrugged. 'Our task is to fight slavery and to support peace so perhaps you could call us missionaries.'

'The photograph,' I said. 'These men are slaves?'

'They *were* slaves. Our brother, Andrew Arnold' – he pointed to the man at the end of the line in the white suit – 'has just secured their release from bondage. As you can see, their chains are being cut.'

I wanted to go immediately to Africa and speak very sharply to the photographer. While Napier saw the image as an eloquent record of the moment of liberation, this was only because he knew what was happening. To anyone without the benefit of his knowledge, the photograph might have shown precisely the opposite: the final bond being fixed before the unfortunate chained men were marched off into captivity. It was a photograph that recorded an event without conveying its unique meaning.

Almost as soon as he had finished speaking, we were joined by Lawrence Stolz.

I should have realised sooner, of course, but when Lawrence Stolz appeared, I was perplexed.

Because Lawrence was a woman, not a man.

She advanced into the room in a way that was – I settled on this word immediately and nothing in our subsequent conversation caused me to question its accuracy – *earnest*. She was about thirty, tall and slim, dressed in a plain grey skirt and a white shirt fixed at the top with an ivory broach. Her fair hair was pulled back in a bun and crowned with two braids that began in the middle of her forehead. She peered at me through a rimless pince-nez.

I stood.

'This is Mr Juan Camarón,' Napier said, pronouncing my name correctly.

'How do you do, Mr Camarón?' Miss Stolz had a voice that was clear and steady and, like everything else about her, earnest.

'As I have explained to Mr Napier,' I began, 'I am a photographer. Three days ago, I was asked to photograph a room in Glasgow where a policeman – forgive me, this is not a pleasant subject – where a policeman was . . . he had been murdered.'

'Oh!' she said. This syllable somehow communicated empathy as well as alarm. She said no more, waiting instead for me to continue. *Disciplined*, I thought, as well as earnest.

'In this room, I found a piece of paper.' I took the paper from my pocket and handed it to her. Napier stepped forward so that he was close enough to read if Miss Stolz elected to show it to him. She did so, simply by turning it in his direction, but when she looked up from the paper she looked at me, not at Napier.

'You spoke of a murder, Mr Camarón?'

Her accent was profoundly French, and mellifluous in the manner that is natural to some French speakers when they soften the hard edges of English.

'A policeman was murdered,' I said.

'Where is this room . . . where the . . . murder . . . was done?'

I named the place. 'It is close to a working men's club, an association of shirt makers.'

Her hand shot up to her mouth and the blood drained from her face.

'Oh!' she said again, 'Is Mr Martin unharmed?'

'Mr Martin?'

'I gave this to Mr Michael Martin.' She handed me back the piece of paper. 'So that he could write to me when he had finished his report.'

I was about to repeat the words 'his report' as an interrogative, but I realised that my apparent inability to respond to any statement without simply saying it over again seemed more than a little hapless, so I said nothing.

'Would you like to sit down, Mr Camarón?' Napier suggested.

I sat. Miss Stolz also sat, perched like an elegant sort of sylph, on the very edge of the sofa. Napier took the other armchair.

'May we know why you are involved in this affair, Mr Camarón?' Napier asked. 'Why were *you* taking photographs in this room?'

'I came to Scotland two months ago. My father was killed during the fighting in Cuba. He was a photographer too. I was his assistant . . .'

'Oh dear,' Napier said, and he too conveyed a sense of empathy.

'In Glasgow I developed a new kind of photography. It involves taking photographs from the same position at regular intervals over a period of several hours and then comparing them, very carefully, to extract information. I was invited by the police to—'

'—to help them identify the killer of those unfortunate people in the Gorbals.' Napier's voice became little more than a whisper. He seemed pleased and at the same time shocked to have made this connection.

'Yes,' I said. 'That was me.'

'And now you are working with the police again?'

'Well, I was invited to come and take photographs of the murder scene, no more than that.'

'But why have you come *here*? Surely it's for the police to come and speak to Miss Stolz if they feel she has something to tell them?'

He asked this in a matter-of-fact way, as though the

picture before him contained an inconsistency that might be resolved with relevant information.

I wished I could answer the question in a way that would reassure both Napier and Miss Stolz.

'I found this piece of paper and . . . I was coming to Edinburgh in any case on business . . . and I . . .' I stopped.

'You are not investigating this case of murder,' Miss Stolz said, 'but you are curious, and' – she looked at me in a way that seemed to carry her characteristic earnestness to a new pitch – 'there has been one murder?'

'Yes,' I said.

'You found this,' she said, pointing to the crumpled paper still in my hand. 'Did you find anything else?'

This surprised me.

'There was an envelope,' I said.

As the words came out of my mouth, the recklessness of what I was now doing became apparent to me.

'Have you brought it with you?'

I had started and so I continued, 'It was taken away by the policeman who is investigating the murder.'

She nodded. 'The room you photographed is behind the offices of the workers' syndicate?'

'The shirt makers'. Yes.'

She nodded again. 'It is a small room, not a pleasant room.'

'You have been there?'

'Yes, I have been there. I have discussed with Mr Martin the details of his report.'

'His report?'

'Mr Martin was preparing a document. He was to send it to me when it was ready.'

Before I could repeat the word 'report' again, she continued speaking.

'I am here in Scotland to help Mr Napier and his brothers in the Society. I am from Antwerp, a city that has benefited greatly from the Africa trade, but the Congo not only provides profit' – she said the word as though it were unseemly – 'for Belgium. Companies from all around the world are making money there. They are making money from the sweat and tears of' – she pointed to the photograph above the table – 'of these people, Mr Camarón.'

'I see,' I said, though I didn't really see.

'I am preparing an article that will be published by the Society,' Miss Stolz continued.

Napier nodded enthusiastically.

'It will describe in detail the profits derived by companies here and in Belgium from the Africa trade. Mr Martin is to provide me with information about a yard in Glasgow that has been commissioned to build a gunship for King Leopold. It is a vessel with unique specifications that will allow it to navigate the upper Congo river. It will enable my countrymen to intensify their cultivation of rubber and it will strengthen their power over the people who live in that part of Africa.'

'Which yard?'

'Auchinleck,' she said.

CHAPTER THIRTEEN

After I left the offices of the Friends of the African Slave, I travelled to the eastern part of the city, where I had an appointment with Gregor McCallum, the manager of the Lothian Carriage and Wheelwright Company. My acquisition of the Lumière Cinematographe, now marooned in Le Havre, was premised on an idea that Alan and I had developed together. We proposed to film workers as they emerged from factories and then show these films in nearby theatres for a ha'penny a time. We believed this could be very profitable. Mr McCallum's company was one of several we had approached. He was a small, round man with a firm handshake and a florid face and although he proclaimed himself to be a believer in the benefits of innovation, he resolutely failed to grasp the essence of our moving pictures proposal. I explained that the exercise would require nothing on Mr McCallum's part, other than permission to set up the camera outside the factory gate and film his workers. However, he wanted to know what sort of workers should be selected, what they should wear, how they should behave. I told him no one need be selected and the workers should dress and behave as they would normally do. I quickly realised that he would have been more easily persuaded if the proposition had involved some sort of difficulty, some sort of challenge that would require executive authority. It was the very fact that no one had to do anything out of the ordinary that made the proposal appear, in his eyes, unsound. I left the meeting with Mr McCallum's promise that the scheme would be considered, but since I knew perfectly well that there was really nothing to consider, and the hour or so of recording workers leaving the factory was hardly 'a scheme' I did not expect to receive a positive response. The moving picture business, for which I had rather high hopes of joining, was proving difficult to get off the ground.

Shortly after half past four, I took a cab to the Marchmont Boarding House in Leith.

The Marchmont had the appearance of an establishment likely to be patronised by travellers of modest means. The white paint that had been applied to the grey stone was peeling, the sign advertising accommodation was cracked and the pale blue letters were hard to read.

'I wish to speak to Señora LaGuardia,' I said, presenting myself at the reception desk.

Only a portion of the desk was visible, as the cubby hole in which it was located was separated from the lobby by a dozen panes of frosted glass. The lobby was bathed in a depressing gloom, the principal illumination coming from a lamp behind the glass screen. By the faint light I made out a figure behind the desk.

The figure inspected me. 'Señora LaGuardia is not here.'

'I was given to understand that I might meet her here this afternoon.'

The man did not shrug, but he might as well have done. 'I know nothing of that.'

'When will she be back?'

'I could not say, sir. May I know who you are?'

The question was pertinent, but it conveyed, I felt, an unmistakable insolence. I could not see how short or tall the man was, since he was seated, although, he struck me as short. There was a constricted, almost shrivelled quality about his posture. He wore a black beret, perhaps to cover the onset of baldness, though he had a thick moustache and a dark grizzled beard. He peered at me through pebble glasses that were without rims. The beret, the beard and the thick glasses made him seem almost gnomic.

'I have been given Señora LaGuardia's address by her solicitor in Edinburgh. My name is Juan Camarón.'

'Solicitor?'

I should have considered the ramifications of announcing

a legal connection in a house such as this. I blundered on, untruthfully. 'She has inherited a sum of money.'

He seemed surprised. 'Why has the solicitor sent *you*?'

Having embarked on an untruth, I was obliged to continue. 'Señora LaGuardia had a business connection with my father.'

This was not an answer to the question he had asked. It was an assertion that would require another lie in order to be sustained. 'Look,' I said, with an impatience that was genuine rather than feigned, 'do you know when Señora LaGuardia will be here?'

He became more obliging. 'She was due back today, but she may have been delayed. She sometimes is.'

There was a noise from the interior of the building, the sound of a door being closed and two voices speaking in a corridor.

'Back?' I asked.

'From the continent, but there are no more boats tonight.'

Two women, perhaps a little older than me, emerged into the lobby. To my astonishment, I heard them speaking to one another in the unmistakable accent of Havana. I turned and watched as they climbed down the steps in front of the house. I wondered if I might find out more about Señora LaGuardia from these two than from the concierge.

'I will call on Señora LaGuardia again,' I said, and I began to move towards the door.

'Is there a message for her?'

I did not want to lose sight of the two Cuban women. 'No message,' I said. 'I will call again.'

I ran down the steps and looked towards the promenade, but there was no sign of the girls. In the opposite direction, the road went uphill and into the town: no sign of them there either.

I muttered an oath. In the direction of the town there was an opening twenty yards away where a street ran off to the left. I hurried towards it and peered along the side street. It was deserted. I ran back down the hill, glancing up at the boarding house as I passed. The faint illumination in the cubby hole was even fainter seen from here. In the gathering dark, the peeling paint on the grey walls looked even more forlorn.

At the promenade, I turned to the right with the intention of walking towards a bridge where I had seen a row of waiting cabs. There was a tea room on the second block along and as I approached I detected an aroma of fried potatoes and meat. I had not realised until then that I was hungry. I saw through the downstairs window that there were people sitting at tables. I walked to the end of a narrow hall and through the door on my right, where there was a large room with a dozen tables, about half of which were taken.

In the corner were the two girls from Havana. I almost cried out.

'Is it dinner you're after, sir?' The woman who spoke was stout and middle-aged, and her pale, flat face made me think she must have come from the Baltic. She led me to an empty table on the opposite side of the room from the two girls.

'May I sit over there?' I asked.

She hardly hesitated before turning and escorting me to the other side, where I sat at the table next to the girls.

There was liver and onions with fried potatoes. This was all that was served.

I sat facing into the room and began to eavesdrop. From time to time, I glanced over. I could see the back of one head, a glossy profusion of tresses that reached to below the shoulders of a cream-coloured jacket, which had the cut and the colour of the Caribbean. It could not possibly be warm enough for late summer in Scotland – she must either be inured to the cool weather or unable to afford warmer clothes.

To see the other girl, I had to turn my head, which I did sparingly as I did not wish to attract attention. She was pretty, with an engaging expression; her mouth was a little open when she listened to her friend and her teeth were white and even.

The advantage of a tea room with just one dish is that the food comes quickly. I ate quickly, too, concentrating on the conversation behind me rather than on the food on my plate.

The two girls were speaking about boys – one boy in particular. His name was Hector and he was staying with his parents at the Marchmont. They wondered why he was unmarried. The girl with her back to me had witnessed an incident in which Hector, who I gathered was something of a Scottish Adonis, had been reprimanded by his mother for some small infraction. He had borne this humiliation, the witness felt, with too much resignation. He was not a man who could be looked to for strength or solace. The other girl took an opposite view: Hector's forbearance testified to strength of character, and a certain winning gentleness and this placed him very firmly in the category of *material por el matrimonio*.

When I had finished the main course, the woman brought me a cup and saucer on a little tray with milk and sugar and a small enamel teapot. 'I have Dundee cake,' she said.

I asked her to bring three slices and then I got up and took two steps to the next table.

'I'm sorry,' I began, speaking, like them, in the Havana dialect, 'I was not eavesdropping, but I couldn't help but hear you both and I believe we are from the same part of the world. May I join you for tea? I've ordered cake.'

They glanced at one another before the one who had had her back to me said, 'You are a little forward, Señor, but we will take that as gallantry, especially since you have cake!'

Like her partner, she was pretty, but in a more delicate and aristocratic way. Her name was Elsa and the other girl was Patricia. They were not from Havana but from Matanzas, about fifty miles along the coast. They had been teachers in a girls' school financed by the government in Madrid and had shipped out from Spain three years before the final phase of fighting. When Madrid cut off the funds, the school closed, and the two were left to find their own way home. They had made it as far as Glasgow and had travelled to Leith in hopes of securing passage, ideally to Vigo.

I liked Elsa and Patricia. They were still resourceful and cheerful despite having been left in the lurch on the other side of the world and rejected by the people they had come to live among, people whose accent and clothes they had adopted. I told them how I had come to be in Scotland.

'But it was very bad in Santiago,' Elsa said.

There is sometimes a peculiar competitiveness among those who have undergone a common hardship, a resentment if one party has a greater claim to the bulk of the hardship. Elsa and Patricia were not like this. They wanted to know how bad it had been in Santiago and whether or not the terrible accounts they had read were close to the truth. I told them about the shortage of fresh water and food, and the fear of typhus. I told them about the manner of my father's death.

'This is very sad,' Elsa said, reaching out and touching the sleeve of my jacket.

The process of speaking to them was cathartic.

'A photographer,' Patricia said. 'Can you take pictures anywhere?' It was the attention to practical contingency that goes with having to fall back on your own resources.

'I have a camera and some bits and pieces. That's all that's needed,' I said, and then I told them how I had assembled the pieces of a puzzle, with the help of serial photographs taken in Glasgow over a period of several days that summer.

'We were there,' Elsa said. 'In Glasgow when the murders were happening.' She shivered.

'The woman who fired the fatal shot,' Elsa asked, an expression of empathy on her face, 'she was working at the hotel?'

Perhaps my tone changed a fraction. The roof of my

mouth was suddenly dry. I took a sip of tea.

'She was my friend,' I said, 'Well, my fiancée . . . now.'

Elsa and Patricia exchanged another glance. I watched this happen and could not understand what it meant.

I had done nothing wrong. Yet I felt that I had.

'And what are you doing here in Edinburgh when you should be with your young lady in Glasgow?' Patricia asked. Her tone may have been slightly acerbic.

'My father's photographs,' I said, trying to sound as though I had not noted any cooling in what had been until then a lively, almost intimate conversation. 'The publisher has received a letter claiming that someone else took the photographs. The letter originated with Señora LaGuardia.'

Again, Patricia and Elsa exchanged a glance, but this time, instead of being more distant, they became more animated.

Patricia nodded and said, 'Señora LaGuardia! I might have known!'

'Really?'

'We don't like her,' Elsa said.

I turned around and asked the waitress if we could have more cake.

'We're closing now,' she said.

I looked at the girls. 'Is there somewhere nearby?'

'Shouldn't you be getting back to Glasgow?' Elsa asked, a little archly.

'We don't generally do more than have tea in the evenings,' Patricia said.

'Let me treat you.'

'There's a place with a nice little snug, just before the start of Commercial Street.' Patricia had already got to her feet.

In the snug there was space for three of us on a bench with a small table in front of it. I would rather have sat facing them. I feared we would now have to go through the time-consuming process of bringing the subject of Señora LaGuardia back to the point where we had left it, so that they could tell me everything about her and why they didn't like her. But instead, to my surprise, as soon as I had fetched a glass of gin for each of us and sat down next to them, Patricia said, 'Her husband was executed by the Spanish.'

I did not at first know who she was talking about.

'Señora LaGuardia,' she said, suddenly on her guard, as though I ought to have grasped who she was referring to since I was the one who had raised the topic in the first place.

I took a sip of gin and said, 'Of course.'

She hesitated but then she continued, 'He was killed in the south. It may have been in Santiago.'

'He was with the rebels?'

'So she says.'

'She's always asking us about our business,' Elsa said. 'The other day she wanted to know if I had found a place at a school in Spain. I didn't tell her. I think she would write and tell them something nasty about me.'

'But why?'

If Señora LaGuardia was a mean-spirited harpy inclined to write damaging letters about people she encountered, perhaps I was no more than a random victim, an accidental target for her spite. But this, I realised, was a rather desperate hope.

'She hates us because we are Spanish. She never lets us forget that she's not Spanish, she's Cuban, as though anyone could tell the difference.'

'But what's she doing here, then? Why isn't she in Cuba?'

'I think she's a spy,' Patricia said.

Patricia struck me as the less serious of the two. I waited for her to elaborate, which she duly did. 'She disappears for days, sometimes coming and going in travelling clothes.'

'She goes abroad,' Elsa added. 'The ferry to Zeebrugge. We think she's spying on people like us – people like you – who were on the wrong side in Cuba.'

'But has she ever spoken of this, or spoken in a way that would make you suspect she's actively trying to do harm?'

'We try not to speak to her,' Patricia said. 'Once I asked her if something bad had happened to her during the conflict, other than the death of her husband. She wouldn't confide in me, though.'

'Why did you think something might have happened to her?'

'She walks with a limp,' Elsa said.

CHAPTER FOURTEEN

I spent longer with Elsa and Patricia than had been my original intention and because of this, after I had found a cab that would take me first to the hotel to collect my suitcase and then to Waverley Station, I caught a later train. I wanted to return to Glasgow because Jane was waiting for me there, and because I felt that if I waited a day or two before going back to the Marchmont, there was a better chance I would find Senora LaGuardia there.

I reached the platform just as the train was leaving, so I opened the first carriage door and jumped inside. As I put my case on the netting above the seat, I realised I had selected a first-class compartment. At the same time, I realised that there was just one other occupant, a woman sitting on the middle portion of the bench opposite the one above which I had placed my case. With some sort of ancient instinct that applies to the optimal configuration of two people thrown into one another's company for a limited period of time, I sat beneath my suitcase and opposite the only other passenger.

She looked at me with an expression of faint amusement.

'I'm sorry,' I said. 'I thought I would miss the train. I hope I have not disturbed you.'

'Not at all.' When she smiled, the little crow's feet around her eyes crinkled, rather fetchingly. She was about forty years old, perhaps a little younger or a little older. I had a lifetime's experience of studying faces and the crow's feet were a characteristic that could be elided from finished portraits with a clever arrangement of lighting. Some sitters would be delighted with the youthfulness this gave their appearance. Yet I did not think that erasing the crow's feet from the face that now looked at me with slightly disconcerting candour would have added to its beauty. The woman had blue eyes and what might have been described in certain types of literature as 'a button nose'. When she smiled, there seemed to me to be an almost tangible intelligence in her expression, as though she had grasped every aspect of this encounter; my harassed and hurried entry and my embarrassment, and the fact that we might now spend an hour in one another's company, possibly even without interruption, as the train was an express, with just one stop between here and Glasgow.

And as I absorbed the detail of this woman's features,

together with her elegant velvet travelling jacket and skirt, I grasped from the vowel sounds that attached to her refutation of any disturbance that she was, like me, a foreigner.

'Why were you late for the train?' she asked, with the half-smile on her intelligent face that made the question somehow engaging rather than intrusive.

'I had a dinner,' I said, 'that went on for longer than I had planned. I had to pick up my suitcase and got here just in time. I'm very glad I did.'

One of her eyebrows rose, as if I had said something amusing.

'I would have had to wait more than an hour for the next train,' I explained.

I felt somehow that she was appraising my suit and tie. Her gaze went down to my shoes and I experienced a curious sense of relief that they were smartly polished. Curious because there was no reason I should have cared what this woman thought of my shoes.

'Your dinner was with a young lady?' she asked.

I found myself speaking recklessly. 'Two young ladies, actually.'

The woman started to laugh. 'My goodness!'

I opened my mouth to explain that they were two girls I had not met before, and of course this would have sounded even more preposterous, so I said nothing. My mouth may have remained open, in the manner of an enraptured schoolboy.

'My name is Nadia Natasha Orlova,' the woman said. 'May I know with whom I have the honour to share a compartment?'

'Juan Francisco Camarón,' I replied, inserting my middle

name and announcing myself in the proper way, as Madame Orlova had done. I sensed that the one thing she would find tedious was a want of confidence.

I should perhaps have asked myself why the sensibilities, or the approval, of Madame Orlova should have been a matter of the least concern to me, but of course I made no such internal enquiry. I simply admired her beauty, which was made even more dazzling by her forthright manner.

'You are visiting Scotland, Señor Camarón?'

'I arrived from Cuba some time ago.'

'From Cuba?'

'My father and I were photographers. We made a photographic record of Spanish architecture on the island. He was killed in June last year in Santiago, as he made the last of the photographs.'

Madame Orlova leaned forward, placed her hand on my arm and said, 'Señor Camarón, I am very sorry to hear this.'

It was not simply the tactile nature of her unexpected gesture, or the fact that she looked me in the eye as she spoke, her face assuming an expression of honest sympathy, it was the way in which she spoke; measured, steady and clear. People tend to mumble when they express condolences. As I thanked her, I felt a sudden and unfamiliar sense that I was in the presence of a kindred spirit.

'And you continue to work as a photographer?' she asked, sitting back and resuming her tone of frank interrogation.

'I do. I was able to assist the police in Glasgow recently in quite a well-known murder case.'

'You are *that* photographer, the one who makes many, many photographs all of the same place?'

I have read in the newspapers that some people dislike the recognition that comes from being in the public eye, even when this recognition is expressed through approbation. I cannot pretend that this was my own response to the modest amount of fame my role in helping to solve the Crown Street murders had attached to me. I was gratified by the fact that Madame Orlova had heard of me, even if being described as a photographer 'who makes many, many photographs of the same place' did not, I felt, accurately reflect the originality or indeed the scientific rigour of my method.

'I am,' I said. 'May I know if you too are a visitor in these parts?'

The question was an attempt to establish a measure of equilibrium in the conversation. If we had been playing tennis, I thought, it might have been seen as the equivalent of batting the ball back over the net to Madame Orlova's side of the court.

But I hadn't applied sufficient force or sufficient skill to my volley, because Madame Orlova smiled indulgently as though I had said something tremendously gauche.

'I am a visitor everywhere,' she said.

I was momentarily alarmed by this. I wondered if I had stumbled into a carriage with the sort of dangerous adventuress who pops up in the penny dreadfuls, the kind of woman who produces a pistol and robs other passengers of money and valuables.

I think perhaps my alarm was visible, because Madame Orlova smiled even more indulgently, 'I am an *artiste*,' she said, using the French pronunciation, 'I will sing tomorrow at the Theatre Royal.'

'A singer!' The excitement with which I said this really did make me sound like an infatuated schoolboy. 'Are you a soloist?'

Madame Orlova chuckled. She appeared to find me remarkably amusing. I resolved to strive for more gravitas.

'I am a soloist,' she acknowledged with a little nod of her head. 'I can say that I am even quite a *celebrated* soloist. I think, though, that you are not an opera lover, Juan.'

That she had called me by my first name seemed a delightful deviation from convention. I had, however, sufficient presence of mind to check what I now recognised as an unbecoming enthusiasm on my part. I replied in a judicious manner, 'I have not heard a great deal of opera.' She looked at me as though this was surely not the extent of what I was prepared to share in the matter of my familiarity or otherwise with her artistic world, so I continued. 'When I was very small, I think it may have been about 1886, my father took me to a performance of Federico Chueca's *La Gran Vía* in Granada.'

'*Charmante!*' Madame Orlova said, speaking as though I had opened up a whole new aspect of my life's experience.

'I was very small,' I repeated, 'but I remember how the stage seemed to me to be . . . magical . . . the lights and the brilliant colours' – I remembered Madame Orlova's profession – '. . . and the singing, of course.'

'Of course,' she said, smiling as though to indicate that she was prepared to forgive me for making the music an afterthought.

'It was in the springtime or the summertime, I can't remember exactly, but I do remember walking with my father after the performance was over. We walked under the trees to the river. There were lots of people sitting on the banks. They sat by the river and made music. I remember there was dancing under the stars.'

I had never spoken of this to anyone. Perhaps until that very moment, I had not had any occasion to recall this fragment of my childhood. I found myself looking at the beautiful opera singer sitting opposite and praying that she would rescue me from what I could only regard as an uncharacteristic and embarrassing indiscretion.

'Chueca was the friend of a baritone I used to know in Vienna,' she said. 'Well, more precisely, his wife was a friend of my friend. I have heard very little of this Spanish style of operetta but I liked it very much. It has a delicacy, a closeness to the music of speech. This is very . . . *Iberian* . . . I think. Now, tell me, Juan, the music of Cuba, is it . . . exciting?'

I had to confess that I had never considered this question. I said, 'Like the music of Spain, I think.' Then I added, 'Though it has a certain' – I stopped and thought – 'a certain *rhythm*, which may be distinct from the rhythm of Spanish music.' I threw up my hands. 'I know little of music.'

'Nonsense! You remember the Zarzuela from your childhood, and you remember the music by the river, the music that comes from the moment, from the heart's desire. Every human being knows about music, even when they do not know that they know. It is God's gift!' She opened the carpet bag that sat on one of the vacant seats and produced a small case, revealing a flask and two china cups. 'When you travel, as I do, Juan, you must savour the journey and the best way to do that is with good companions, so I have two cups, not one. You will join me in a little Armagnac. It is good for the voice and good for the soul. She presented me with a cup in each hand and I took them both. Then she unscrewed the top of the flask and poured. She put the flask beside her on the carpet bag and accepted one of the cups. She raised it and said, '*Salud.*'

'*Salud*,' I said, and then I added, '*Vashe zdorov'ye.*'

She beamed at me and said, '*Ochen harasho, spazebo.*'

'I know only the first part of the toast,' I said.

'It is very gallant, nonetheless.'

'Are you from Moscow? Saint Petersburg?'

'My father was from Smolensk and my mother from so far beyond the last paved road that we do not even know what to call the place where she was born. I grew up in Yalta. I moved to Saint Petersburg when I was fifteen, and when I was eighteen, I left Russia. I have lived in Dresden and Paris and Milan.'

We drank several more cups of Armagnac and she told me about the peripatetic life of an opera singer who had enjoyed some success, without, I gathered, quite reaching the pinnacle of her profession. She said she had been fortunate, because the music was her passion, even though she was increasingly called upon to perform in concert halls rather than opera houses – 'I am paid less, but I work more often.' She had a fund of stories. 'Of course, Maestro Verdi is not of this world,' she said. 'He is of the *theatre*. He lives and breathes for the stage. When I was presented, he asked me to sing, at that very moment, the upper register, if you please. As though he were asking me where I came from, whether I liked olives or parmesan.' She was fond of Maestro Puccini, she said, 'but I would never go in his motor car – he is very careless on the road!'

'Maestro Puccini has a motorcar?' It struck me as odd, for no good reason, that Puccini, one of the few composers whose name I recognized, should be a motorist.

'The very first ever to be driven in Lucca and he had it brought to Milan. He and a handful of other fanatics have taken to racing their machines in the *parco dei genitori* on Sunday mornings. It is a source of conversation, and not a little scandal!'

'Have you sung in London?' I asked.

'Of course, *caro*. I played Mimi in *La Bohème*. Maestro Beecham led. The production won considerable praise, though the *directeur* is rather *vljubčivyj* – how do you say this? . . . rather *naughty*.'

'I do have something perhaps a little interesting,' I said, 'something that happened just recently. I have been working with a Doctor Breitling from Vienna. He is a photographer too, and one of his particular themes, which he has explored with some success, is to photograph musicians and the places where they have created music. He has made wonderful portraits of Johannes Brahms, for example, and, as he is visiting Glasgow, I accompanied him this week to a house in the north of the city where Sir Arthur Sullivan composed the Buttercup aria, from *HMS Pinafore*.'

'Oh, Juan,' Madame Orlova said, 'that is sweet. You speak of Sullivan and Brahms in the same breath! You have a soul that is . . . generous.'

When the train stopped in Falkirk, we watched the door. No one opened it. After a long minute there was a jolt and a screech, and we began to move again.

'I would like you to make my portrait,' Madame Orlova said.

I do not believe I have ever agreed to a request more readily. This was not because I was infatuated, but because making a portrait was a logical continuation of everything we had discussed. I was unsure of very many things, but I was certain of my art. I was as confident of my photography as Madame Orlova was of her voice. It *was* my voice, the instrument that allowed me to communicate. I believed I could photograph Madame Orlova in a way that would capture not just her physical beauty but her artistic beauty, too.

So, it was with a certain amount of dismay that I greeted Madame Orlova's next proposal. 'And you will produce a portfolio!' she said. 'Yes! A portfolio that will bring to life the entire cast!'

'The entire cast?'

'I have performed with many of the people who will share the stage in Glasgow. Oh, they are a varied collection of *artistes*!'

'A varied collection?'

Madame Orlova looked at me with a scintilla of impatience and I realised that my response may have appeared to fall short of wholehearted artistic solidarity. I was not matching her enthusiasm.

'The performance brings together music and dance and poetry, of course, but there are other attractions too. A pair of Englishmen, Mr Temple and Mr Hall, one is very short and the other very tall; they are comical, very stupid in the English way, and how the people adore it when they exchange nonsense with each other! The Family Fellini, an acrobatic troupe from Calabria; Baron Norbert von Herzog, the mesmerist; and a juggler from Nîmes whose name I do not quite remember. In fact, it may be that I have never actually known his name. I address him simply as Monsieur le Jongleur.'

I temporised. I was in dispute with the publisher of my father's work, the very reason I had been in Edinburgh. I had a number of issues to resolve. While it would be an honour to make a portrait of Madame Orlova, I did not feel I was in a position to undertake the sort of documentary record that she proposed.

She looked at me with what I might have described as 'tempestuous' disappointment.

'As you wish,' she said and became silent. More than silent. I believe the proper term might be 'morose'. Madame Orlova had had a book in her hand when I arrived in the carriage. She had placed it to one side when we began to talk. The title on the spine was printed in an odd sort of script, with letters that

I could not decipher. Now, she took up her book again, and we exchanged just a handful of sentences in the quarter of an hour before we arrived at Glasgow.

As the train shuddered to a halt at platform three, the rhythmic tap of the wheels on the rail joints was replaced by the cacophony of raised voices and steam vents echoing beneath the station's glass roof. I got out of the carriage and reached up to hand Madame Orlova down on to the platform. She accepted this assistance, and when she was safely at the same level as myself she astonished me by planting a kiss on my cheek. She turned and began to walk in a very stately fashion along the platform. There was a crowd of people on the other side of the ticket barrier and as Madame Orlova approached the barrier, this crowd began to cheer. I was very slow in making the connection between the elegant figure of the arriving diva and the large concentration of her devotees. As she passed through the barrier, the porter on duty raised his cap. A child and a young woman each presented Madame Orlova with a bouquet of flowers.

The sense that a glamorous event was underway rippled back to where I stood on the platform. People passed me, walking towards the barrier. 'Who is that?' I heard someone ask. 'The Russian soprano,' another said. 'They say she's sung for the Tsar.' By some curious collective instinct, she had walked along the platform practically alone, as though an invisible cordon prevented ordinary mortals from coming too close within her ambit. Just one figure remained detached from the excitement miraculously and mysteriously generated by the presence of Madame Orlova; this was a woman dressed entirely in grey, who had stepped down from the train several carriages ahead of us. She stood in Madame Orlova's path. Such was the influence exerted by the opera singer that I expected the woman to step aside and allow Madame Orlova to maintain her stately progress, but she remained where she was, and the diva had to swerve around her as she bore down on the admirers and the waiting bouquets of flowers.

When I came close to where the woman stood, she turned away suddenly and began to walk very slowly and with an uneven gait towards the barrier. I might have reached it before her, but my attention was drawn to the crowd where Madame Orlova had been received, and I stopped and waited. I did not want to go through the barrier and pass my travelling companion without some sort of greeting, and as we appeared to have had a contretemps followed by an unexpectedly tender leave-taking, I felt it would be redundant and perhaps even awkward to have a second farewell. I waited for the admirers to move off with the object of their affection. However, something unexpected then happened. In the middle of the crowd there was some sort of consultation – I saw Madame Orlova's pale blue hat bob up and down, then the little boy who had been the bearer of one of the bouquets began to run towards the barrier, head down. He ran pell-mell along the platform and came to a halt in front of me, holding out a folded piece of notepaper. When I had accepted the note, the boy saluted and ran back the way he had come, keen to catch up with the procession by means of which Madame Orlova was being escorted from the station.

The notepaper bore the name Nadia Natasha Orlova in embossed letters. Below, in elegant handwriting, was the message: *Come and see me at the theatre. I would like you to make my portrait. Your friend, N*

CHAPTER FIFTEEN

At the main entrance to the station, Madame Orlova and her party stopped in front of two photographers, who had set up their cameras and tripods in the optimal place, with a view of the concourse behind. The photographers were creating a stir with their magnesium ribbons, startling passers-by.

Outside the station I began to walk towards Waterloo Street.

I had been enthralled by Madame Orlova's tales of Puccini and Verdi and other titans of the theatre. Who would not have been enthralled? The woman was full of charm and full of life; she possessed a beauty that might have been celebrated by one of the great Renaissance painters.

This way of thinking made me feel guilty. It was as though one part of my brain had placed another part in the dock, as though I were on trial. I remembered what Jane had written about the 'personality' and how the same person might have several personalities or at least several *levels* of personality. Perhaps my personalities were at war with one another. As I turned the corner, I felt uneasy and dissatisfied with my conduct that day.

Waterloo Street was not in its normal state. A crowd had gathered. Crowds exude a chimera, a disposition: the spirit of this crowd was apprehensive. I thought about the onlookers at the close next to the shirt makers', and the people watching from the back-court windows: humans have a nose for catastrophe.

Even before I knew, I knew.

The crowd had congregated outside the Fletcher Gallery.

I crossed the street. There were perhaps a hundred people. I began to make a path through them, beginning with those on the edge who were standing on tiptoe and trying to catch a glimpse of what was going on at the entrance to the building. I eased past elbows and shoulders, meeting greater resistance in proportion to the greater density of bodies towards the front of the crowd.

'Let me through!' I repeated, and then, by way of offering some sort of logical reason for anyone to stand aside, 'This is my building.'

The untruthful assertion of a connection to the scene enabled me to squeeze between grudgingly yielding hips and shoulders as far as the front of the line. There, a policeman, whose attention had been drawn to my progress by a number of '*Hey!*'s and '*Where do you think you're going?*'s, stood facing me, arms folded. The pressure of the crowd forced me up against him. He prevented me from stepping forward as conclusively as a granite pillar would have done. He was at least six inches taller than me, which meant that, at uncomfortably close quarters, I was obliged to look up at him and make my case. As I spoke, he stared down at me impassively.

'My name is Juan Camarón. I am a friend of the owner of this gallery and my fiancée is his niece. She works here. Please, let me through.'

The people on either side murmured. I felt a lessening of the pressure of bodies. My connection to the gallery had earned a certain notice, but perhaps also there was an instinctive separation from a figure whose association with whatever had happened to draw the police here might not be entirely innocent.

The policeman said, 'Stay where you are.' He spun round in a movement that was faster than seemed possible in one so large, and took just three steps towards the coterie in the middle of the clearing. I disobeyed his instruction and stepped forward. All I heard him say, as he spoke in a voice intended not to be heard by the crowd, was 'This man . . .' He pointed at me. The others in the little group looked up, and I recognised the figure in the middle.

Captain Smith reacted as though my appearance were anticipated and unwelcome.

'What has happened?' I moved towards him. The policeman reached out to stop me, but Smith waved him aside.

'My fiancée works here,' I said. 'This is her uncle's gallery.'

'Then you had better come inside.'

Smith led, and I followed. The other officers brought up the rear.

Two thirds of the way to the desk at the back of the room, a body was sprawled on the floor.

Every corpse is naked, even when fully clothed. The dead have no defence against scrutiny. They have no means of directing attention or imposing themselves on the viewer. They cannot create an impression, false or true. They are caught for ever with the final expression, the final configuration of limbs, the final arrangement of physical presence, fixed and on view.

The corpse lying on the floor of the Fletcher Gallery was male.

As I absorbed with unspeakable relief that the deceased was not my fiancée, I reconfigured the significance of what Jane had written. She suspected that Breitling was involved in some sort of scheme and she believed that Alan too might be involved, willingly or otherwise.

It wasn't Alan's body on the floor. The jacket was a loud check, a sort of yellow on black, and it was matched with a pair of checked trousers. Doctor Breitling's clothes.

Breitling's face was pressed against the floor. I guessed that the body had been lying here for at least an hour because the skin on the face had collected in a sort of wrinkled pocket on the surface of the carpet.

Someone was speaking. It took me several seconds before I realised that the words were addressed to me.

I was being asked if I knew the deceased.

'His name is Breitling,' I said. 'He was visiting from Vienna. He is – was – a photographer. He and Mr Fletcher were organising an exhibition. Doctor Breitling has produced a portfolio of portraits, pictures of the Vienna slums. Where is Mr Fletcher? Where is Miss Macgregor?'

'We don't know, but we intend to find out. The more you can tell us, the sooner we'll be able to get to the bottom of things.'

'You don't know where they are? Are they not at home? Have you been to their home?'

'I must ask you to be calm, Mr Camarón.' This was the same man who had urged me to go back to my hotel two days before and get over my 'excitement'.

'Calm? I have returned from Edinburgh to find a body – the body of a man I was with just days ago – and my fiancée and her uncle have disappeared. It is hard to be calm. Do you know anything about how this' – I gestured down to where Breitling's remains lay on the carpet – 'how this ghastly deed was done?'

When he spoke, his tone was obstinate. 'Your fiancée and her uncle have disappeared. Miss Macgregor was seen running from the gallery. We haven't caught her yet, but we will.'

I did something I had never done before. I sat down without being conscious until I was seated that this was what I had done. I believe it may be said that I simply collapsed into a chair. I realised that I was no longer looking at Smith's face but at the buttons on the front of his waistcoat. I struggled to recover my composure.

'Running from the gallery?' I addressed Smith, but my words were uttered so quietly that they were little more than an absent-minded articulation of my thoughts. 'Running from the gallery?' I repeated. I tried to stand but for the moment I realised I must remain seated. 'This cannot be. You are mistaken.'

Breitling lay in a manner that suggested he had not simply fallen over, as although he was face down, his arms were splayed out on either side of his hips, one of which was slightly raised as his knee had been brought up. If he had fallen forward on his own, one or both of his arms would surely have been raised, as his instinct, even in the case of a sudden loss of consciousness would have been to try and break his fall.

Perhaps Smith followed my gaze; he turned and began to look at the body.

Slowly, I got to my feet and took a step forward. I stood next to Smith and we looked down together. He pointed to the neck. I saw, above the crushed collar of Breitling's shirt, a long, very dark blue ridge on the white skin. 'He was strangled,' Smith said.

He pointed to a brass candlestick on the carpet between the body and the policemen standing opposite. 'And he may have been beaten with that.'

I stepped round and stood above the candlestick. I did this still in a state of acute amazement: it was as though there was no one else in the room. I simply wanted to see the candlestick more clearly, so I walked to where it lay and got down on one knee and examined it carefully.

The men on either side made way for me. Perhaps they looked to Smith to gauge how much or how little freedom I was to be allowed. If so, he must have signalled that I should be allowed to do as I wished.

My skill in detection, such as it is, depends upon images. I looked at the body, the carpet, the candlestick, but without my camera I was of little use here.

Smith walked round the body and past the others. 'Come with me,' he said. I stood up and followed him through the little anteroom where the stairs ended, and into the studio at the back of the gallery.

When we were alone, Smith said, 'The dead man had taken pictures of the Vienna slums, you say?'

I nodded.

'There are plenty of slums in Glasgow. Why would he come all the way here to show his pictures from Vienna?'

'Each city's slums are different,' I said. He looked at me as if I'd spoken in a foreign language. 'Alan – Mr Fletcher – produced photography on this theme a decade ago. He photographed some of the districts that were cleared when the city improvement scheme was at its height. He photographed the buildings, and the people too. These images are important; they document living souls; they document the conditions in which these souls had to subsist. This affects everyone.'

Captain Smith gave no indication that he found any of this helpful.

'There is a possibility that Alan's pictures will be shown in Vienna,' I said. 'Breitling was helping him through his contacts on the continent.'

I had no authority to discuss Alan's business.

'What does this . . . case . . . have to do with the case I photographed?' I asked.

'Why do you think they are connected?'

'*You* are here. That's the only connection that I can see. And *I* am here.'

'Your fiancée was seen running away.'

'Running away from danger,' I said.

'Was Mr Fletcher in debt? Did he have creditors? Impatient creditors maybe?'

'I could not say. He is a businessman.'

'Domestic problems? Affairs? That sort of thing?'

'I do not know enough about the family.'

'But you are going to marry into the family.'

I looked around the studio. 'You have examined everything?'

'Mr Macintyre!' Smith shouted. His voice was so unexpectedly loud that I was startled. I wondered if Smith would conclude that I was nervous because he had asked me about an affair.

One of the plainclothes men came through.

'Did you find anything unusual when you examined the premises?' Smith asked.

Macintyre shrugged. 'We don't know what's usual here.'

Voices were raised among the crowd outside. I guessed the mortuary van had arrived. Sure enough, a few moments later we heard the men in the next room conferring in the way they do when a corpse is to be moved from one place to another: there is a businesslike tone that is resolutely defiant of death's presumption.

I gathered that I was not going to be asked to take photographs, and, quite unreasonably, I resented this. Jane had disappeared and everything in my world should have been predicated on addressing this fact. But the mind behaves in strange ways. I found myself wondering if the gallery could possibly recover from what had happened. Perhaps this peculiar preoccupation with commercial prospects was because on one of the levels of my personality – as Jane might have put it – I did not wish to dwell on the issue of my fiancée's disappearance.

'What do you think happened?' I asked Smith.

He looked at me with irritation, as though what had happened was obvious: Breitling had been murdered.

'Where are Alan and Miss Macgregor?' I said, giving way to my own impatience.

He blew air into his mouth so that his cheeks expanded, then he expelled the air and shrugged. 'I am as much in the dark as you appear to be, Señor Camarón.'

I was annoyed by the expression 'appear to be'.

I looked around the studio again. I knew what was usual here – cameras, shelves built to accommodate the dimensions and weight of photographic plates, a heavy curtain closing off the darkroom, a row of cabinets. Nothing indicated a disturbance. Smith followed my gaze. I turned slowly on the same spot, working my way along one wall and then the next.

'May I look inside the drawers?' I asked, nodding towards the cabinets.

He shrugged as if to say I was as free as anyone else.

In the cabinet where Alan kept his large prints, there were about twenty drawers. I opened each a few inches. There were views of streets and squares around the city; group portraits, of paupers in back courts and prosperous burghers, some of them wearing their municipal regalia. There were individual portraits too.

But there was nothing, as far as I could see, that was out of the ordinary.

'This Doctor Breitling,' Smith said, 'has been associated with some very colourful characters.'

'Oh?'

'Did he speak of his connections to you?'

'No.'

'In Edinburgh, you met people known to Doctor Breitling?'

'No. I was in Edinburgh on my own account. A commercial matter.'

'A commercial matter?'

'I visited the offices of a lawyer, Croft & Croft in the Cowgate. The matter concerns a book of photographs . . . on the architecture of Cuba.'

'And in Edinburgh you met no one from the Land and

Labour League?'

'The what?'

He shook his head. 'It doesn't matter,' he said, and then, with characteristic discourtesy, 'You may go now, Señor Camarón.'

CHAPTER SIXTEEN

When I called on Mary it was already after nine o'clock. The door was opened by a woman I had not met before. She greeted me with a look of disappointment – she had hoped, I suppose, that I would have been either Alan or Jane, or both.

'I'm Juan,' I said, 'Jane's fiancé.'

Her defensive posture became less so. She stood to one side and indicated that I should come in.

'We have had the police and the newspapers,' she said. 'I thought perhaps you were another reporter. I'm Janet, Mary's sister.'

Mary was sitting at the end of the sofa in the sitting room.

'Juan!' she said, jumping up and coming over to meet me.

She held out both hands and took hold of mine. 'Have you news? Do you know where they are?'

I led her back to the sofa and sat down beside her.

I shook my head. 'I came back from Edinburgh, went to the gallery, then came straight here.'

'Doctor Breitling?' she asked. For one terrible moment I thought that she did not know that the doctor was dead. I had blundered into her company without first finding out what the police had or had not told her, but she continued, 'Do they know . . . do they know for sure that he was . . . that he was *murdered*?'

I nodded. 'They took away the body while I was there.' Perhaps I told her this only because shaking and nodding my head seemed inadequate. Yet, it was information that could not in any light have been expected to offer her comfort.

Janet sat in one of the armchairs opposite. 'Is there anything you can tell us, Juan?'

Mary and her sister were physically alike, but quite different in the impression they made. Janet was straightforward and, I sensed, tougher. She would take a realistic view of what might or might not have happened. I could imagine her making the case for a grand coincidence of unfortunate circumstances, a heart attack, for example, or a hurried departure by Jane to fetch help. By this time, however – with the police and press on the scent of the fugitives – there was no getting away from a more brutal truth.

What was this truth? Jane had suspected that Alan and Breitling were involved in a scheme of some sort.

I shook my head.

'The police wanted to know what you were doing in Edinburgh,' Janet said. 'Neither of us knew what to tell them.'

'Alan tells me nothing of *his* business,' Mary said with sudden bitterness. She looked absently at the fireplace.

'I have spoken to the police,' I said by way of reply to Janet. 'They mentioned the Land and Labour League in Edinburgh.'

Janet nodded. 'They asked us about that too. They think Breitling was mixed up in it. Started by an anarchist, apparently – an Austrian living over here.'

I took Captain Smith's card from my pocket. 'The man I spoke to belongs to something called the Special Branch.'

Again, Janet nodded. She was a good deal more self-possessed than her sister. 'I've read about them in the papers. They are a little bit like the police, and a little bit like the army, and they deal with foreigners, which is why they're interested in Breitling . . . and anarchists.'

My bafflement was complete. 'Breitling didn't seem like the sort of fellow who would throw a bomb.'

Mary gasped and her hand shot up to her mouth.

'I'm terribly sorry,' I said.

'Where is Alan? Where is Jane?' Mary began to cry.

Janet hurried over and sat on the other side of her sister.

I stood up. 'I'm sorry,' I said again.

Outside, I walked in the direction of the cabs on the main road near the Fletchers'.

Alan could not be trusted. This was at the heart of Mary's agony. She did not know if her husband had done something desperate, something wicked and she could not say with certainty that he had *not*.

Life chips away at the truth. There are things that we wish to believe that may be true, but we make them absolutely and incontrovertibly true because we *wish* to believe them. Mary wished to believe in her husband's goodness, but she no longer could and the absence of belief was not replaced simply by doubt but by all the demons that can enter the human soul when doubt makes a path for them.

Jane spoke about the layers of personality, the ways in which we change, over the course of our lives, over the course of a single day.

The recollection of this frightened me.

There were no cabs on the corner. I took out my pocket watch and looked at it by the light of a street lamp. It was a quarter to ten. Great Western Road stretched into the far horizon, the gas lamps making a necklace in the night. I glanced at the little service roads to the right and the left of me, the narrow, terraced platforms that gave access to the townhouses separated from the road by ash and oak trees, swirling now in the night breeze. I looked behind me, as if Jane might be there.

Perhaps it was because I had looked far into the distance and then on either side that I became convinced I was being watched. Or perhaps it was because I had lost all sense of reality. I looked behind me a second time and then a third, and when, at the end of the next block, just before the deep canyon flows under the road at Kelvinbridge, I came upon a line of cabs, I called up to the driver and jumped into the first one.

The pattern on the red and green interior was illuminated and then darkened as the cab moved beneath the street lamps. I stared at this, first a mesh of waves and then nothing. There was a clatter of hooves and a sound of steel upon cobble that grew and grew. A carriage passed in the opposite direction and the noise it made diminished as steadily as it had risen when it had approached. I realised that I was listening with a kind of manic intensity to whatever noise might indicate that a vehicle of some sort was following behind. Even as I realised this, the absurdity of my thoughts bore down on me: we were on a main road so there were bound to be carriages in front and carriages behind. I was reading into things a significance that was surely beyond reason.

When we crossed the river, I looked at the masts and funnels of the ships below, picked out by lamps that swayed on the water. The carriage slowed on the upward slope of the bridge and then as we moved down towards the south bank, we gathered speed again and began to navigate the warren of streets where the tenements and warehouses were laid out by the river.

When I climbed down in front of the shirt makers' and paid the driver, I looked back along the road. It was just after ten and there were cabs and carriages travelling in both directions. My own cab moved towards the middle of the road and turned to go back into the city. The carriage behind slowed down. There were two men inside. I glimpsed the rims of their bowler hats, though they sat well back in the high seats, so I could not see more. The hats were caught for just a moment in the glimmer of a street lamp. When my cab moved out of its way, the carriage continued for twenty yards and then turned into a side street.

I hurried into the shirt makers'. One man stood at the reading frame, inclining his head to examine a notice at the bottom of the *Glasgow Herald*. Two others sat at a corner of the study table. One of them was Arthur Knox. He stood up and without explanation led me along the corridor to the office at the back of the building.

'I may have been followed,' I said when we had sat down on either side of his desk.

A gas jet on the wall opposite the door to the back court glared over the room. In daylight, this had struck me as an agreeable place to work, but now it seemed unutterably bleak.

'Followed?'

'I should be frank, Mr Knox. A man has been murdered at the gallery of my fiancée's uncle. Now they have disappeared. I do not know where they are or what this is about, but I believe it may be connected to the photographs I took over there.' I nodded towards the shed in the back court. 'And when I was here before, and you invited me to inspect the furniture, I was threatened by a man. He pulled a knife—'

I was about to describe the gorilla with the bowler hat, but Knox cut me short.

'I too should speak frankly, Mr Camarón. I have made enquiries about you. I did not think I could speak freely before . . .'

I was assailed by a feeling of the most acute exasperation. The people with whom I had recently come into contact seemed to choose whether or not to tell the truth. I was not inclined to trust Knox or Smith. I no longer knew if I could trust those who were dear to me.

He continued, 'When you helped in the investigation of the terrible murders in Crown Street, you encountered corruption. I spoke to people who know about the case. Because of what they told me, I know that you stayed upon the path of truth. I know that *you* will understand better than others that this can be a dangerous path.'

'You know where Michael Martin is!' I said.

Knox was visibly alarmed perhaps because I knew the name or simply because I had spoken it out loud.

'You said the tenant was travelling, but he was hiding, wasn't he?' I leaned forward. 'He is still hiding. It's because of what he found out, what he found out about the Auchinleck yard.'

He lifted his hands from the desk as if he were playing an imaginary piano. We had reached that juncture where the terms of engagement had shifted in a significant way.

'Michael Martin is a fugitive,' he said. 'He did not murder the policeman but it would be convenient for many people if he were to hang for the crime.'

I was unable to disguise my exasperation. 'I do not know what this has to do with me or with . . .' I did not want to say Jane's name out loud, or Alan's.

'You are respected, Mr Camarón. You are involved in the investigation. You may know something – you may know something, yet you do not know that you know it!' He inflected the last handful of words in a rather forlorn effort to introduce an element of levity to what he was saying. Then he added with the utmost seriousness. 'Michael is afraid, and I fear he has reason to be. He believes, and I believe, that you may be able to help, even if at this point you do not see how you can do that. He trusts no one, but I believe if he were to place his confidence in anyone, then he might sensibly place it in you.'

'Mr Knox,' I said, 'be so good as to tell me why I should place my confidence in Mr Martin or anyone else.'

'You showed discernment, Mr Camarón, and courage too, when you stood up for the truth. I believe you can recognise here' – he opened his arms to indicate the shirt makers' – 'an honest struggle for what is true, for what is just.'

I would have done anything to understand the events that were taking place around me. I was inclined to believe that Knox could help me do that.

'Wait here for just a little while,' he said as he got to his feet.

He hurried out of the office. I sat down, and as I did so I realised I was sitting in the chair that had been in the murder room.

When he returned, Knox opened the door to the back court and said, 'Go to the carriageway. Someone is waiting there.'

I stood up.

'Hurry!' Knox said. 'You are right. You were followed.'

Outside, I inhaled the odd mixture of hops and refuse and damp. There was a night-time coolness, but the air here was not fresh. I picked my way along the path. When I reached the carriageway I recognised the man who was standing there. He had been sitting with Knox at the table when I entered the shirt makers'. He caught hold of my elbow and, putting a finger to his lips, pushed me towards the back of a peddler's cart that was covered with a heavy tarpaulin.

'Get inside,' he whispered. He lifted the tarpaulin and said, 'Inside now, sir.'

There was a smell of sawdust and cotton. When the canvas flap was pulled down and tied, the darkness was total. I felt the cart move out of the carriageway. There was nothing to hold onto and I had to brace myself against the side of the cart so as not to slide forward and back each time the horse changed pace. I do not know if I spent five minutes or ten minutes like this. When the cart stopped, the canvas was untied and the man told me, still in something close to a whisper, to climb out, I found myself on the corner of a main road, lamplit, with tram lines.

'Go in there,' the man said. He pointed to a public house. 'Someone will come for you.'

There were chairs all the way around the outer wall, and tables and chairs in the space in front of the long bar, where three men were serving. The place was crowded, and dense with tobacco smoke and alcohol fumes. I found a space at the bar and ordered whisky. The men on one side of me were speaking in the almost impenetrable dialect of the city. I struggled to make sense of what was said – it could not be described as a conversation, indeed, it sounded more like a quarrel. One of the men in the group had been guilty of an infraction of some sort. His principal accuser, speaking in a voice of the utmost indignation, rejected the other man's explanation while the rest of the group observed morosely, intervening from time to time only to express agreement that the infraction had been inexcusable.

On the other side, two men, better dressed, with bowler hats and city suits, were sipping whisky and speaking calmly about a meeting at which one of them intended to make clear his dissatisfaction with a decision that had been made.

Bars are about real life, yet they are separate from it. They are places where men take refuge from their troubles by dwelling upon them.

Here, there was an all-pervading gloom that had little to do with the dim light from the gas jets. There were faces and figures of every description and men of every station. All manner of emotions were expressed, but there was a uniformity to the resignation that sat like a weight upon this place. Disparate conversations melded to create a continuous sound. It was a sound that articulated sadness and resignation in the face of all that waited on the other side of the frosted glass doors.

'Mr Cameron?' a voice beside me asked.

I do not know how the man contrived to appear next to me. I had been standing with my back to the bar surveying the room, yet he was suddenly there. He was well dressed, like a solicitor or a merchant or a medical man, middle-aged with a grey moustache and an air of authority. He had not removed his bowler hat.

'Go outside and cross the road.'

I opened my mouth to speak, but he said, 'Go now, Mr Cameron. There is no time to lose.' He turned to the bar and called, in a voice that found its way across a chorus of competing voices, 'A brandy, if you please!'

I had entered from the side street but, as directed, I exited by the main door. Stepping into the night air, I felt as though I were floating. I smelled coal dust and, from somewhere, rose blossom.

A man stood on the other side of the road, facing me. He watched as I crossed and then he turned and began to walk. I was not for a single moment in any doubt that I must follow him. The sounds around me fell away, the clatter of wheels, the screech of a tram, the distant rise and fall of voices from the bar. I was conscious of the darkness, the tenement walls, a window box filled with roses above a tobacconist shop and the points of light where the lamps cast a yellow pall across the pavement and the road.

The man turned into a carriageway. I increased my pace. The last few steps before the entrance, I moved almost at a run.

In the back court, he walked to a space between two sheds. I followed.

With his back to a brick wall, he turned and as I stepped towards him, he raised his right arm ready to strike if I did not maintain a certain distance.

We could see one another in the faint light from a window on the second storey of the tenement behind us. I heard a thud and then the sound of a rat scratching a path over open

189

ground towards the safety of a gutter.

'Michael Martin?'

He was still standing in the manner of a boxer, his arms slightly raised.

'I am Juan Camarón. I met Lawrence Stolz and Alexander Napier in Edinburgh and I have spoken to Arthur Knox.'

'Has Miss Stolz been harmed?' His whole demeanour changed. His features escaped for a moment from the rictus of fear and hopelessness. I hadn't taken much note of his appearance until now. He had wavy red hair and freckles. He was older than me, but he wasn't old. I had an epiphany which did not alter the difficulty of our circumstances, but nonetheless enabled a small change of perspective: Michael Martin was the lover of Lawrence Stolz. They were, I thought, rather a good match.

'No, she has not been harmed,' I said. 'She is with Mr Napier, at the office of the Friends of the African Slave.'

He nodded. 'You are not a policeman?'

'I'm a photographer. I photographed the man who was murdered in your room.'

'I didn't murder him!'

His voice rose. In the darkness, where the brick walls made it seem as though we were in a room, not in the open air, his protest sounded like a scream.

'I photographed your room,' I said. 'I guessed that the chair had been moved so that you could stand up and reach the little ledge at the top of the stovepipe. I found Miss Stolz's address there and I went to see her. She told me that you were writing a report.'

He nodded vigorously. 'They tried to get it from me.'

'That's what the policeman was looking for, the one who was killed?'

'Auchinleck sent his man, who I think killed the policeman. Auchinleck wanted the report.'

'But why was the policeman in your room?'

'I don't know but they follow people like me. A year ago, I attended some meetings at the Land and Labour League.'

'The Land and Labour League . . .'

Perhaps I repeated the name with too much familiarity. His expression changed to one that seemed to be suddenly suffused with a kind of hatred. 'If you are a policeman—'

'I am *not* a policeman,' I said. 'Someone who is known to me has been murdered, and people close to me have disappeared. I want to know the truth.'

'The police have asked about me,' he said. 'They came to my work; they came to my family. They have a special department. The officers are not from here . . .'

'From London?'

'How do you know that?'

'Auchinleck doesn't have your report,' I said. 'One of those officers from Special Branch. I think he has it.'

He gave me a stricken look and there was a silence between us. I listened for the sound of rats.

'How do you know that?' he asked again, now speaking almost in a whisper.

'There was a document under the bed when I came to take photographs.'

He looked as though I had shattered whatever hope had prompted him to meet me.

'Look,' I said, 'I want to help you . . . Other people want to help you too – Mr Napier and Miss Stolz, the shirt makers—'

He seemed to recover something inside himself. He spoke in a more determined and a more measured way. 'The police think that something will happen to the Prince.'

'The one from the Black Sea?'

He nodded.

'But what does that have to do with you?'

'I work at the yard that made the torpedo boat.'

I remembered Lucheni and Angiolillo. 'And were you – *are* you – planning to do something radical?'

His expression changed to one of indignant disbelief. 'No, of course not!'

'Then . . .'

He took a deep breath. 'I went to work for Archibald Auchinleck two years ago. I've never met him, of course. He rarely comes to the yard, but it was clear to me from the beginning that this is a man of the future.' He saw my incomprehension and carried on quickly. 'The yard is a new one. Its business is new. That's why they deal with anyone. Not just Prince Danilo. They are finishing a vessel for King Leopold. Leopold didn't come to Auchinleck – in the past, he has placed orders with a yard in France and another smaller firm in Antwerp – Auchinleck went to Leopold. He offered the plans for a vessel that will not only navigate the Upper

Congo but has sufficient draught to carry large numbers of passengers.'

'Passengers?'

'Field labour, being moved from plantation to plantation, sometimes across considerable distances. There are rails along the open decks and manacles can be attached to them. There are cages below deck that can accommodate more than a hundred people.'

'This is what you were going to send to Miss Stolz?'

He nodded. 'But there is something else . . .'

He hesitated.

'Something to do with Vienna?' I said. I remembered what Breitling said about the charismatic mayor who was stoking resentment among citizens.

Martin made an impatient clucking sound with his tongue. 'Auchinleck's weak point isn't Vienna,' he said. 'It's Berlin.' He began to speak more quickly. 'The new canal has created a problem that wasn't foreseen, due to the transition from seawater to fresh water and back again. The propeller shafts on the smaller vessels are building up alkaline deposits. The canal was supposed to make the Kaiser's navy a match for ours.'

'Alkaline?' The leap from our present predicament to propeller shafts was too abrupt to be absorbed quickly.

'If you take a penny and you dip it in the sea,' he said, 'nothing will happen.'

I waited.

'If there's a river nearby and you take the same penny that you've just dipped in saltwater and then dip it in the fresh water, it will turn white. That's the beginning of an alkaline reaction. Pennies are made of copper; they will stain but they won't be damaged. Ships are made of steel. Alkaline generates rust.'

The passage between Kiel and Brunsbüttel had been operating for at least three years. There didn't seem to me to be a problem for ships going in and out of the Baltic. 'How does this affect the Kaiser?'

'Because most merchant ships have vertical propeller shafts, but the new destroyers have a shallow draught and a horizontal propeller shaft and they can't use the canal. To move a large part of his fleet from the Baltic to the North Sea, the Kaiser still has to sail around Denmark.'

'What has this to do with—?'

'Auchinleck has an answer to the problem. The Glasgow yards are already using aluminium for ship's hulls, but it has drawbacks in enclosed areas that require a very high degree of displacement precision, like propeller shafts. Auchinleck has developed a method of inhibiting corrosion by placing a sodium-chloride-resistant oxide shield in an aluminium casing over the steel core of the propeller shaft and it can be fitted to ships of up to two thousand tons. It will make it possible for the Imperial fleet to use the new canal as intended. Auchinleck has already reached an agreement for the delivery of fifty propeller shafts which will be worth infinitely more than King Leopold's slave ship or Prince Danilo's torpedo boat.'

'Propellers for the German navy!'

'Auchinleck could hang for this,' Martin said.

'Who knows about it?'

'Auchinleck and me, and now you, and whoever has the report that I prepared for Miss Stolz. I put the plans for the new propeller shaft and the draft agreement with the *Kaiserliche Marine* in the same envelope. I was going to—'

Martin stopped speaking. As the sound of his voice died in the darkness, it was displaced by the report of a gunshot and the spattering ricochet of a bullet that had pierced the brick enclosure. I felt something on my face, like dew in the early morning. The light from the window above and behind me was too weak for me to see anything other than Martin's face.

'You brought them here!' he said.

And then he disappeared.

I was standing in the same place, but I was alone. I took a step forward and for the first time I understood why Martin had brought me to this strange meeting place. It wasn't a sealed cul-de-sac. In one corner, there was a hole in the wall. He had used this to make his escape.

A second shot hit the bricks beside me, followed at once by the spattering sound of a violent ricochet. Again, I felt a puff of fine moist grit as a cloud of dust and dirt descended on my face. I heard footsteps in the carriageway, and I saw lights in the tenements and then a police whistle.

I ran out of the cul-de-sac. I would rather have been shot than miss an opportunity to see who had tried to kill Martin and then me.

But the person had vanished. The police whistle became louder. I ran in the opposite direction. As I barged through the darkness, I nearly bowled over a man who had emerged from one of the sheds in the middle of the back court. His eyes were wide and frightened in the faint light.

When I had exited the back court by the nearest close, I discovered to my astonishment that I was in Crown Street. A tram was moving past me, travelling towards the river. I ran after it and jumped aboard.

CHAPTER SEVENTEEN

When I lay down in my room, my thoughts moved in crazy undulating patterns over unrelated images – Breitling, face down on a threadbare carpet; the policeman, face up. I remembered the rage in Martin's face. *You have brought them here.*

I remembered the packed earth of the stable floor where my father's cousin and his wife lay, and I remembered, too, the cobblestones of the piazza in front of the cathedral in Santiago de Cuba, where my father was murdered at the very moment of creation.

And then there was a necklace of soft sound that lulled me deeper into sleep before it wakened me, and I realised there was daylight in the room and someone was knocking on the door. I rolled out of bed and stepped into my slippers. The coolness of the leather rose up from my feet through my body. The knocking persisted. I pulled on my dressing gown and stepped towards the door. I reached down and turned the key. The bolt drew back from the hasp, the handle turned, the door opened.

It was Jane.

She took my hand, and I drew her inside. She closed the door. We faced one another.

She was without a hat and stray wisps of hair created a kind of halo around her head. Her face was drawn, her jacket was crushed and there was dust on one of the shoulders.

I took cognisance of all of these things before I drew her towards me and said, 'You are safe!'

I felt her hands on my elbows and then her arms around my neck. We moved across the room and sat on the bed.

I looked down and saw that her skirt was creased and there was mud on her shoes.

'Have you slept?' I asked. 'Have you eaten?'

She shook her head. I didn't know if she was responding to my questions or dismissing them as irrelevant.

'I'll bring coffee,' I said

She held my hand very tight. 'No one must know I'm here.'

'Are you certain no one saw you when you came in?'

'I waited until I was sure,' she said. Then she added, 'Yes, I am hungry.'

I stood up. 'I'll bring food then.'

'No one must—'

I raised a hand. 'I know.'

The dining room was empty. I heard the clatter of pots and pans in the kitchen and went through. The woman there had water boiling on the hob; there were loaves of bread on the table next to her.

I asked if I could take coffee, bread and ham to my room.

'No, sir. Breakfast is from seven, in the dining room.'

There is a language that is never spoken, but which is often more effective than words. In the woman's tone, in her steady but expectant expression, I gathered that this was not the end of the matter.

She was a matronly figure, dark blouse and dark skirt under her starched white pinny. Her grey hair was brushed back severely but her expression was more intelligent than austere.

I produced a shilling. 'I would be very much obliged.'

'It's irregular, sir.'

Just at that moment, the door at the back of the kitchen opened. 'Coal's in the bunker!' a man shouted. He closed the door and I saw him through the window climb up on top of his cart, where another man shimmied the reins and the giant vehicle lumbered off to the next delivery.

'One of the girls will bring it up,' the woman said, accepting the shilling.

'I'll take it up myself.'

She shook her head and said with great emphasis, 'That would not do at all, sir.'

I produced another shilling.

Minutes later, after flitting across a corner of the main lobby – as far as I could tell, unnoticed – I climbed the stairs, two at a time. The door of my room was locked. I knocked. There was a sound of someone scurrying.

'Who is it?'

'It's me!'

The door opened. I stepped in and put the tray on the desk by the window. There was a chair at the desk, I dragged another chair from next to the wardrobe.

Jane sat and I poured milk from the jug into the single coffee cup and then poured coffee into the cup and into the jug. I took the jug and sat down at the side of the desk, so that we were sitting next to one another.

'I couldn't ask for two cups.'

'But you asked for two sandwiches?'

'I said I was hungry.'

Jane sipped her coffee, holding the cup in both hands. After several more sips, she took a bite of her sandwich.

We drank and ate in silence.

I wanted her to start in her own time, but this seemed to take for ever, so I said, 'Jane, what happened?'

She put the cup down. She had drunk most of the coffee. I took the pot and filled her cup again.

'I wrote to you,' she said. 'I expressed my concern. My uncle and Breitling seemed to have an understanding that went beyond the arrangement of the exhibition. You asked me once if my uncle is a member of a particular group of men who endeavour to support what I believe are very commendable principles of progress for all mankind. I was angry with you then, Juan. It was the first time that I was angry with you.'

Jane said this without any expression of regret; it was an almost absent-minded observation.

'Well, my uncle isn't a mason. I've no idea if Breitling is, but they *were* being secretive about something. It was sinister.'

She took a sip of coffee and I did the same. This was rather awkward, as the jug wasn't designed to be used as a cup.

'When I arrived at the gallery yesterday afternoon, Breitling was agitated. He and Alan were poring over the pictures we took at the villa in Milngavie. When I came into the studio, they put the pictures away very quickly. I pretended not to notice. I had no reason to be suspicious then. When I left the studio, I heard one of the cabinet drawers being opened and then closed again. I presumed the pictures were being stored. Now, why would Alan and Doctor Breitling not wish me to see photographs that had been made in my own presence? What could possibly have been in them?'

I waited for her to continue.

'They then went out, leaving me on my own in the gallery. They did not say where they were going, and naturally I did not ask, but I did enquire if my services might be needed, as interpreter. "No need," my uncle said.' Jane looked at me with an expression of sudden fragility. 'I was still not on my guard, Juan.'

I reached out and placed my hand on top of hers and I felt

her fingers curl up in mine. For several seconds we sat like this, and then she withdrew her hand and lifted her cup and took a sip of coffee before continuing.

'There was a single reference and it is odd because I did not pay attention to it when I first heard it, but it must have lodged in one of the layers of my mind.' She glanced at me and gave a weak smile when she used the word 'layers'. 'When they had been speaking to one another in the studio, when I interrupted them – my uncle mentioned 'the captain'. As you know, my uncle's German is not like his French. It is a schoolboy version of the language. He repeated the words in order to be sure that he had understood Doctor Breitling properly: "*Der Kapitän! Der Kapitän!*"'

'The captain?'

She nodded.

'I waited all afternoon for them to return. I could have closed the gallery and gone home, but by then I was quite certain that something was very much amiss.'

I reached out to take her hand again, but she did not respond in the same way. She continued to hold her cup. I did not know if she did this as a gesture of rejection or if she was simply so tired and so focused on what she was telling me that she had not noticed my hand.

'My uncle is a brilliant man,' she said. 'He is an artist. I know that there is a profound dissatisfaction in his nature and he feels that he has betrayed his art by failing to produce anything memorable. I have told him, of course, as have

202

others that many of his photographs must be viewed as an eloquent . . . as a powerful testament to the inequity of our times. But he has that unanswerable way of thinking that he has never created the one work that would make him feel his life has been worthwhile. And because of this, he is reckless, he is bitter, and he is sometimes cruel.'

I knew that Mary's deep, deep sadness was a function of that cruelty. Not physical cruelty but a kind of emotional mistreatment – his sarcasm, his hubris, even his cleverness all served to exclude his wife from the intimacy and tenderness that she craved.

'After two hours, perhaps a little more, I went into the studio. I opened several of the drawers before I came to the pictures of the villa on the loch. I recognised them immediately, of course, because when Doctor Breitling developed them, I acted as his assistant. He has a strange approach, Juan, not like yours, not like my uncle's. He works very slowly.'

'It's because he doesn't use an emulsifier,' I said. 'There is less danger that the contrast will be diminished by a concentration of the chemical in one part of the developing liquid, so the paper can remain in the liquid for longer.'

She looked at me with sudden contentment, as though this brief reversion to our ordinary world with its comprehensible mechanisms and clear explanations offered a sort of respite.

'He made them larger than the ones that you customarily make, I think a foot and a half by a foot.'

I nodded. 'That's common on the continent.'

'I found the pictures and I took them out and examined them.'

She stopped speaking and looked at me.

'And?'

'And there was nothing! Nothing that I could discern. Nothing untoward. Just the empty rooms that we photographed.' She stood up and walked to the bed where she had left her bag and took out a manila envelope. 'They are here,' she said.

I joined her and took the photographs from the envelope and laid them on the bed.

'There are only six here!' I said. 'Breitling took eight.'

'There *were* eight,' she said. 'Two were removed.'

'Removed?'

'That is the next part of my story.' She walked back to the desk and poured herself the last little bit of coffee. She stopped in the middle of doing this and indicated that there was some for me. I shook my head and she finished pouring into her own cup. Then she took a long sip and put the cup down.

'Jane, have you slept?'

'No, I have not slept, Juan, but this is not to the point now.' She said this with a trace of irritation.

'I was still looking at the photographs,' she continued, 'when I heard the little bell at the main door of the gallery. I put the photographs back in the drawer and went out. Breitling had entered the gallery in the company of another man I didn't recognise. They were walking towards me. I do not know why I behaved the way I did, yet I believe it may in some way have been for the best. I went up to the landing on the stairs and let them pass through the anteroom and into the studio. If either of them had looked up they would have seen me.'

'But they didn't?'

'They were preoccupied with one another.'

'Preoccupied?'

'Juan, I did not announce my presence because I sensed that something was terribly wrong. There was . . . violence . . . in the air. It was almost as if you could touch it.' She stopped speaking and I realised that she was no longer looking at me but into the middle distance. I wanted to reach out, but she was in a sort of trance and I thought it better simply to stand close to her and allow her to finish telling her story.

'When they were in the studio, I heard Breitling say, "The photograph is not here!"' She glanced at me. 'That's what he said: "The photograph is not here!"'

'What did he look like, the man who was with Breitling?'

She nodded and carried on speaking. 'I will tell you. I will tell you when I have told you what happened first. I stood on the landing and heard a terrible sound. It was the sound of violence, Juan. I *know* that sound.'

I stepped forward and took her in my arms. 'Do not speak of it.'

She pushed me away, very firmly and at the same time without any hint of her earlier irritation. She continued looking into the middle distance.

'I heard Breitling shout, "Have it, then!" The drawer was opened. The two men came out of the lobby, Breitling in front, the other man hurrying behind. It was as though Breitling were trying to make his escape. And then' – she paused and looked at me for a moment – 'and then I heard a scream. Not properly a scream. It was like the *beginning* of a scream, but it seemed to die in the throat. I heard a struggle.'

She was staring at me.

'What did you do?'

'I cast around for a weapon.'

'A candlestick?'

She was startled.

'It lay on the floor beside his body when I went to the gallery,' I said.

Jane put her hand up to her mouth. 'Oh, Juan!'

'You were very brave,' I said.

This sounded foolish. Jane's expression changed to one of disappointment, as though the notion of valour were beside the point.

'I came to the bottom of the stairs holding the candlestick.'

'Where did you find it?' I sounded like a policeman now.

'It was in the corner of the landing. There's a high sort of table there and the candlestick sits on top of it. I tiptoed down to the bottom of the stairs and looked into the gallery. Breitling was lying on the carpet.'

She stopped speaking, and her face became a mask, a mask of horror, as though she were again feeling as she had felt during the events she described.

'What did you do?'

'I did the only think that I thought it right to do. I advanced into the gallery. I had the candlestick in front of me and I was ready to use it as a club if the stranger attacked.'

'Oh, Jane!'

She looked at me indulgently. 'Juan, I did not need to exercise this rather fanciful stratagem. The man had fled. I knelt down and examined Doctor Breitling. He was dead. I stood up and went back into the studio.'

'And the candlestick?'

She looked at me as though my preoccupation with the candlestick were somehow baffling. 'I left it, I suppose.'

I nodded.

'I took the photographs from the studio and I ran back through the gallery and out into the street. The stranger was already twenty yards away. I saw him climb into a carriage. I ran as fast as I could and when I reached the corner I climbed into a cab and told the driver to follow the carriage.'

'That was resourceful!' I sounded condescending now and Jane gave me a look that seemed to reflect this.

'The only course of action,' she said, 'was to ensure that the murderer did not slip away. I also believed, though I cannot say I thought as clearly at the time, that the man in the carriage would lead me to my uncle, and I believed that these photographs were in some way the key to the scheme in which Breitling and my uncle and the stranger were embroiled.'

'Where did he go?'

'To the Theatre Royal. The carriage stopped at the stage door. The murderer entered the building. I did not see his face, but I know he was the man who committed the murder.'

'How do you know that?'

'Because he wore a yellow raincoat and a brown trilby with a red band. It's not a very common combination.'

'You were remarkably astute,' I said. 'You kept your head.'

'I don't know about that – all I did was catch a cab. It wasn't terribly gallant or clever.'

I was going to argue but she cut me off. 'I got out of the cab and went to the stage door . . .'

She waited just long enough for me to say, 'And?'

'It was locked.'

I walked back to the desk and put the jug down next to the pot. Jane remained at the bed holding her cup in both hands. She had laid the pictures out on top of the blanket. 'I told the cabbie to wait and I went around to the front of the building. People were coming out of the evening performance. I scanned the crowd to see if my man in the yellow coat and the trilby would appear.' She took a final sip of her coffee and then said, 'But he didn't.'

She stepped across the room, placed the empty cup next to the empty jug and then we both returned to where the pictures lay.

'I took the cab back to the gallery,' she continued, 'but when we pulled up outside the building there were people standing at the entrance, including a policeman. My driver shouted across to the policeman to ask him what had happened. The policeman said, "There's been an incident." The cabbie said, "This one ran out of the building not twenty minutes ago." I had started climbing down. I looked up and saw that the cabbie was pointing at me.'

'What did you do?'

'I climbed back into the cab and out the other side, then I ran across Waterloo Street. The policeman followed me, of course. I ducked into one side street and then another, and when I emerged into Sauchiehall Street, I walked as calmly as I could for several steps and got into a cab that was coming back into the centre of town.'

'But why did you—?'

'Because the cabbie was telling the truth. He *had* seen me running from the building. They would have arrested me.'

Perhaps she recognised in my look a certain scepticism.

'Will *you* go to the police, Juan?'

I had no response to this.

'I must know what has happened,' she said. 'I must speak to my uncle.'

I experienced a sudden wave of anger, which was directed not at Jane but at Alan. Whatever he was involved in would be the undoing of his niece.

But before I could begin to speak, there was a knock at the door.

It might have been a maid sent up by the cook to collect the breakfast things – but it was not that sort of knock.

'Who's there?'

'Police! Open up!'

Jane had only to move half a pace and, as I opened the door, she had stepped behind it.

The policeman practically filled the doorway. He must

have been a foot taller than me and he was broader too. He stepped aside to make way for a man closer to my own size.

'Señor Camarón,' Captain Smith said. 'You were already up?'

He was looking over my shoulder at the desk, where the empty breakfast things lay on the tray.

'And have you had company?'

'Company?'

Oddly, I experienced more indignation than alarm when he said this. The insinuation was impertinent.

I had to follow Smith's gaze again to understand the logic of his observation. 'Two chairs,' he said helpfully. 'Two chairs at the desk.'

'The gas jet is temperamental,' I said. 'It sometimes needs to be coaxed.' The chair was below the lamp holder and might plausibly have served as a step from which to reach up and adjust the jet.

'Mr Camarón, have either of the fugitives been in contact with you?'

I had become 'Mister', instead of 'Señor'. This struck me as an ill omen.

'Fugitives?'

I should not have said this. Smith knew that I knew who the fugitives were. I wondered if, when I had the sense of being watched as I walked along Great Western Road, I was being watched by someone Smith had set to follow me.

And I wondered if he already knew that Jane was in the room.

A lie is a commitment; it changes a man's status. Things that would not have been possible before the falsehood become possible, and even necessary, after it.

Smith stared at me.

'No one has been in contact with me,' I said.

When he hesitated, I realised that he did not know that Jane was there.

'Have you spoken to any member of Mr Fletcher's family?'

If this was an attempt to catch me out, it was very clumsy.

'Yes,' I said, trying not to sound too relieved as I moved back to the safer territory of truth, 'I visited Mrs Fletcher last night after I spoke to you at the gallery. She too has heard nothing from her husband . . .' I wondered if I should add 'and her niece' but decided not to. Just to refer to Jane seemed to tempt fate. She was utterly still and silent, something that could only have been achieved by a monumental effort of will. If she had moved her arm or changed the weight of her body, even the slightest sound would have been audible on the other side of the door.

'She was alone?'

'Who?' I had been distracted by my consideration of how finely this encounter hung in the balance.

'Mrs Fletcher.'

'No, she was with her sister, Janet.'

'And after you visited Mrs Fletcher?'

'I went to the shirt makers' association.'

He was surprised.

'I have been more and more angry,' I said, moving suddenly into the heart of a new and calamitous lie, 'over what that man did to me – the one who nearly killed me on the roof. I want to know who he is. I want *you* to apprehend him.'

Smith's reaction was gratifying. He became officious. 'Señor Camarón, you cannot conduct your own investigations. These are matters for the police.'

I did not respond.

He nodded. 'I will let you return to your coffee, then.' He glanced again at the desk and the two chairs were configured for two people to sit together.

I was about to close the door, but he stepped suddenly forward. 'I want you to understand that if you render any assistance to Fletcher or his niece, you will be deemed an accessory to murder.'

He had placed his foot in such a way that the door could not be closed completely. Perhaps this is a policeman's trick. It was very effective.

'Do you understand?'

'I understand,' I said.

He removed his foot, and I closed the door.

CHAPTER EIGHTEEN

Neither of us spoke. We looked down at the pictures on the bed. As we examined the photographs, I sensed that the physical distance between us reflected an emotional distance. It was small but tangible.

'What happened, Juan? Someone nearly killed you? On a roof? Why did that policeman come here?'

I shook my head. 'It was nothing, a small incident of no importance that happened near the place where I made photographs the day that Breitling arrived. That' – I nodded towards the doorway recently vacated by Smith – 'was the policeman who took me to the place. He was at the gallery when I went there from the station. He's not, in fact, a policeman, or at least not a regular one. He belongs to some new department that spies on trade unions and socialists.'

'What on earth?'

'Well,' I said, 'Breitling was some sort of socialist, wasn't he? He had all sorts of ideas about violence and politics, and he seems to have very—he *seemed* to have very decided views on what the mayor of Vienna is up to . . . and the Black Sea.'

The emotions that raced among and between my thoughts were overwhelming. Jane's hair had come loose with a kind of exquisite abandon. I wanted with every atom of my being to lose myself in those dark eyes.

'Five days ago,' I said, 'I had a dream, a vivid dream. I walked in a quiet street; it was misty, very dark. A man walked in front of me. He wore a bowler hat, and there were just two of us in the street. We entered one of those courtyards behind the tenements. There was a place with three brick walls and cinder on the ground and I remembered the same place where we found . . . where one of the victims was found . . .'

I should have told Jane then about Michael Martin, but instead I said, 'After I caught the cab in Kelvinbridge, I remembered that dream. It was like a premonition. It struck me very powerfully. I have a sense of chasing the truth, but never getting hold of it.'

I sat down on the bed. Jane moved the photographs to one side and sat beside me.

'Sometimes evil things stay with us,' she said. 'Sometimes we think they have been left behind, but they are waiting

214

for us, in our thoughts.'

After we had sat in silence for what seemed to me a very long time, I asked, 'What shall we do?'

'I need to find out who that man is.'

'The man in the yellow coat?'

'Yes.' Jane said. 'We could go to the theatre and ask about him, but why would anyone tell us anything?'

'There *is* a way. How did you get into the hotel?'

'A guest was coming in through the main door – drunk, I think, top hat and tails, not altogether steady on his feet. I slipped in behind him and the porter didn't see me.'

'We'll have to sneak out. I'm going to go down and check out the lie of the land.'

'But where are we going?'

I had already scooped up the tray and opened the door. 'I'll tell you when I come back.' I closed the door and hurried along the corridor and down the stairs. The lobby was beginning to fill up now as breakfast got underway.

In the kitchen, the woman who had obliged me earlier was standing at the end of the huge table in the middle of the room, kneading dough. She was not happy to see me.

'I would have sent the girl up for that,' she said, glancing around. There were two girls at a huge sink in the corner next to the back door. They were peeling potatoes.

'I didn't want to trouble you.' I put the tray down on the table. The woman wiped her hands and hurried round to pick it up and carry it to a different sink, where she placed everything quickly inside.

Satisfied that there were few people in the kitchen, I went back out to the lobby. Across the lobby I saw a policeman on the other side of the main door, loitering on the pavement.

In the room I told Jane we must hurry.

'But where?'

'To the theatre. I know how we can have the run of the place. I met someone on the train from Edinburgh last night.'

'You met someone?'

'An opera singer. She wants me to take her photograph. She wants me to take *everyone's* photograph. I'll tell you more about it when we are safely out of the hotel.'

'The police—'

'We will slip out through the back of the building, now' – I hurried over to the wardrobe and inside I found a cotton cap with a visor. I brought it back and put it on Jane's head – 'it's a little large, but that's even better,' I said. 'Pull it down over your face.'

Disassembling the tripod and placing the Eclipse in its travelling case, I added two lenses, for individual and group photography, and some magnesium ribbons.

I presented Jane with the tripod. 'You will be my assistant.'

The tripod was heavier than she had imagined, and her arms stretched when she took it from me. I reached out and supported the weight while she steadied her grip. 'I will carry it when we are outside, but when we walk through the hotel, hold it like this.' I showed her how to take the weight in both hands and carry it in such a way that the bracket was at the height of her face. 'Use it to shield yourself. It may be enough, together with the cap, if someone is watching.'

'They will know it's me!'

'Perhaps they will,' I said, surprised by my own rather brusque tone, 'but we are going to try, because the alternative is to sit here and cry.'

I stepped out into the corridor and Jane followed. As we moved to the top of the stairs, a man and a woman walked towards us in the opposite direction. They were rather young, and their manner, I thought, was that of newly-weds. The woman giggled as they passed. Jane raised the tripod so that the bracket partially obscured her face. We met no one on the stairs but when we reached the lobby, we encountered the last thing in the world I had expected to find there. A large and voluble family group had begun to assemble on the bottom steps in front of a photographer, who had set up his tripod and camera in front of the reception desk.

We were trapped on the wrong side of a group portrait, perhaps fifteen people.

'Coming through!' I said, conscious that Jane and I were now the centre of attention. Jane's disguise would not serve much purpose here.

'Can't you wait?' someone asked.

'We can,' I said, loud enough for the photographer to hear, 'but then we'll be in your picture.'

Perhaps the photographer saw my camera case, or the tripod that Jane was holding up like a beacon. He opted for the quickest solution.

'Make way there,' he said in the gently coaxing voice that

photographers deploy when people have to be corralled.

Two of the party stepped forward and made way.

'Couldn't even wait,' someone said. 'How rude!' said someone else.

I glanced at the main door. The constable was still at his post in the street outside. I led Jane across the lobby and along the corridor to the kitchen.

The cook looked up and saw me, her face reddened and she opened her mouth, no doubt to complain that I really was taking intolerable liberties, but I headed this off by whispering as I hurried past her and Jane followed. 'We'll be out of your way before you know it!'

Out in the lane, I took the tripod from Jane and we moved quickly to the main road behind the hotel.

There is a particular atmosphere in a theatre at the start of the day, as if the cleaning and mending and delivering that fill the passages and offices and corridors cannot entirely displace the residual spell of a full auditorium, tobacco smoke and evening gowns, greasepaint and footlights and jewellery, and the rising, falling hum of human voices.

In the foyer I put the tripod down on the thick pile of the red carpet in front of the box office. Two men in overalls emerged from a corridor and walked past us on their way out to the street. As they left, we heard one tell the other that the empty barrels could be left until later. This was spoken with an accent I could not have deciphered when I first came to Glasgow.

A tall man with longish grey hair and a grey goatee came towards us from the box office and asked what our business might be.

'Madame Orlova asked me to come,' I told him. 'I am a photographer.'

He looked down at me as if everything I had just said should be absorbed and carefully assessed.

'I am to make a portrait of Madame Orlova,' I added.

His attention turned to Jane.

'I am the assistant,' she said.

Once, it seemed a long time ago now, I asked Jane to become my assistant and she turned me down, proposing that we get married instead. I was momentarily troubled by her enthusiastic assumption of the title now.

'Your name is?' the man asked me.

I told him. He looked from me to Jane, but he didn't ask her to identify herself. I was certain her name would have been in the papers by now.

'Madame Orlova invited you to come to the theatre?'

His accent was foreign, clipped.

'She did,' I said. 'We met last night, on the train from Edinburgh.'

'She has not told me about a portrait.'

I disliked being obliged to give an account of myself. 'Perhaps, you could let Madame Orlova know that we are here.'

'Madame Orlova cannot to be disturbed before rehearsal.'

'Then perhaps the manager—'

'My name is Müller,' he said. '*I* am the manager.'

'*Wilhelm* Müller?' Jane asked in a bright voice, as though meeting this particular Müller was an unexpected honour.

'That is correct.' His head bowed very slightly and his heels came together, not quite in a formal military clicking but in something rather close to it.

'My father attended you,' Jane said, 'soon after you arrived from Hamburg. You had measles.'

If I had had to predict a likely conversation on entering this theatre it would not have involved German ports or infectious diseases.

'You are Doctor Macgregor's daughter?'

Jane acknowledged that she was, and again I considered the fact that her name must surely have appeared in the papers.

Müller, apparently, had not seen it there. His manner became solicitous. 'I was very sorry . . . to hear—'

'Thank you,' Jane said, and then she spoke in German, for which there was no need, as Müller clearly spoke excellent English. I gathered that the objective was to gain the man's confidence.

After they had spoken for some time, Müller turned to me and said, 'Please bring your equipment to my office.'

I picked up the tripod and began to follow him across the foyer.

'The first rehearsal finishes at ten,' Jane whispered.

As we deposited the camera case and the tripod in a corner of Müller's office, he said again, 'Madame Orlova didn't tell me anything about a portrait.' This time he sounded more disposed to hearing details.

'She had the idea,' I said, straightening up, 'as we were discussing her appearance here, that it would be possible to create *a portfolio* – a portrait of Madame Orlova, of course, but also of others in the cast.'

'Juan and his father travelled all the way across Cuba making portraits,' Jane said. 'He has been very successful.'

I disliked being spoken for. And at the same time, I disliked the resentment that welled up inside me. It was petty and spiteful and utterly without any basis in reason. Jane was establishing our bona fides. We had to have the run of the theatre in order to find the man with the yellow raincoat – it was *my* idea to put this unlikely plan into action.

Jane's appearance, at least, lent credibility to her role as photographer's assistant, with her cap and her dusty jacket and skirt.

'Please, take a seat,' Müller said.

There was a circular table in the corner of the office to one side of the house manager's desk. It had four chairs around it and a polished marble top. Müller stepped outside for a moment and we heard him asking for tea to be brought and for someone to be fetched.

'Madame Orlova thought that I might make portraits of . . . She mentioned several . . .' I racked my brain to remember. 'Baron von Herzberg,' I said.

'Herzog,' Müller corrected, coming back from the door and taking a seat next to Jane.

'Yes, Baron von Herzog, and the family of jugglers from Naples, the Pollinis.'

'The Fellinis,' Müller said, 'they are acrobats.'

'And Messrs Temple and Saul.'

'Temple and Hall.'

'He has a mind like a sieve,' Jane said.

'A portrait of the theatre!' Müller was suddenly enthusiastic.

'Well,' I said, 'portraits of the performers.'

'But the theatre itself will be a character!'

Whether this was a momentary inspiration or a prescription laid down by the house, I could not tell. Either way, the portrait of Madame Orlova, which was no more than a pretext, appeared to be spiralling into some sort of serious endeavour.

'We can use the theatre as a backdrop,' Jane said. 'We can make the portraits in different places – in the auditorium, in the wings, in the dressing rooms, on the stage.'

'Ah,' Müller said, 'here is the tea.'

A woman our age came in carrying a tray, which she placed on the table. She wore a grey skirt and a white shirt, with a red kerchief round her neck. She was slim and tall and her fine features; small nose, pale blue eyes, delicate lips were complemented by auburn hair tied in a careless bun. Wisps fell down on either side of her pretty face and I noticed that on her kerchief and her shirt there were streaks and blotches of colour, as though she had been working at an easel.

Not an easel, as it turned out, but a stage set depicting a city street illuminated by gas lamps that made the cobbles gleam in the twilight, the backdrop for a sentimental serenade.

'Miss Macgregor and Mr Camarón, this is Natalia

Aleksandrova,' Müller said, and then he added, 'Natalia, Miss Macgregor and Mr Camarón are going to make a portrait of the Theatre Royal, a *photographic* portrait. I would be grateful if you could assist them.'

I felt a sudden urge to assert myself. Müller introduced Jane and then me and described what we were going to do, as though we had suddenly become employees of the theatre. Before I could speak, he added, 'Natalia is our angel. She has breathed life into our artwork.'

Natalia smiled, sat down at the table and took one of the cups of tea she had poured, and said to Jane, 'We have met before perhaps? Your face is familiar to me.' Her accent was clipped and correct, like Müller's.

Jane explained, without any circumspection, where she worked. This was not inconsistent with her assumed role as my assistant, yet I was certain we would not be able to continue much longer without being unmasked as fugitives.

'Natalia is one of the Kunstgewerbeschule's brightest students,' Müller said. 'The Kunstgewerbeschule in Vienna,' he added, apparently in case Jane or I might be thinking about a different craft school. 'I persuaded her to spend a season at the Theatre Royal and to learn about art in the real world.'

He said this, I thought, with the fondness of an infatuated middle-aged man.

'You are making a portrait of the theatre?' Natalia asked Jane.

'Well, we have been asked to make a portrait of Madame Orlova,' I said, 'and Madame Orlova suggested we photograph the other cast members, too.'

'The Fellinis,' Müller explained, 'and the English comedians.'

'And Baron von Herzog,' Natalia said quickly. It wasn't clear to me whether this was a question or a suggestion. Either way, Natalia added, looking at Müller and then at us, 'and Monsieur Meunier.'

I raised my eyebrows at the last name. It meant nothing.

'The juggler,' Natalia said. 'He is very skilful . . . from Nîmes.' She mentioned his place of origin as if it might have some bearing on his skilfulness.

After two or three sips of strong tea I felt as though some of the dullness in my thoughts had been lifted. Once, when we were in Cuba, we stopped at a town in the mountains on the fifteenth of August and watched from the terrace of the main cafe as a statue of the Virgin Mary was carried through the main street. I remember the noise of the brass band and the crowd. A girl brought little bow-shaped pastries covered in sugar. We watched the procession and drank coffee. When I bit into the pastry, I had the strange sensation that we were not in the Cuban sierra but sitting in the Carrera de la Virgen in Granada, where the cafe opposite the basilica serves exactly the same cake, with the same milky vanilla and crisp layers of golden pastry topped with sugar.

'Juan!' Jane said.

I gathered that she had said my name once or twice already. I had been dreaming.

'Yes?'

All three of them were looking at me.

'If you would like to wait in the auditorium until Madame Orlova has finished her first rehearsal,' Müller said, 'Natalia will make sure that she knows you are here.'

'That is very kind,' Jane said. 'We will stay well out of your way.'

'An assistant would not have been so forward,' I whispered when we were seated in the auditorium. To my surprise, there were at least twenty people dotted around the stalls when the rehearsal began at eight o'clock sharp.

'But I'm not really your assistant, am I?' she replied. 'Unless that's all you want me to be.'

I glanced at her.

Her hand rose and then rested on my wrist. 'I'm sorry, Juan. I didn't mean to speak so plainly.'

The sudden pain her first response had caused receded with the touch of her fingers on my arm.

But then she removed her hand and said, 'But you have changed, so much and in such a short time.'

'What do you mean?'

There were people sitting further along the same row, and people several rows in front and behind. Jane and I had to carry on our conversation, or perhaps I should better describe it as 'an exchange' rather than 'a conversation', in whispers. And when the rehearsal began, our whispers were barely more than breathless monosyllables.

'I have done nothing wrong,' Jane said.

'I know that.'

'How do I *know* that you know that?'

I raised my hands, palms outward, in an expression of the utmost exasperation. 'Because I have *told* you that I know. Surely this is enough.'

We were both silent.

When Madame Orlova walked out from the wings, I noticed several things. Despite the fact that the stage itself was untidy, with pieces of furniture, including a set of step ladders and an overturned chair, interspersed among different bits of scenery suspended from the overheard rigging, and despite the fact that we sat towards the back of the stalls, the eye followed Madame Orlova: the distractions of colour and form around her faded away to nothing. She was somehow taller than I remembered, but every bit as pretty. Perhaps it was because I was preoccupied with the appearance of Madame Orlova that I hadn't noticed a small man take his place at the upright piano about a third of the way from the wings. He struck up a chord and stopped, and as soon as he stopped, Madame Orlova began. She sang three arpeggios, the first in the same chord as the pianist had played, and the second and third a modulation from that.

When Madame Orlova had concluded the third of her arpeggios, the pianist began to play a dramatic introduction to the first number. While he did this, Madame Orlova scrutinised the stalls from left to right. When her gaze fell on me, she gave no sign of recognition.

And then she began to sing. I had, I suppose, expected something girlish and whimsical, but this was nothing of the sort. She began on a high note, which was so loud that I wondered how someone so slim and fragile could produce a sound robust to the point of being frightening. From this note, she descended with such precipitate and spectacular assurance that for a second or two I found myself imagining that the sound must actually penetrate the floorboards beneath her. This focused the attention; for the rest of the aria, Madame Orlova and the pianist appeared to be in a sort of competition, edging round one another and over and under one another as first the piano and then the voice created patterns of sound that communicated, I am almost certain, a young woman's dramatic response to being told that she cannot after all marry her young man.

'You have changed too,' I whispered to Jane, apropos of nothing.

I had whispered before I knew it. It was as though my thoughts had decided on their own to communicate with the woman next to me.

'I have not,' she said.

'When I told you about the woman in Edinburgh and the things she said—'

'Juan. I said nothing.'

'You doubted me. By saying nothing you expressed that doubt.'

She glanced at me. 'That makes no sense.'

I did not return her glance. She was right. It made no sense.

Madame Orlova stopped singing. I raised my hands to begin clapping. No one else did. Jane's hand was on my wrist again, not this time to express tenderness but to prevent me from making a fool of myself by applauding one of the performers during a rehearsal. This was not, I gathered, the done thing.

The pianist struck up the next number. This was as I had expected the first aria to be, one of those songs where the singer assumes a coquettish persona and enunciates the phrases with musical adornments that make the high notes sound like squealing and the low notes like the careless chat of market vendors bantering with their customers. Madame Orlova walked one way across the stage and made a sort of comical curtsey and then the other way, ending her little promenade with another curtsey. She wore the same clothes, but she became a completely different person.

'Juan,' Jane said. 'Juan!'

I hadn't heard her the first time. I looked around. 'Yes?'

'You are being very unfair.'

I could think of nothing by way of a response to this. I thought silence would be the prudent policy, so I turned and gave my complete attention to Madame Orlova's performance.

'Juan,' Jane said.

'What?' I turned and faced her again.

'Oh, never mind.'

I was filled with the most profound unease. I sensed that what had now taken place between us could not be papered over with tender expressions of remorse or of love.

Madame Orlova stopped again, and after a few seconds, the pianist struck up a new number.

This one I had heard before. It was from *La Bohème*. On

the train, Madame Orlova told me that she had sung the part of Mimi in London.

There was nothing of the coquette; there were no little jokes or playful wanderings about the stage. Madame Orlova stood by the piano, absolutely still. She seemed to me now a rather small figure, and her voice, though loud and clearly heard in every part of the auditorium, conveyed a tenderness that could not have been evoked so beautifully by any other medium.

Perhaps the best way I can describe the effect of this music is to observe that during the course of the aria, I forgot entirely that Madame Orlova was the singer. The music itself assumed a kind of hold over the listener, and not just me. A change took place in the theatre. Mimi cast a spell. Beside me, Jane relaxed a little and gazed at the stage.

And then the music stopped, and the spell was broken.

Madame Orlova walked into the wings.

'Is that it?' I asked. 'Shall we go and see if we can find her?'

'*I* don't know,' Jane said. 'She's *your* friend.'

The issue was quickly resolved. Natalia appeared in a doorway to the left of the stage. Her appearance had a certain drama to it, because the door made a loud noise when it was opened and light from the corridor flooded into the relative darkness of the auditorium, so that Natalia's red kerchief and auburn hair were like a vivid tableau against the surrounding gloom, as in a Caravaggio canvas.

She waved to us and I waved back.

'Juan,' Jane said, 'you really are a child.'

As we walked down the aisle, I took Jane's arm. She maintained a certain distance, however, and I sensed that my gesture was an intrusion rather than a help, so, after several seconds, I withdrew my hand.

We walked on a thick red carpet along a dimly lit corridor with walls that were covered in maroon flock paper. The effect of the deep colour in the enclosed, gloomy space was peculiar and it was as if we passed through a dreamscape. This effect dissipated abruptly when we entered a large and brightly lit area where fifteen or twenty sets were stored in a giant frame fixed to a brick wall. There were windows all the way along the top of the wall opposite. Half a dozen men were manhandling a screen out of the frame. Patterns of dust swirled in the sunlit air. Two of the men were at the top of stepladders, standing at either end of the screen. They were unfastening some sort of clasp, and they exchanged instructions apparently with a view to releasing the clasps at the same time so that the screen could be lowered safely to the four men standing below.

It takes ropes and pulleys to manufacture magic. I wondered if, for the men shouting to one another in their impenetrable Glaswegian, working in a theatre was very different from working in a warehouse or a factory.

'Juan!' Madame Orlova said when we entered her dressing room. 'You have come!'

'I have.'

Madame Orlova surprised me with an embrace. The scent she wore was different from the one I remembered from the railway carriage. The dressing room smelled of talcum powder and eau de cologne. At one end of the room there was a sofa, and there were two wardrobes along the wall. Opposite the wardrobes was an armchair over which several dresses were draped. A trunk had been placed next to the armchair and the lid was up, revealing a variety of differently coloured silks. Behind Madame Orlova there was a dressing table with a mirror so large that when I glanced at it, I saw the back of Madame Orlova and the front of Jane and me. The diva wore a silk kimono, her hair was tied up rather carelessly with a scarf and a profusion of black ringlets spilled over the scarf and under it, giving her an appropriately Bohemian appearance.

'Allow me to introduce my fiancée,' I said.

'Juan, you didn't tell me you had a fiancée.'

I was obliged to notice that Madame Orlova did no more than glance at Jane – the whole motion of her head and body took just a second – and she nodded in a somewhat cursory way.

'You have come to take my photograph after all.'

'If there is time,' I said. 'Perhaps even this morning?'

'But I am very busy.' She spoke in the way an indulgent mother might dismiss a proposal made by a small child.

'You mentioned too that I might consider making some sort of portfolio with pictures of the other members of the cast.'

Madame Orlova seemed surprised. 'I remember,' she said. 'Do you think it a good idea?'

'An excellent idea, especially as it came from you.'

Jane's posture changed when I said this. Her back

straightened and her body swivelled, first in my direction and then away from me. She tutted. Madame Orlova glanced at her again.

I had by now grasped the nature of Madame Orlova's interaction with others, or at least with me. But I was not such a naif as to be seduced by it. Rather, I wanted to turn Madame Orlova's rather harmless flirtatiousness to our advantage. That is why I spoke as I did.

My fiancée, however, appeared to take me for a gullible fool and this irritated me. I ignored her expression of impatience, though I could see that Madame Orlova had noticed it.

'You mentioned the Family Fellini, the English comedians, the German mesmerist?'

'As a matter of fact, that is why I am busy this morning,' Madame Orlova said, 'But won't you sit down?'

She sat on the low chair in front of her dressing table, perched sideways so that she was still facing us. I indicated to Jane that she should sit on the armchair.

'Would you rather I go and attend to the camera?' Jane asked.

'Please sit,' I said. I was surprised when Jane did as I asked.

'I am to see a man recommended by Norbert,' Madame Orlova told me.

'Norbert?'

'Baron von Herzog.'

Madame Orlova looked at Jane and then at me. 'Have you had coffee, *cheri*?'

'We have, thank you,' I said. 'I'd like to get straight down to work.' Her expression clouded over – this was too direct. I changed tack. 'You are going to see a friend of Baron von Herzog?'

'Well, they are not, as it were, friends, but colleagues. Doctor Ambrose has recently returned from Vienna, where he first made the acquaintance of the Baron. He is a student of the new school of mind medicine.'

'Mind medicine?'

'Yes!' Her eyes opened wide and I gathered that we were in the presence of a convert. 'You see, when there are broken limbs, we think it natural to bind them and help them mend, but we don't do the same with the mind.'

'I suppose we don't,' I said.

'Doctor Ambrose has studied a new discipline that seeks to understand the mind better. He is an expert in what is called "the personality".'

Jane sat forward.

'A person is never the same,' Madame Orlova said. There are,' she continued, telling me for the second time in as many days about a new way of looking at the human mind, 'different *layers* to the personality.'

'Different layers,' I repeated. I glanced at Jane.

'Yes, and you see it's possible that one layer may be hurt; it may be injured, and this will affect the other layers.'

'And why are you going to see Doctor Ambrose?' Jane asked.

I did not detect in Jane's tone any trace of her earlier irritation.

Perhaps mollified by the pertinent and polite way in which Jane addressed her, Madame Orlova, too, seemed inclined to be more indulgent, though she directed her answer to me rather than to Jane.

'I have been a singer since I was a little girl. I first performed in public at the age of nine, at a concert given for the Grand Duke Alexei of Novgorod. It was in the Winter Palace, the Marijnsky rooms.' She looked at Jane when she gave this detail. I could not decide whether this was to indicate a certain level of condescension, as Jane was unlikely to be familiar with the Marijnsky rooms, or whether it was to indicate that Jane had now been brought into the circle of people whose presence Madame Orlova elected to recognise. 'I was aware from the beginning that I have been given a gift – the gift to make music,' she continued. 'When the musician is in possession of such a gift, it is a small thing to turn a rough bauble into a fine jewel.' She paused and looked first at Jane, then at me and then at Jane again. 'About a month ago I experienced something that never in my life have I experienced before.' She paused. I gathered that, in the manner of any seasoned performer, Madame Orlova had the knack of teasing her audience. Jane sat a little further forward and I leaned forward too, keen to catch whatever Madame Orlova would now say. She may even have lowered her voice in order to tweak our attention. Outside, I heard one of the workmen call along the corridor. He wanted to know if anyone had seen his wrench. I wished he would be quiet. 'I was standing in the wings of the Metropole Theatre in Manchester. It is a delightful house.

Have you been there?' Jane and I shook our heads. 'To my astonishment, in the moments before I took the stage, I experienced a disturbance in my breast.' Perhaps we looked mystified. 'A heartbeat,' Madame Orlova said. 'A *pounding* of the heart. And when I stepped onto the stage, listening to the applause – it was a full house – I realised that I was trembling.' She looked at us with an expression that combined concern and exasperation. 'I have sung at La Scala in Milan with Maestro Puccini in the front row! I have performed for the Tsar of all the Russias! Can you tell me why my heart was pounding? Can you tell me why I trembled as I took to the stage of the Metropole Theatre in Manchester? It is a jewel, but it is not one of the world's *great* houses!'

Jane and I could not tell her.

'And what do you think happened when I opened my mouth to sing?' She looked even more unhappy as she said, 'I could not. I could not begin. I could not sing!'

'I'm very sorry,' Jane said. Her sympathy was characteristic and spontaneous.

Madame Orlova nodded. 'Thank you. It is a condition I know that others have experienced, a very painful illness of the mind.'

'Stage fright,' Jane said.

Madame Orlova nodded.

'But you have performed since then,' I said.

She nodded again. 'In Manchester, I waited. And the audience waited. The orchestra, too. Oh, there was a minute's worth of waiting.'

She stopped.

And then she continued, 'In the course of this minute, my beating heart beat faster. The condition itself is fuel for the condition. As the body struggles, so it compounds the difficulty, like a man attempting to extricate himself from quicksand.'

I did not immediately grasp this comparison, but Jane seemed to understand. 'And what happened after a minute?' she asked.

'The beating of my heart stopped, just as suddenly as it had begun. I no longer trembled. I began to sing.'

We sat in silence and I wondered if that was the end of what I considered to be a rather odd and unexpected digression from the business on which we had come to the theatre.

'And Doctor Ambrose has the answer?' Jane asked.

I was unaware that there had been a question, let alone an answer.

Madame Orlova nodded. I felt resentful that a rapport had now sprung up between Jane and Madame Orlova. This resentment was, of course, quite unbecoming and entirely illogical.

'He believes that if we explore the layers of our personality, we can discover why our thoughts run in this direction or that.'

'But how is the personality explored?' Jane asked.

'We talk.'

'Talk?' It was I who asked the question.

Madame Orlova smiled. 'I have met Doctor Ambrose

twice now. We have spoken at some length.'

'But what have you spoken about?' I asked. 'Surely you can't *talk* away the problem?'

'That is exactly what you *can* do,' Madame Orlova said. 'Or something very like it.' Then she stood up and said, 'Juan, you have kept me here long enough. I shall be late for my appointment. Go and photograph the others.'

'Mr Müller has been very kind—' I began.

Madame Orlova waved her hand to indicate that further discussion was redundant. 'I have told him you are my friends.' I noted that Madame Orlova's approval had been conferred on Jane as well as me. 'Go now! You will make my portrait in the afternoon. I think the auditorium will be the best place, yes? The dress circle. Choose something lavish. For the others, you will decide what is best.'

'Well,' I said as we walked back along the corridor towards the part of the building where Müller's office was located, 'now we have the run of the place, let's find out who the man in the yellow raincoat was.'

Jane stopped suddenly and faced me. 'Juan,' she said, and I could tell that this was not to be a moment of happy intimacy, 'you spent an hour and a half in that woman's company on the train from Edinburgh and you didn't think to tell her that you are engaged to be married.'

My mouth opened and I began to speak, but, rather like Madame Orlova at the Metropole Theatre, no sound came.

Jane's face darkened and she began to shake her head. 'I wonder if you want to be married at all,' she said.

'Jane.' I managed this only because she had begun to walk away.

She didn't stop and I was obliged to hurry after her. 'Jane,' I said again. 'Wait!'

I caught up. We had entered the area where the huge screens were kept. The men who had been moving the sets were now assembling the elements of a drawing room with armchairs and sofas flowing towards the stage.

I spoke in an undertone. 'I did not tell Madame Orlova that I am to be married because this is something that is sacred to me, something that is not discussed with strangers.'

'Oh,' Jane said. I felt her fingers in mine, and then, just as quickly as she had held my hand, she let it go again. 'Then let us see what we can find out.'

CHAPTER NINETEEN

A theatre is like a village. There were carpenters and painters and stage hands and make-up ladies and set changers and wardrobe assistants and porters and cleaners and cooks and front-of-house staff including an army of commissionaires, not to mention the house manager and his band of bookkeepers and secretaries and clerks. And then the choreographers, designers, musicians, actors and singers.

Messrs Temple and Hall, Baron von Herzog and the other cast members were the dignitaries in this village. We went in pursuit of them, escorted by Natalia. There were expressions of dismay as the proposal to make portraits had arisen from nowhere, but no one turned down the prospect of a flattering image.

Temple and Hall were enthusiastic, but apparently less in tune with one another off-stage than when they were performing their double act. We set up the camera in the stalls, where I planned to have Hall sit in one row and Temple sit in another so an impression of distance would be created, but the two figures would clearly be a duo. Temple failed to appear, and Hall went to look for him. Then Temple turned up before Hall had returned, so he went off again to look for Hall, who came back without Temple.

In the meantime, we photographed Baron von Herzog. It was clear to me that the Baron was not remotely baronial. Those with a legitimate claim to something rarely feel the need to assert it, but the Baron insisted on protocol. 'Please address me as Your Excellency,' he told me, twice.

He wore a dark suit of faintly continental cut and his longish grey hair was swept back from a high forehead. He did have a distinguished-looking face, though the skin was pasty, suggesting a fondness for brandy. He was probably not more than forty years old, physically imposing but running to fat.

I didn't like the Baron, and my dislike undoubtedly coloured the way I conceived his portrait. I was focused on creating the finest possible images, even though we were in the theatre on a mere pretext, and I wanted to do justice to the Baron, but I am obliged to admit that I did not entirely succeed. He had perfected the mannerisms, or what he imagined these mannerisms to be, of wealth and privilege. He inclined his head and nodded with approbation when I explained that I wanted to convey the essence of his art as a mesmerist. It was the sort of approbation, I thought, that is easily dispensed because it is not genuine; it is part of an act. I wanted him to pose in front of the stage curtain, since that was where he performed his feats of mind manipulation with members of the public. He stood before a packed auditorium and cast a spell without the benefit of props or scenery. He did this by using the power of suggestion. I could see how his mannerisms would contribute to his stage technique: his affectation of aristocratic indulgence was irritating in person, but it would no doubt engage an audience. His mane of silver hair and 'stately' bearing were consistent with the popular notion of patrician gravitas. I found myself wondering if his friend, Doctor Ambrose, who was treating Madame Orlova with some sort of talking cure, was equally bogus.

But I checked these thoughts: they were instinctive and surely unreasonable. The likelihood that the Baron was not a baron was hardly shocking in a world where people made up stories for a living. Still, when he insisted that we photograph him against a screen showing the interior of a sumptuous ballroom, with French windows opening onto a balcony drenched in the light of a full moon, I gave way to my irrational dislike.

'That has nothing to do with your performance,' I said. 'A plain backdrop—'

'Your Excellency,' Jane interrupted me, speaking in a way that made it unclear if she supplied the honorific to compensate for my own failure to do so, or if she was simply starting the sentence with his preferred manner of address,

'Juan wants to show you to your best advantage. The plain background would illustrate how your work is with *the mind*, with *ethereal*, not *material* things. But the ballroom is superb. If you would prefer the ballroom . . .'

Preoccupations about artistic merit were, of course, beside the point. We were there only to find the man in the yellow raincoat. Nothing else mattered. Certainly not my concerns about the right setting for a picture of the Baron, or, indeed, my dislike for the man, which was now very great.

He looked at Jane with an expression of surprise. She was self-assured and well spoken, perhaps to a degree that did not fit her role as photographer's assistant. The paradox was not lost on me: we were all pretending. Again, I wondered how long it would be before everyone in the theatre knew that the police were looking for us.

'The ballroom is more . . . in keeping,' he said.

'Then let us use the ballroom,' Jane said.

It was necessary to have the screen taken down from its steel frame and placed against the wall below the windows. Natalia took charge and gave instructions to the set changers. I did not envy Natalia her position in the theatre. She was the manager's protégée, a foreigner and she was very young. I had no doubt that she would be a subject of gossip. If a theatre is like a village, it is replete with village jealousies. I was quite sure that the gifts she had shown at the Kunstgewerbeschule would count for little beyond a very small coterie of dignitaries at the Theatre Royal. I wondered if she was Müller's mistress.

'Señor Camarón,' she said, as we watched the screen being

taken down, 'will you also photograph Herr Müller?'

She spoke lightly and her expression was relaxed, but I sensed that the question was more important to her than she pretended.

Jane and Herzog were standing a little way away. The Baron had spoken only a few words of German with Jane, preferring to converse in his own heavily accented English. I suspected that the accent was an affectation and his German was not of the native variety.

'I hadn't planned to,' I told Natalia.

'Oh,' she said, 'he would make a fine subject. He is highly regarded in Hamburg, you know, and in Vienna too.'

'I'm sure we can make his portrait,' I said. 'Where is the best backdrop?'

'In the gods,' she replied without a moment's hesitation, 'with the house behind him.'

The light that flooded the area where the screens were stored made it ideal for portrait making. I acknowledged this only reluctantly and only to myself, such was my dislike of the mesmerist – but with the ample space and the light from above, it would be possible to show Baron von Herzog perhaps even more effectively than would have been the case if we had adhered to my idea of making the portrait against the plain backdrop of the stage curtain.

'I've heard that mesmerists plant people in the audience,' Jane told the Baron. 'Then they invite them up on stage and pretend they've never met them before.'

I thought this rather provocative, except that Jane said it in a light, friendly tone that seemed to invite Herzog to make a full-throated rebuttal.

I was even more surprised when the Baron said, 'That is correct. This is how the session must begin.'

'You plant people in the audience?' I spoke, I realised, in an accusatory tone.

The Baron glanced at me, but when he answered he directed his remarks to Jane. 'Mesmerism is a delicate art. It requires the right conditions. The audience must understand what is happening; they must know what to expect and so, I have one or two associates on whom I call at the beginning of the performance. They come up on stage and we demonstrate how a person may be brought into a trance. After this, I call on people I do not know, but by then the audience is primed and ready. They understand what will take place even though, of course, no one can predict what the subject will say or do.'

I was disarmed by his frankness, but unpersuaded of his good faith. 'And transmigration?' I asked

Jane looked at me as though I had said something inconceivably stupid.

'What about transmigration?' The Baron was unruffled.

'Some mesmerists pretend that they can spirit people away and make them reappear in different parts of the theatre.'

He chuckled. 'Oh, Señor Camarón, my profession is a colourful one and there are charlatans – people who claim to be mesmerists who are merely showmen. I am sure, as you say, there are performers who pretend to make a subject disappear and then reappear at the top of the house, but I am not one of those!'

When Temple and Hall were finally reunited, I proposed again that we make the photograph of them sitting in the stalls, which were now almost empty.

'It will look like us on an average night in Birmingham,' Hall said.

'We've never had a crowd this big in Birmingham,' Temple replied.

Temple and Hall continued like this, trading asides as though they were on stage. When Temple said, 'Oh oh! Have you been up to no good?' and nudged Hall theatrically, pointing towards one of the entrances, I didn't bother to look away from the viewfinder. But then I heard Jane gasp. I looked up. Two policemen were walking towards us.

They walked slowly. Amid the gilt motifs, the filigree light fittings and the burgundy seats, their drab black uniforms stood out. I thought of pall-bearers. The one in front was a sergeant, middle-aged. He looked like a man who was accustomed to being out of place and accustomed to regarding this with indifference. He walked with ease, a representative of order who knew he rightly, and always, had the upper hand. Any pretensions that might be advanced by art or illusion would evaporate in the face of the dull, dispiriting presence of this figure of the law.

Jane and I stood, transfixed, and watched our nemeses approach. Temple and Hall were suddenly quiet and they craned their necks to watch the officers. Workmen had been scurrying between the stage and the orchestra pit, manoeuvring some sort of platform. The scurrying stopped. The platform remained halfway between the pit and the stage. Behind us a group of ushers, young women who seemed to go everywhere in groups of three or four, had been chattering by the curtained entrance to the foyer. The chatter ceased, as the policemen's progress became the focus of everyone in the auditorium.

The constable was a lanky youth. His uniform was ill-fitting, and he lacked even a whisper of the sergeant's authority. He seemed to require two steps for his superior's one. His baton swung in a distracting, ungainly way from his leather belt and, though his buttons and boots were polished, his trousers were at half-mast. He might have looked comical, except that, with every step, this man and his master intimated our demise.

Jane's fingers tightened in mine as the men approached.

And then, to our astonishment, they tipped their helmets and continued past us, walking up the aisle to where the ushers stood.

'The building has to be inspected before tonight's performance,' Natalia said. 'There will be dignitaries.'

I had begun to shake. I wondered if Jane noticed. I sensed not the remotest tremble on her part when I held her hand.

'It was even worse when we played the Lyceum before His Royal Highness on Regatta Day,' Hall said, '. . . and he's a *real* prince, not one of your jumped-up pashas!'

To reach the stage door, we had to walk back along the corridor towards the dressing rooms. Halfway along, instead of continuing to the end, where Madame Orlova's dressing room was located, Natalia led us down a flight of steep stone stairs. This led to a long corridor with a bevelled brick ceiling and gas lamps that were lit even in the daytime. There was a smell of plaster and sawdust that reminded me of the crypt in the church in Granada where I practised judo as a teenager. The corridor opened onto a broader and busier lobby at the end of which was our objective: the stage door.

'Mr Hamilton,' Natalia said, 'this is Miss Macgregor and Mr Camarón; they are taking pictures of some of the performers.'

Hamilton was in his fifties. He wore a waistcoat and a collarless shirt that may or may not have been washed since the beginning of the year. He had a grey-black walrus moustache so profuse and luxuriant that the principal purpose of the face that lay behind it might have been to serve as a backdrop for the moustache. He puffed on a cigarette. 'I've not sat for my portrait since that time Her Majesty wanted to try out her new camera,' he said, looking first at Jane and then at me, poker-faced.

'Well, I hope Her Majesty was on form,' Jane said. 'I'm sure your portrait is a very distinguished one.' She giggled. 'I wondered if last night there was a man who came in here, about half past seven, through the stage door. He wore a yellow raincoat and a hat, a trilby with a red band.'

'Might have been,' Hamilton said, 'but I'm not the one to ask, dear. I wasn't here last night.'

'Oh,' Jane said.

'Oh,' I agreed. 'Who was here?'

'Billy,' Hamilton said. 'He'll be here again this evening.'

'A man with a yellow raincoat and a trilby with a red band?' Natalia asked.

Jane and I spun round and at the same time we said, 'Yes.'

She shook her head. 'Is he a friend?'

'Not a friend,' Jane said.

'Actually, he's a friend of a friend,' I lied.

'What's his name?' Natalia asked.

I glanced at Hamilton, only because he was watching this exchange in the engaged way that people adopt when they have no reason to be in a conversation but find themselves in one anyway.

'We don't know his name,' Jane said, 'but my uncle saw him last night and that's what he was wearing. My uncle owes him money.'

There was no reason for this to sound plausible, yet Natalia seemed to believe it. She thought for a moment and then she said, 'Shall we go back to the auditorium now?'

'The way we have just come,' I said, looking between Hamilton and Natalia, 'from the stage down the steps and along this corridor, is that the only way from here into the theatre?'

'No,' Natalia said, 'there's another way. Would you like me to show you?'

'Yes, please,' Jane spoke with such evident pleasure that I almost thought she was going to take Natalia by the arm and skip off with her.

'So, you aren't going to take my portrait after all?' Hamilton called after us.

At the end of the lobby there was a double swing door. Along the centre of the marble floor in the corridor on the other side was a thin carpet with a red and green pattern that had been worn through in places so that the marble underneath was visible. I caught up with Jane and Natalia at the bottom of the stairs.

'This leads to Mr Müller's office,' Jane told me.

'And that?' I asked. A door was open at the end of the corridor, except that it wasn't a proper door but rather a section of the wall that could be swung out on hinges.

'The back stairs,' Natalia said.

The back stairs were narrow and steep; there was room for just one person to go up or come down. 'For the technicians,' Natalia explained, 'and sometimes for performances, too.'

'The other night,' I reminded Jane, 'when one of the cast appeared next to us in the dress circle.'

'That's right,' Natalia said.

'So, there,' Jane said, 'the Baron could play one of these tricks if he wanted to, but he chooses not to.'

There was a note of rebuke in this.

'I didn't mean—' I began.

'Oh, Juan,' Jane looked up at me, 'sometimes you are quite intolerant.'

'The Baron wouldn't play tricks like that,' Natalia said in an amiable voice that I thought was designed to paper over the embarrassment of watching two people bicker.

'Shall we take the regular stairs?' I said, moving back into the corridor.

When we stepped out, Natalia closed the door so that it blended into the wall. You could see the shape of it if you knew it was there, but otherwise it was almost invisible.

'How does it open?' I asked. There was no handle.

Natalia reached up and pressed the top right-hand corner. There was a click and the door opened a few inches. She pushed it closed again. Another click.

Using the regular stairs, we climbed to a small lobby on the ground floor.

'We are back where we started,' Natalia said, 'but I don't think Mr Müller is in his office. He has visitors. He will be showing them around.'

'And from here to the front door?' Jane asked.

We continued through a heavy swing door to the foyer. At this point, Jane, who was at the head of our party of three, brought the line to a standstill and then reversed, so that Natalia and I had to step back behind the doors or Jane would have barrelled into us.

'That's him!' Jane whispered to me.

I looked over her shoulder. In the lobby stood a tall man in a yellow raincoat. He was accompanied by another man and they were speaking to Müller.

'By Jove!' I said. I was astonished not because we had found the man in the yellow raincoat but because I recognised the man who accompanied him.

'That's him,' Jane said, still whispering so that Natalia wouldn't hear, 'the one who murdered Doctor Breitling!'

'The other,' I replied, my lips so close to her that we almost kissed, 'is the officer who came to the room this morning.'

The man in the yellow raincoat was speaking with a sort of genial authority to Wilhelm Müller and Captain Smith. They had reached the point of concluding handshakes.

The man in the raincoat put on his hat, a trilby with a maroon band, and pushed open the front door. He and Smith left the theatre.

We hurried across the lobby.

'Mr Müller,' I said, looking at the exit, where the door was still swinging on its heavy oiled hinges. 'I think I just missed Captain Smith! I would have greeted him.'

'You know Captain Smith?'

'Yes,' I said, 'and do please forgive my curiosity, but who was the other gentleman? I believe I may know him, but perhaps I'm mistaken. I wanted quickly to go and pay my respects.'

'Captain Barkov,' Müller said, 'Prince Danilo's man.'

I hurried across the lobby and peered through the pebble glass in the heavy swing doors.

Captain Barkov was climbing into a phaeton. Captain Smith climbed in beside him.

'No, I was mistaken,' I said. 'I don't believe I know Captain Barkov after all.'

'Prince Danilo,' Jane said, looking at Müller. 'He is staying with Mr Auchinleck? I think I read that in the paper.'

Müller nodded. 'In Milngavie.'

Natalia had hung back a little, but now she came forward and said to Müller, 'Mr Camarón would like to make your portrait.'

'After lunch,' I said, and as I spoke, I knew that I had torn the fabric of confidence we had built up carefully over the course of the morning. 'We will come back after lunch.'

'You have arranged with the others? Madame Orlova? They are expecting you?' Müller looked at me as though a veil had been drawn from his eyes and he knew he had been deceived.

'Madame Orlova has been kind enough to speak to the Fellinis,' Jane said. 'We are just pondering the right place to photograph all of the family to best advantage.' She reached for the swing door and pushed it open. 'Until this afternoon, then.'

I was struck by the ease with which Jane conjured up this convincing but entirely fabricated account of Madame Orlova's intervention with the Fellinis. My equipment, I concluded, would be safe enough, and the priority of the moment, clearly, was to follow the two men in the phaeton, so, I followed Jane out onto the steps and we walked quickly from the theatre towards Sauchiehall Street.

'There are cabs on the corner,' Jane said.

When we reached the line of cabs, she climbed into the first one and I called up to the driver. 'Auchinleck House!' I said.

'In Milngavie?'

'That's the one!'

CHAPTER TWENTY

It was one of the new, larger cabs, which meant that we were able to share the bench in such a way that our bodies did not touch. Jane looked out the window on her side and I looked out the window on mine. The cab moved first for several blocks to the west and then made an abrupt turn north. When we moved into the northbound flow of carts and carriages, we swayed from side to side as if aboard a ship. The traffic at one point was dense and it took the cabbie some time to find an opening in order to cross a busy junction, but presently we began to make steady progress.

'What shall we do when we get there?' I asked.

Jane turned abruptly, as though I had wakened her.

'Let's just see the lie of the land.' She spoke gently.

After several minutes, I said, 'This is the same road we took when we came with Doctor Breitling.'

Jane shuddered. 'Doctor Breitling,' she said in a low, steady voice, as though testing whether or not the name could be invoked without summoning demons.

I put my arm around her. Her body seemed to move with the rhythm of the carriage, first a little faster and then a little slower. I realised that she was sobbing. I took a handkerchief from my pocket and she dabbed her eyes. Then she sat up straight.

'We must not be sentimental,' she said.

I brought my arm from around her shoulder. She sat with one hand on her knee. So, I took this hand and squeezed it. She allowed me to do this for a few moments and then we both looked out the window again.

'He's turning,' Jane said. 'When we came with Breitling we carried straight on.'

We moved into a long, narrow road that had a stone wall along one side and houses interspersed among trees on the other. Above us, the cables of a tram line indicated that we were still within the municipal boundary. The wall continued unbroken for about a mile, while the houses on the other side gave way to woodland. The carriage slowed and we joined a road that was narrower but still cobbled. We continued for another half-mile, passing just two or three entrances along the way. Then the carriage stopped and Jane and I peered out at a monumental gateway, with stone posts on either side. Lions rampant stood on top of each of the posts. The heavy black iron gates were closed. Beyond the gates a gravel drive led into a wood. Auchinleck House was hidden from the road.

'Not the sort of place that's easy to get into without an invitation,' I said.

'Particularly when important guests are staying.' Jane was leaning very close to me and she nodded through the window further along the road, where a blue police van sat. Two constables loitered by the side of the van while a third fed the horses.

I called up to the driver and asked him to take us back to the main road. We drove on past the three constables so that the cabbie could find a place to turn. He did so about fifty yards further on. The constables were tall, and the new model cab was slung lower than its predecessors, which meant that as we trotted past for the second time, they were able to peer in. Involuntarily, I locked eyes with one of them.

As we drove back along the road beside the long stone wall, I said, 'Maybe we'll find out more if we retrace our steps.'

Jane nodded. I called up to the driver again, this time giving him directions to the villa on the loch. At the junction with the main road, instead of turning right to return to the city, he turned left and followed the route we had taken three days earlier.

The Larch View gateway had seemed imposing when we first visited, but it was a very modest affair compared to the lion-topped entrance to Auchinleck House.

We climbed down from the cab and Jane crossed the road. The driver declined to wait.

I crossed the road to join Jane. The gate swung open on hinges that were less well-oiled than those in the Theatre Royal. There was a low groaning noise as the heavy iron moved a foot or two and we stepped through to the gravel path.

At the front door I rang the bell.

'What shall we say?'

I shrugged. 'Brazen it out.'

There was no answer. I rang twice more.

'Mrs Anderson only comes in three times a week,' Jane said. 'That is what they told me when I arranged Doctor Breitling's visit.'

'If no one is here,' I said, 'there's a way in.'

We walked round to the back of the house. At the French windows, I reached down and found the wooden ball that could be pulled forward and sideways to release the lock. It moved smoothly and I heard a click. 'Try the handle,' I told Jane. She turned it and pushed. The door opened inward.

'How did you do that?'

'I saw how it worked when we were here last time.'

We stepped into the room that had been the composer's bedroom. I walked through to the sitting room and then to the hall. Jane followed. 'Where are you going?'

'To make sure there's no one here.'

I started to climb the stairs. 'Juan,' Jane said in an agitated whisper. 'We were not upstairs. It can have no connection to us.'

'We do not know what is connected to us,' I said in a tone that surprised me. I sounded angry. 'I want to make sure we are entirely alone.'

I continued to climb and after a few seconds I heard Jane begin to follow.

There is a point, when you have committed yourself to something dangerous or foolhardy, when risk ceases to be much of a consideration, since you have already placed yourself in a position of the utmost vulnerability. Perhaps Jane and I had passed this point much earlier, but I was conscious of it now, as we entered the bedroom of the absent Doctor Ratković. We had already broken into his house and stepping into his private apartments seemed but a small additional infraction.

The bedroom was above Sir Arthur's bedroom, but in this case, there was a bed, a dresser and a wardrobe. The sitting room, likewise, was properly furnished. We walked into the study. There was a heavy desk facing away from the window, and against the opposite wall a chest of drawers. Lithographs on the walls showed scenes from the Highlands, with men in kilts and berets standing on promontories.

Jane moved quickly to the desk and began to go through the papers.

'What are you doing?'

She looked up and said, matter-of-factly, 'We're here, aren't we? Let's find out what we can.'

'What's that?' I said. She was peering at a sheet of notepaper.

'I don't know. I can't read it.'

I took the paper from her. 'I've seen this before,' I said. 'At least, I think I have.'

Jane waited for me to explain.

'When I first met her, when I got into her carriage on the

train, Madame Orlova was reading a book with these sorts of letters.'

Jane's eyebrows rose. 'It's in Russian then?'

'Or something similar. What else is there?'

We began to sift through the papers together.

'Look at this.' I lifted a sheet of notepaper that bore the Simpson-Burley letterhead – the same letters that were emblazoned across the facade of the paint factory on the river. The writing was copperplate but cramped, and because of the quality of the paper and perhaps also the poor quality of the nib that had been used, it was difficult to read.

'Medium grade, emulsion,' I said. 'Fourteen quarts. Blue, green, red, grey.'

I studied the note a little more.

'Look where the delivery is to be.' I pointed to the bottom of the paper.

'Where?'

I pointed to the bottom of the paper.

'The Theatre Royal.' Jane looked at the document and then at me.

I walked over to the window.

'Come and see this,' I said.

'Auchinleck House,' Jane whispered as soon as she was beside me.

'Ratković spends time on the water, Mrs Anderson said.'

I returned to the desk and took the photographs from my satchel and laid them out. They covered the assortment of papers.

'The rooms downstairs,' I said.

'Yes?'

'The two pictures that are missing?'

Jane nodded. 'The view into the garden!'

I scooped up the photographs and put them back. By the time I had closed the satchel, Jane had already left the room. I followed her out and hurried down the stairs and across the hall to the composer's bedroom. Jane was fiddling with the wooden lever above the skirting board.

'How did you do this?' she asked.

I bent down beside her. Our foreheads touched.

'Like this,' I said. I pulled the wooden bulb gently but firmly and then moved it to one side. Jane stood up, stepped to the door and turned the handle.

With the door open, we both stood at the spot where Breitling had placed his tripod. Each of us leaned forward and screwed up our faces as though we were looking through an imaginary camera lens.

'What can you see?' Jane asked, as if my imaginary viewfinder might be more illuminating than hers.

'The tree,' I said, 'on one side; the edge of the door on the other. A little bit of water . . .'

She leaned in beside me. The degree to which our attention was fixed on a camera that didn't exist should have been preposterous but I don't believe it struck either of us as such.

'Did he change the lens?'

'Why?'

'The photographs he had taken until then were interiors.'

I thought a little more. 'I don't believe he changed the lens.'

'So, he would have had greater definition further away from the camera. It's just after midday, but when he took the picture from here it was later in the afternoon. The sun was lower but it wasn't cloudy.'

'There would have been more definition in the distance.' I peered again through the imaginary lens and Jane peered beside me.

Then Jane said, 'This isn't what he saw.'

'Of course!' I was conscious of the fact that Jane appeared to reach every significant conclusion before I did. 'The branch of the tree!'

Jane bent her knees and lowered the level of her eye by six inches. I did the same. If anyone had interrupted us at that point, they might have imagined that we were adherents of some occult religion performing a secret rite.

'I can see the other side of the loch,' Jane said softly.

'Where Auchinleck is entertaining his royal guest.'

'What shall we do?'

'Investigate,' I said.

I may have wished to seize the initiative. If this was the case, then I admit it with some shame, because Jane had shown that she was easily more accomplished than me when it came to teasing out the meaning of disparate facts. I should have been proud of her investigative acumen, her keen intelligence. Instead, I felt that my position was being undermined. It was as though loving Jane was bringing out the worst in me.

'Where are we going?' she asked as I stepped through

the French windows. She came onto the veranda and I closed the door, feeling the bolt click into place as I did so.

'To the other side,' I said, and I began to walk across the lawn to the little jetty where the rowing boat was tethered.

The boat was there, which resolved the first potential complication, and the oars lay across the gunwales below the centre thwart. I climbed from the jetty and slid the oars up from under me and attached them to the rowlocks.

'Untie it there,' I told Jane, pointing to the post at the end of the jetty where the second line was tethered. She did as instructed, then hurried back and climbed down into the stern. She sat on the bench facing me. I pushed away from the jetty and began to turn the boat around. Then I started to row.

From the French windows to the moment we departed the jetty, the time that elapsed could not have been more than a minute and the words that passed between us were fewer than a dozen. In such a way are important decisions made.

'I'm sorry I was cross before,' I said.

Jane had been peering towards the other side, but now she looked at me. We had not looked at one another like this, I think, since before I went to Edinburgh, or rather, since before I had my disagreeable interview with Benjamin Jackson.

'Juan, I was jealous of your . . .' She seemed to hesitate over the correct terminology. I believe if she had used the person's proper name it might have reintroduced one of the several clouds that hovered over us, so she contented herself with the name of the profession, '. . . opera singer.'

I shook my head. 'Jane, I will never give you reason to be jealous.'

'I know, Juan. I am sorry too.'

'Am I going in the right direction?' I asked.

Jane seemed for a moment to be unsure if I was speaking metaphysically, but then she grasped that I was asking about something more prosaic.

'Take us a little that way.' She stretched out her arm and pointed to the south. I noticed again, as I had noticed earlier in the day, that the sleeve of her jacket was crushed.

'We should not be doing this,' I said. 'I'm going to go back.'

'What do you mean?'

'This is dangerous,' I said. 'You have already come within an inch of your life. You have been obliged to spend a night alone in the city, and now I'm taking you to a place where we have every reason to believe you will be in danger again. I'm not going to do that.'

I had already started to turn the boat around.

'Juan! Stop!' Jane said.

I stopped.

'You are perfectly right,' she said. 'All of these things are true, and they argue for turning back. But there is one much more powerful argument for going forward, and that is that I believe my uncle is there.' She pointed over my shoulder to Auchinleck House, the upper storeys and crenelated roof of which were just then coming into view over the brow of a long and well-kept lawn that stretched down to the waterside. 'We have come this far; we must continue.'

Then she looked at me with an odd expression and said, 'But if you wish to stay on the other side . . . I do not want to place you in danger. I will make this journey on my own. After all, this is my affair.'

She could not have offended me more deeply if she had accused me of infidelity.

'Jane,' I said, 'how could you think . . . ?'

I turned the boat back in the direction she had indicated and I rowed with so much energy that the remaining distance was covered quickly.

The lawn came right to the water's edge, where the bank had been cut so that small boats could come alongside. I retracted the oars and clutched a clump of long grass, while Jane scrambled ashore. She reached down and took my hand, steadying me as I climbed from the boat. During this awkward manoeuvre, our eyes met, and in that moment, it was as though we were the only two living souls in the universe.

I laid the oars on the grass and tethered the boat to them, trusting that the weight would be sufficient to prevent the vessel from drifting away from the bank.

Jane and I began to walk towards the house.

CHAPTER TWENTY-ONE

We did not take the most direct route, which would have been to walk straight up the middle of the lawn. Rather, we moved diagonally while we had some cover from the natural undulation of the land running down to the water. In this way, it would have been difficult for anyone watching from the ground floor or the first floor of the house to see us.

The wood by the side of the lawn had been left to grow wild. I did not think that any but the most determined intruder could have cut a path through the trees and foliage to reach the point where we stood now. There was, however, a path running just inside the first treeline.

The path hugged the edge of the lawn, but after twenty

yards it veered deeper into the wood, and I feared that it would not lead to the house at all until I saw what looked like an opening in the thicket.

'That goes to the house,' I told Jane.

She had been walking a little way behind, and as she caught up and stopped to examine the narrow opening in the undergrowth, I heard her breathing. I glanced at her. Her hair was even more unruly than it had been when she arrived at the hotel that morning. She had not slept. She had drunk coffee and eaten a makeshift breakfast during which we spoke about unpleasant things.

'That's not a path, Juan.'

'It is,' I said, and I began to move towards it.

I felt Jane's hand catch my elbow. Her grip was tight, almost fierce. I looked round, irritated. Neither of us was thinking or behaving as we would have done in normal circumstances.

'What the devil—?' I began.

Jane let me go, but then she hurried to the side of the thicket and picked up a handful of pebbles and a stick. She stepped to the place where I believed there might be a path and threw the pebbles into the thicket. Nothing happened. For several seconds Jane gave the impression of a shaman casting a spell, where the mystical invocation is accompanied by actions so mundane as to confuse the observer. She lifted up the stick and threw it hard into the thicket.

We heard the sound of a steel trap snapping its jaws. I stepped forward and looked over Jane's shoulder. Just a few feet into the thicket, we could see the stick impaled by the jagged teeth of the trap.

'The opening was made to tempt foxes,' Jane said, and then she glanced round and added, 'or people.'

We stood in the middle of a little clearing. The path behind us led back to the loch. I wanted to abandon what now seemed to me an idiotic attempt to force our way into the shipbuilder's mansion. And I was impatient with a skein of uncertainty as dense as this wood.

'Jane,' I said, 'what do you believe your uncle's role in this affair is?'

Now it was Jane who was irritated. 'Why are you asking me now?'

'Because we have placed ourselves in danger. When you wrote to me, you expressed concern about your uncle. I understand that. Alan is charming but he is . . . reckless.'

She began to shake her head. It was not a gesture of disagreement or denial, but rather the gesture of a woman who is considering a difficult question for the hundredth time and is unable to arrive at anything but the same answer.

'I cannot believe that he would be so foolish, or so wicked, as to be willingly mixed up in a crime,' and then she added, a little morosely, 'or, at least, a *serious* crime.'

I experienced the odd sensation that occurs when someone has articulated one's own thoughts exactly.

'Then let's go on,' I said. I began to walk along the path. Over my shoulder I asked, 'What are we going to do when we get to the house?'

Jane caught up. She had started to smile. 'Well, you were

very resourceful at the last house. Let's see if you can find a way for us to get into this one.'

I do not think the rather decisive course I now followed was entirely a response to Jane's flattery.

Small houses have a front door and a back door. Large houses have half a dozen doors. The facade of the mansion facing the loch had no doors at all, just a series of bay windows on the ground floor. Along the side that came into view as Jane and I continued on the path, there was a low extension that might be a kitchen or a laundry. I could see two doors here, and plenty of windows, several of which were open.

'There's our way in,' I told Jane. We stopped and crouched to peer through the foliage – rather, I thought, like two Indian braves lying in wait for a bison. When I was about twelve my father took me to a Wild West Show in Madrid and the images of cowboys and Indians have never left me. 'I'm going to go over and see what can be done,' I said. 'Stay here till I tell you.'

I do not know if Jane did not hear me, or if she did not understand me, or if she heard and understood and saw no reason to obey, but when I stood up and stepped out onto the gravel that surrounded the house, Jane stood up and stepped out beside me. I was going to remonstrate but this was not the time to engage in a dispute over tactics. We crunched over the gravel together.

Without the cover of the trees and making a very clear sound on the gravel, I felt as though we might as well have gone to the front door and rung the bell.

We heard a man's voice and a woman's voice from inside the extension. I put a finger to my lips.

Jane pointed to the side of the building. I didn't understand what it was she wanted to convey.

'What?' I whispered.

'That way,' she said. 'Quickly!'

Perhaps my slow train of thought was a product of the anxiety which our present predicament naturally induced, but I found myself simply staring at Jane.

Rather gracelessly, I felt, she barged past me and I had no option but to follow. She ran around the corner of the extension and I lost sight of her for several seconds. When I turned the corner, I saw what she had apparently seen from the path. A drainpipe, offering a route to the roof, which might provide access to the house via one of the windows on the first floor.

It was a solid pipe, securely fixed to the wall: every foot and a half, there was an iron bracket that could be used as if it were the rung of a ladder. No more than thirty seconds were required to arrive at the top. Here, the challenge was trickier. The pipe had been fed through a hole in the eaves so that it could carry water from the gutter. In order to climb onto the roof, I had to cling to the pipe with my knees and at the same time reach up and backward and catch hold of the rim of the gutter. Then, using all my strength, I had to push myself away from the wall and swing sideways, far enough to get one foot over the edge and pull the rest of my body up. I did this without stopping to think whether or not it was feasible. If I had thought about it, I believe I would have concluded that it was *not* feasible. I got hold of the wall, pushed myself out, swung myself up and failed to get purchase on the roof. Instead, I bruised my ankle, such was the force with which I brought it into contact with the sharp slate. I swung back and for the briefest moment, I found my footing on the bracket, but I did not rest there, because my hands were tiring and I knew that I only had sufficient strength for one more try. I pushed out and swung upward and this time, with the advantage of having attempted the same thing once before, I managed to place my ankle in such a way that it could be used as the fixed point from which to lever up the rest of my body. It was as though the ankle knew where it had to be, how long it had to remain there and how it had to act when it was in position. The body, like the mind, follows its own impulses. I released the tension in my muscles, rolled back and looked up at the sky. I did not remain in this position for more than four or five seconds, however, as I had grasped that while *I* had been able to make it onto the roof, it would be quite impossible for Jane to do the same. She was wearing unsuitable clothes and she certainly did not have the strength to swing up from the drainpipe. I was not sure if she even had the necessary agility to climb to the top of the drainpipe.

'Juan!'

I looked round and scrambled to my feet. Jane's hands were clutching the edge of the roof. I leaned over to see her looking up at me.

'Take my hand,' she said.

She removed her right hand from the surface of the sharp corner of the slate and I caught hold of it. In a moment I felt tremendous force, as though Jane were pulling me off the roof and because it was so unexpected and so powerful I almost lost my balance, but I managed to adjust my posture and held on as she swung her right leg up, followed quickly by the rest of her. She rolled over, got to her knees, then to her feet and said, 'Now, is there an open window?'

Jane tiptoed across the roof and I tiptoed beside her. She had slung her bag over her shoulder and fastened it with the leather belt round her waist in order to climb the drainpipe, and now, I thought, she looked like Calamity Jane, girded for battle. When we reached the wall, we stood facing outward. The wood looked different from here. It was possible to see over the tops of the trees, though the view was not entirely uninterrupted because the larches and some of the elms sprouted above the canopy, but we could see what lay at the other side. The wood in front of the house was more extensive than at the back. Along the side, where we had walked, it tapered away so that at the water's edge there was a stretch of only about twenty yards before the trees gave way to a path that followed the edge of the loch in front of the neighbouring houses.

Jane stood next to me. Looking out at the treetops, listening to her breathe, I felt in some strange way closer to her than I had ever been.

She moved to the edge of the nearest window. Gingerly, easing her body forward she brought her head round very slowly so that she could see through. The speed with which she retracted her head was all the more striking because of the very slow manner in which she had first brought it in front of the window.

'He's there,' she whispered.

'Who's there?'

'My uncle . . . and Captain Barkov.'

I moved to where Jane stood. I wanted to see for myself. She caught my elbow. I thought this was to prevent me from stepping into view in front of the window, but instead she turned me around to look in the opposite direction.

A man was climbing onto the roof. He didn't do this by means of the drainpipe, but by using a ladder, and stepped onto the slate. As he began to walk towards us, I saw the head of another man appear. I recognised him. It was the second time we had met on a rooftop – and the last time he had caused me to jump off.

Sometimes things are seen before they are registered and registered before they are fully understood. So it was now. I did not realise until after it had happened that the window had been opened. Barkov looked out and addressed us.

Jane allowed herself to be assisted by the captain as he helped her climb into the room, and then I felt myself being taken again by the elbow.

CHAPTER TWENTY-TWO

I was hustled rather than helped over the windowsill. The man who had shown such deft footwork three days earlier, when we fought on the rooftop overlooking the shirt makers', now showed the strength and delicacy of the gorilla I first took him to be. I staggered. The gorilla climbed in and stood behind me, with his partner following him, walking round Jane and Alan to take up a position in front of the door. His chin up, arms clasped in front of him, feet splayed out, he looked like a prison warden.

Barkov was large but he was not imposing. He was well-dressed yet there was an air of shabbiness about him. I might have had him down as a gambler, someone who had dispensed with the safe or the sensible option and was ill-served by his own carelessness. As with Baron von Herzog, I identified a florid flush that suggested a fondness for drink. He had a pencil moustache and dark brown eyes. He would have made a good portrait.

Alan held Jane in an embrace that was affectionate and that was intended, in a manifestly ineffective and therefore touching way, to offer protection. I was glad he was alive. I was glad too that he was evidently a prisoner, and not a conspirator.

Barkov looked at each of us. He seemed to hesitate, as though he wanted to be sure of the right tone. Finally, he said, 'Miss Macgregor, please sit. You have been running. This must tire you. The police want to know why you murdered that man from Vienna. You are hunted.'

I began to move towards Jane; she had turned pale. However, I was prevented from completing the step I had initiated. Two powerful hands were placed on my shoulder. I would like to report that I exercised some skilful manoeuvre, some application of the oriental art of judo, and threw the man across the well-appointed sitting room. But I didn't do this. I felt his hands take hold of my shoulders and, for a second, I had the sensation of being lifted off my feet. I allowed myself to be brought back to my original position.

I took note of Barkov's stilted delivery. He sought to appear relaxed and in command, but his not-quite-perfect English undermined this. *You have been running* was surely a clumsy allusion to being on the run. *This must tire you* struck an equally awkward note. When he said *You are hunted*, his voice rose on the word 'are' and then fell abruptly on the first syllable of 'hunted'.

'The police know that Miss Macgregor didn't murder Doctor Breitling,' I lied. 'They are looking for the man who did, a man with the height and strength to strangle someone the doctor's size.'

Alan's face had turned the colour of parchment. He sat down, or rather he fell back into the armchair behind him and stared into the middle distance. Jane detached the bag from her belt and placed it on the sofa and then sat down quickly on the edge of the chair and put her arm round her uncle's shoulder.

'Breitling,' he whispered.

He glanced at Jane and then he looked at me. His eyes slowly came into focus, as though his expression were catching up with his thoughts. He looked the way people look when they are obliged to confront something they have known all along but have until now successfully persuaded themselves that they do *not* know.

'Doctor Breitling was murdered,' I said. 'His body was left in the gallery.'

'But . . .' Alan looked at Jane.

'The police will catch the man who did it,' I told Alan. Then I turned to Barkov. 'They will catch the man in due course . . . Captain Barkov.'

I had the satisfaction of seeing the lines around his eyes deepen and the retinas contract. He took a step towards me. He was not as tall as the gorilla who was resting his hands on my shoulders, though he was taller than me. He wanted to intimidate, yet I did not think he intended to strike a blow. Jane had not arrived at the same conclusion, however. As Barkov stepped forward, she leapt up from the side of the armchair and threw herself in front of me, shouting, 'Do not hurt him!'

The force of Jane's body made me step back, but I was unable to complete this trajectory because of the granite-like presence behind me. We thus presented a very curious spectacle, with the gorilla standing like a pillar; me leaning against him; Jane holding me while turning her face and the upper part of her body towards Barkov; and Barkov facing the three of us with an expression that seemed to register the absurdity of the scene.

He stepped back and began to walk towards the door. 'You will not leave,' he said. And then he left.

The gorilla released his grip. Jane had been holding me so fiercely that it impaired the capacity to breathe. Now she turned and embraced me. I felt her untidy hair against the side of my face, the crushed fabric of her jacket and skirt against my own clothes, and her hands around my neck. I could feel, too, the beating of her heart and the warmth of her body.

Alan asked, 'What are we going to do?'

Jane separated herself from me and we sat on the sofa next to the armchair where Alan had sunk into the cushions.

The gorilla and the other man moved to a corner and watched us from there.

'What happened?' Jane asked Alan. Her voice was insistent.

'The villa you went to photograph—'

'We just came from there,' Jane said.

'You came from there?'

'It's on the other side of the loch, just across from here.'

Alan's expression became animated. '*That's* what they meant,' he said. 'That's why they wanted the photograph.'

'Uncle Alan!' Jane's voice was loud enough for the two men in the corner to hear. We looked in their direction, and they looked back at us, poker-faced. Jane lowered her voice again, 'Why did they want the photograph?'

'Ratković said in his note that Breitling had broken the agreement. The photographs were supposed to have been taken inside the house only.'

Jane nodded. 'It's possible to see across the loch to this house.'

'Breitling was frightened,' Alan said. 'He was so scared, he made *me* scared. It's like an illness, you can *catch* fear from someone who's infected.' He stopped and considered this before adding, 'Ratković said "the captain" would pay for the photographs.'

'Captain Barkov,' I said.

Alan nodded. 'I saw him for the first time today, only about an hour ago. I hadn't seen him before then. Very unpleasant. He told me you two were in all sorts of trouble. He said you'd appeared at the Theatre Royal under false pretences.'

'By Jove!' I muttered.

'How did he know?' Jane asked this in a whisper. Then she returned to Alan's story.

'You didn't bring the photographs. You left them in the studio.'

Alan nodded. 'I made Breitling leave them behind but I offered to go with him.'

'Why?'

'Why did I come with him?'

'Why did you make him leave the pictures behind?'

'I thought people had no business demanding photographs. I didn't believe Breitling should give in to that sort of thing.'

'Uncle Alan, did you think you could bargain with these men? Did you want to sell the pictures for a good price?'

'I thought Breitling might be able to sell them for a better price if he didn't take them with him.'

This was a truth, I thought, that Alan had striven to suppress even from himself.

'Anyway,' he said, 'I thought it more than a little foolhardy to go and meet people of this sort without taking some sort of precaution. I thought if he left the pictures at the studio they would serve as a kind of security.'

'Do you know whose house you're in?'

He shook his head. I couldn't read his emotions when he next spoke. It seemed to me that, despite the gravity of what he described, his uppermost feeling was one of embarrassment.

'When we arrived at the rendezvous and climbed into the carriage we were blindfolded.'

'Oh, Uncle Alan!' Jane said. She reached across and took his hand.

He sighed. 'I was stupid, I know.'

'You were brought here?' I asked.

'Into this room. That's when they removed the blindfold.'

'And Breitling?'

'He was summoned away. They said he was to go and collect the photographs and I would be released when the pictures had been returned.'

He sat back and released Jane's hand, and then, abruptly, he sat forward and took her hand again, then said, 'Mary will be beside herself!'

'I have been to see her,' I said. 'Her sister, Janet, is with her. They are anxious, of course.'

'Janet!' Alan's features reconfigured, as though he were trying, not quite successfully, to smile. 'Mary won't be allowed any nonsense.'

I stood up and walked to the corner.

'We met before,' I told the gorilla.

He shrugged. 'You were lucky, sir. You are here to tell about it.'

'My fiancée has had a shock,' I said. 'Can she have a glass of water?'

He shrugged again, and nodded to the other man, indicating that he should go out for the water.

I returned to the sofa and sat down.

'Breitling came back with the captain,' Jane told Alan. 'I was there when they came into the gallery. They argued, then they went to the studio and Breitling handed over two of the photographs from the villa, but then there was a struggle. Breitling cried out. Barkov ran off. I followed him to the Theatre Royal.'

Alan was utterly mystified. 'The Theatre Royal . . .'

All three of us were silent until Jane asked, 'Uncle Alan, what was in the photographs?'

'Two men.'

'On this side of the loch?'

He nodded.

'I'll wager one of them was Barkov,' I said.

'The other was this Ratković,' Alan said.

I nodded. 'He liked "to go out on the water".'

Jane raised her hands, palms up. 'What does it mean?'

I was pleased because I had arrived at a solution before Jane. 'Ratković rented a villa on the other side of the loch. He could go back and forth, but he didn't *stay* in this house.'

But Jane was ahead of me.

'Remember what we found on his desk . . .'

'What?'

'A receipt from Simpson-Burley.'

'So . . .'

'For the delivery of paint . . . to the Theatre Royal.'

'Our man communicates with this house and arranges for a delivery to the Theatre Royal. He's photographed with Captain Barkov. The captain is so upset that he's prepared to kill in order to get hold of the photograph. The Crown Prince went off to see his battleship this afternoon, and tonight he is to be at the theatre. Barkov was there this morning.' Jane stopped. She got up and walked to the window and then she came back again.

'Uncle Alan, do you remember when Mr Peacock visited?'

'Mr Peacock?'

'He had been to the Black Sea, to Yalta and Trebizond and points in between.'

'I remember.'

'He had spent time among the Rumelian clans.'

'But what has this to do with—?'

'In the eastern Balkans.'

'Jane, I cannot imagine why you are—'

'Uncle Alan, Mr Peacock gave us a full account of his dinner at the British legation.' She sat down and her voice dropped. 'The Crown Prince has caused tremendous animosity by abandoning his father's policy, by purchasing this warship.'

'The theatre!' I said.

Jane nodded. 'Why would you be prepared to kill someone for a photograph? Perhaps if you planned some outrage—'

The door opened, and the man who had been sent to fetch water came in. He placed the glass on the low table in front of the sofa and joined the gorilla in the corner.

'Come to the window,' Jane whispered to me.

When we were standing alone, Jane said, 'There is a part of the story I have not shared with you, Juan. I haven't been entirely honest.'

Is it true what people say – the deeper the love, the more painful the betrayal? The very fact that this question arose in my thoughts does not reflect well on my character, but it arose.

'There was a policeman at the end of the street when you came to see my aunt last night.'

My surprise must have been quite evident.

She nodded. 'I was there.'

'But—'

'I could not go in, because the house was being watched.'

'I didn't see any policeman.'

I was dissatisfied with this response; it was rather beside the point.

'He was following you when you arrived at the house and he followed you when you left.'

'But—'

She made a face as if I were being very dense. 'I followed him. That is why I know that he followed you. He shadowed you along Great Western Road until you caught a cab at Kelvinbridge. Then he whistled for a cab and he continued to follow.'

'You followed me?'

'I had to go to my aunt's house. I could not immediately enter. There was another policeman there, standing watch. I followed you because I thought you were in danger. After you climbed into the cab I returned to my aunt's.'

'You visited your aunt . . .'

She made another face, this time apparently to suggest that the words I had chosen did not precisely describe the nature of her presence the previous evening at Alan and Mary's house.

'I could not go in by the front door, because the house was being watched,' she said. 'But, of course, there is a back door. To get there, I had to climb over the wall in the lane. Didn't you wonder why my clothes were dirty?'

I was unable to answer.

Jane carried on speaking. 'I couldn't stay, of course. If

the police had come back to the house, Mary wouldn't have known what to do. She might have told them I was there.'

'But why did you go there, then?' I sounded petulant.

Jane was anything but petulant. She was very calm. 'I'm going to tell you, Juan, but let me just . . .'

She walked over to the table, lifted the glass, turned to come back and tripped on the carpet. The glass spun across the table, scattering water, and then shattered on the parquet floor.

Jane regained her balance, then bent down and started to pick up dripping shards of glass.

The gorilla hurried over.

'Please, do not trouble,' Jane said, as though the principal consideration at this point was the fuss that is created when someone smashes a glass in an unfamiliar sitting room.

'Leave it!' the gorilla barked.

Jane had already scooped up several pieces.

'I will get a cloth,' she said.

The gorilla made a face as if to indicate that such a primitive stratagem was hardly likely to succeed. 'Leave it!' he said again.

Jane continued to stand with her arm outstretched, holding broken glass as though it were a gift.

The gorilla jerked his head, indicating that the other man should take it away.

As the man left, we heard a carriage moving across the gravel and away from the front of the house – the portico reverberated with the sound of a heavy carriage and four horses.

Alan stood up and came to the window.

'They have gone to the theatre,' I said. 'I'm sure of it.'

Jane fetched her bag from the sofa.

'I went back to the house,' she told me, taking up where she had left off, 'because I knew that, one way or another, I was going to need *this*.'

She took her father's service revolver from the bag. Then she advanced to the middle of the room and pointed the weapon at the gorilla.

'Juan,' she said over her shoulder, 'open the window. Quickly!'

I did not at first respond. I simply watched Jane.

'Juan!' she shouted.

I grasped that we had only seconds to act. I also grasped that if Jane had told me that she proposed to point a revolver at one of our captors I would have prevaricated.

Now there was no time for prevarication. The gorilla had raised his arms, but only as far as his shoulders. The ascendancy of the revolver was transitory. If I went to Jane's assistance, I would not be assisting. So, I pulled the window up.

'Alan, come!' I said.

Alan was even slower to respond than me. He stood where he was. I took him by the arm and pushed him out onto the roof.

'Jane! Come!'

She was at the window in three paces.

The door opened and the other man came in. He looked at Jane, or rather more precisely, he looked at the gun. A startled expression crossed his face. Jane fired twice.

As she did this, she reversed into me. I climbed out and pulled her out behind me. I saw the gorilla lying on the floor. I could not see the other man.

Alan stood watching us, a posture which in its absolute want of usefulness filled me with a sudden surge of exasperation. I pulled him to the edge of the roof where the ladder had been. Jane had grabbed him on the other side.

The ladder was no longer there.

'The drainpipe,' I said.

'Follow me,' Jane said.

She knelt down, got hold of the sharp edge of the tiles and swung her body over the side. She disappeared. Not more than ten seconds after this, she reappeared on the ground.

'Uncle Alan! Come quickly!' she shouted up.

'I can't!'

'Then I'm going to fire my father's gun again. And this time, I'm going to kill someone!'

It wasn't clear to me what she meant by this, but it had the desired effect on Alan. He knelt down, took hold of the edge of the roof, swung himself over and disappeared. When he was taking those famous pictures of Glasgow slums, he must have climbed onto myriad roofs and balconies. If such was his experience, then it was invaluable now.

The gorilla climbed out the window and the other man climbed out behind him.

So, Jane had not yet killed anyone.

I stood stupidly on the roof, watching our pursuers.

Realising this, I knelt, grasped the sharp edge of the slate, swung over and slid down. As my toes touched the gravel, there was an unspeakably loud bang.

Jane had fired again.

'Quickly!' she shouted.

The wood offered cover. It was dusk. We knew the path, but I did not think we had enough of a march on our pursuers.

I was right. No sooner had we begun to run through the trees towards the first clearing than I heard the sound of someone running behind me. I looked round. It was the gorilla. I increased the pace. Just at the clearing, I caught up with Alan and Jane. 'This way!' I shrieked. I pulled them into the thicket where there was a narrow opening. I moved carefully, but quickly. I saw the stick still protruding from the steel trap and then I saw a second trap. I edged towards it, taking Jane by the hand. Jane in her turn took Alan's hand. We stepped over the trap and into the wood.

The gorilla saw us and followed.

He held his knife in the same way he had done when he turned to face me three days before. The expression on his face as he moved towards us was one of pure vindictiveness. There was a grotesque sound of steel upon bone as the trap closed. He screamed. I burst onto the lawn and Jane and Alan followed. As we began to run down to the water's edge, we heard police whistles.

I saw men coming around to the front of the house and starting down the lawn. We ran to where I had laid the oars on the grass to tether the rowing boat.

The oars were still there, but the boat wasn't. It was in the middle of the loch. The breeze had loosened the rope.

'Quick!' I said. 'This way!' I began to run to the edge of the wood. I knew the trees were no more than twenty yards deep here, and on the other side there was a path in front of the neighbouring houses.

'I can't run any more,' Alan said.

'Look!' I pointed up to the house, where half a dozen men were racing towards us. 'If they catch us . . .'

Jane was already in the lead. As she reached the wood, she splashed into the water. I pushed Alan in front of me. I felt mud and then water move over the top of my shoes as I clambered along the side of the thicket on the edge of the loch. Ten yards in, I stepped with my left foot, on the landward side, into a hole that plunged my leg into mud up to my knee. When I began to retract my foot, my shoe remained at the bottom of the hole, as though it had been sucked into a drain. I grabbed hold of a branch, swore, bent down, plunged my right hand into the hole, got hold of the leather above the heel of my shoe and wrenched it back out full of water. As I stood up, I felt my shoulder make contact with something that was first soft and then hard, first moving behind me and then moving beside me.

It was one of my pursuers.

If I had tried to tackle the man, I might have had some success. Yet, I was in full flight and even the judo tricks the Jesuit had taught me during my student days might have been of limited use. But there is a tremendous power in the body when it is executing an everyday movement – standing up – without anticipating resistance. I caught my pursuer full in the chest with my shoulder and then full in the face with my elbow. Neither of these blows was intended, but both had a powerful effect. The man shouted and fell backward into the loch. I completed the remaining ten yards to the path in half the time it had taken me to cover the first ten yards.

When I broke out of the wood, I found that Alan and Jane were no longer there.

I heard my name called, and when I looked in the direction from which I was being hailed. I saw the top of Jane's head. She was peeping over the bevelled top of a granite wall. A barrel of the sort in which fish are sometimes kept stood below the wall. I grasped that the means of getting from this side of the wall to the other involved climbing up on the barrel, which I was able to do with greater ease because my shoeless left foot found the rim and clutched it, monkey-like, as I pulled myself up onto the wall and then over, just at the point when the first of our pursuers broke cover and came into the open space.

I lay on the grass and tried to catch my breath without making a sound. Alan and Jane were engaged in the same exercise. The voices on the other side of the wall expressed bewilderment and annoyance. This was very satisfactory.

We were at the bottom of a garden like the Fletchers' in the West End, long and narrow. The house in front of us was unlit, and as dusk turned to evening, the place where we lay was suffused in darkness. The men who had followed us walked the length of the garden wall and at the end they turned into a side street and towards the main road. By the light of a street lamp we watched as, one after the other the four of them passed a gate in the wall that ran along the other side of the garden. Each of our pursuers glanced into the gloom beyond the gate and each failed to see us where we lay in the dark.

Lying there, still afraid to breathe, I saw the means of our salvation. There were two tram wires beyond the wall, and attached to one was a boom.

I nudged Alan and Jane.

'The terminus,' Alan whispered.

We waited five minutes and then, with Alan in front followed by Jane and then me, we moved like a party of polar explorers along the side of the wall on the inside of the garden as far as the gate. I edged past the others and tried the handle of the gate. As I did so, there was a huge clattering noise that seemed to fill the whole street and I thought momentarily that I had somehow created this just by lifting the handle of a rusty bolt and sliding it back.

But it wasn't the gate that created the racket. It was the tram.

The bolt slid only halfway and then it stopped, and we were trapped on the wrong side as the tram began to make its way past us and on to the main road.

'Juan!' Jane hissed. 'Open the gate!'

'I'm trying to!' I said, perhaps with an edge of ill temper in my voice.

'It's getting away!'

'Perhaps if you move it this way,' Alan said.

I hadn't noticed that Alan had come to the other side, so that he could examine the bolt more closely. He reached down and pushed the handle so that it protruded into the street-side. I saw now that the blockage was created by a bracket on the garden side.

'Push it, Juan,' Alan said gently.

'Oh, for heaven's sake!' Jane said.

She reached down and pushed the bolt and pulled the gate, so that all three of us had to jump out of the way as it opened inward.

We hurried out into the street just in time to see the tram disappear around the corner.

'Damn,' I said. I looked at Jane and I was surprised to see that she was smiling.

'This will be faster.' She pointed to a cab waiting at the terminus on the other side of the road.

CHAPTER TWENTY-THREE

There were constables at the main entrance to the Theatre Royal, and there were more at the corner of the building.

Jane's jacket and skirt, which had been crushed even before she climbed in and out of Auchinleck House and ran through a wood and tumbled over a wall, made a striking contrast to the satin and tiaras in evidence among the concert-goers milling outside the theatre. Alan was without a jacket or a tie. My jacket was torn; my trousers and shoes were sodden.

But even properly attired, our entry would have been difficult: the building was guarded like a fortress. There were also police at the stage door, and on the opposite side of the street. When we alighted from the cab, two policemen stood at the corner not five yards away. They were watching the arrival of a particularly splendid phaeton from which emerged one of the city's wealthiest businessmen, together with his wife and daughter, the two women in lamé evening gowns and mink stoles. I ushered Jane and Alan quickly into one of the lanes that led off the main street.

We stood in the dark. Jane put a hand through her hair. There were tresses and curls and wisps. I realised that I was thinking of an image. At first I could not quite settle on its precise nature, and then it dawned on me that Jane's hair was like those found in storybook illustrations of a scarecrow. A beautiful scarecrow, of course. I wondered if she would find this comparison amusing and I was going to share it with her, but she had already started to walk further into the lane.

Alan and I remained where we were.

'Where are we going?' I called into the dark.

'To Cowcaddens.'

The vegetable market in Cowcaddens was still busy despite the lateness of the hour, and the three stalls that sold fresh flowers were all open. There was an evening trade that depended on the music halls and restaurants nearby.

The woman at the first stall looked at us in a manner that was thorough and shrewd. She was not impressed by our appearance, but when Jane began to speak, in the confident and melodic way that I had come to love, the woman's expression changed. There was an identifiable shift, from scepticism to deference, from an assumption that three bedraggled strangers were unlikely to be a source of profit to a contrary calculation.

Jane's confidence conveyed the positive signals that our appearance very definitely did not.

But even as the woman became more disposed towards us, she hesitated when Jane explained what we wanted to do.

'You want to buy *all* my flowers?'

What she actually said was *Ye wid hae aw ma flures?* I understood the meaning without difficulty because I was in a rage to complete the transaction; my agitation must have uncovered some layer of personality where I possessed the language skill to decipher this and subsequent responses as Jane moved forward with the negotiation. We wanted not only all the flowers but the hand cart that was used to carry them across the town. And in addition, we wanted Jeemie, the boy whose job it was to go from theatre to theatre with the flower-laden cart. Jeemie stood to one side, watching. I gathered that the woman was not his mother, though she appeared to exercise a kind of maternal authority. As the negotiations progressed, and as first Alan, then Jane, and then I produced banknotes, Jeemie was instructed to load his cart with *aw* the *flures*.

'Say nothing,' Jane said, as we hurried towards the theatre, where there seemed to be even more police on patrol. 'Your accent will give you away.' Then she added, 'You too, Uncle Alan. You don't know how to speak like a flower seller.'

Jeemie was impressed by our purchase. His evening would be less than usually arduous. I was amazed at how easily he handled the heavy cart, up the narrow ramp from the market and along the lane to the main road, where he deftly navigated the traffic, still brisk at this hour. He manoeuvred the cart into the lane behind the stage door and we walked beside it, listening to the clatter of steel wheels on cobblestones.

Jeemie's jacket and trousers were muddied and though his shoes were dry he was sockless. In appearance, we formed a plausible quartet. The clothes that would have prevented access at the front of the house, facilitated access at the back. We picked up four bouquets each, which meant we had to clutch them in an ungainly fashion, as if embracing the wild profusion of blooms, peering between the stems in order to see where we were going.

'Take the rest to Peter at the Broomielaw,' Jane told Jeemie, part of the bargain, apparently, with the doyenne of the flower market.

What she actually said was, *Gie th'ithers tae wee peasy doon the Broomielaw*. Standing between two constables facing the locked stage door, I absently deciphered Jane's words. My intellect was focused on staring in front of me and trying to appear inconspicuous. I resisted the normal human instinct to look either of the policemen in the eye.

Jeemie began to rearrange the remaining flowers so that they wouldn't roll off the cart when he tipped it up to pull it out of the lane. I glanced back and saw that another, larger cart, pulled by two Clydesdales, was now approaching. It had a canvas cover on the side of which was the name of the firm to which it belonged.

Simpson-Burley.

The carter, whose cropped grey hair and stubble framed a

round, drink-addled face that could never have been handsome, shouted at Jeemie to hurry up. One of the constables sauntered towards the Simpson-Burley cart, in the manner of constables in every part of the world when any untoward activity disturbs the even tenor of the watch.

'Flures fur the Russian wuman,' Jane told the other policeman, 'Madame Borlover.'

The officer hesitated.

I pushed past Jane and hammered the door. Prevarication here would be our undoing.

The bolt was drawn back and the door opened.

It was opened not by an unknown functionary. It was opened by Natalia.

I stepped forward.

Natalia put her hand up. 'You can't come in.'

'Why not?'

She looked at me with an expression that conveyed more than disappointment with our behaviour earlier in the day, when we had left Natalia and her boss abruptly.

'Because you will murder people!'

She seemed as surprised to see me as I was to see her. When she spoke, she wasn't quite able to do so at normal volume.

My response was honest and concise and, of course, utterly ineffective. 'No, we won't!'

For one bizarre moment I thought Natalia might respond with *Oh yes, you will!* Because of this, and because I was standing in wet trousers and ruined shoes, and the policeman had stepped closer so as to hear the exchange,

I smiled and carried on speaking.

'Quite the opposite,' I said. 'If you would take us to Mr Müller or Captain Smith or Captain Barkov, we have something we must tell them.'

Natalia stepped backward and we stepped forward, into the building.

'We haven't murdered anyone,' I said, 'but we must act quickly or someone *will* certainly be murdered in this theatre tonight.'

I was trying to reassure Natalia, but my words seemed to have the opposite effect. They sounded rather like a homicidal threat. I saw in the corner of my eye the constable step through the doorway.

'These people—' Natalia began.

Jane ducked around me and past Natalia and started to move quickly towards the open area where the sets were stored.

'Yes?' The policeman was closest to Alan.

'—are trying to get into the theatre,' Natalia continued.

This was a statement that was neither particularly incriminating nor particularly illuminating, but it induced the policeman to place a hand on Alan's shoulder.

'I think they are the people you are looking for.'

The policeman's other hand now seized Alan by the elbow.

As I stepped past Natalia, she tried to emulate the policeman. I felt a hand on my shoulder and a hand on my elbow, but the hands were small and the grip far from resolute. I shook free and began to run.

I heard Alan remonstrating with the policeman. I was

conscious too, of the porter, Mr Hamilton, leaning out of his little office, holding his pipe in one hand, looking at Alan and the policeman and then at Natalia and me. I noticed many things; perhaps the mind assumes a species of *hyper* vigilance when the body is plunged into stress and uncertainty. This was something about which Baron von Herzog's friend, Doctor Ambrose, would doubtless have an opinion.

There were passageways leading off in different directions, people coming out of rooms and disappearing through swing doors. Young women clutched sheets of music and notepaper and envelopes and the various accoutrements that sustain the workings of a complex and efficient administration; men carried stage props and backdrops. Most of the people in this part of the theatre wore working clothes, but two or three of the men were in tails and white tie and one young woman wore a ballgown and tiara, not, I gathered, a patron of the dress circle but, from the heavy face paint and the rather brilliant sheen of the ballgown's almost industrial fabric, dressed for her role in the chorus.

I plunged through the double doors that led to the lobby with the steep stairs going up to Müller's office. The door swung away as I went through and I heard a young woman utter an imprecation as it swung back towards her. My instinct was to stop and see if she had hurt herself, but gallantry must in this case be a casualty of speed, so I took the stairs two at a time and arrived outside Müller's office. I was profoundly affected by what I experienced there.

Silence.

From the mayhem below, accentuated undoubtedly by the fear and excitement that accompany flight, I was plunged into an ambience in which any sound that penetrated the space enclosed by two doors and four thick walls was absorbed by a plush carpet so deep that I felt my sodden shoes sink into it with almost the same sensation I had experienced when they sank into the mud beside the water in Milngavie.

The pristine silence was shattered by the sound of someone climbing the stairs behind me. I stepped through the double doors and entered the foyer.

Here, again, a different world, perhaps even a different universe. On the floor below, there were lights, along the corridors that projected a harsh paleness onto everything, turning sets and props and boxes into hard configurations of geometric shadow. It was like running through a giant puzzle. The light shed by the foyer chandeliers was a soft orange, and its warmth was accentuated by the rich red carpet. This mellow atmosphere was suffused with the chaotic energy of the crowd. There was an ebullience in the multiple conversations that coalesced all around me: it was the inchoate but instantly recognisable sound of humanity. I heard Glasgow accents and foreign accents, voices raised in the normal undulations of discussion, amplified by the need to speak above the din of competing conversations. There were diamond earrings and gold cufflinks and silver cigarette cases. There were women with almost as much face paint as the singer I had seen below, and there were women with no paint at all, plain and proper. There were girls chaperoned by their sisters and their cousins and their aunts, and boys posing like peacocks in their first grown-up evening attire. Gentlemen puffed on cigars. A man just inside the foyer had his head inclined politely so as to hear what was being said by the woman facing him. He had a walrus moustache and a monocle; he raised a cigar to his lips.

At the very moment I barged into the foyer, as though a stage director had shouted instructions for the conversations to be muted and the disparate points of attention to be focused on one place and one individual, the people in the crowd assumed a new and almost uniform posture, standing on tiptoe and facing the main entrance. The volume of conversations fell from an ocean of sound to a sea and then a lake, until there were just puddles of sentence fragments that evaporated in the atmosphere.

'Your Royal Highness!' I recognised Müller's voice.

I had to stretch and peer around a lady who was wearing a rather extravagant hat. I caught sight of Müller making a deep bow.

Facing the theatre manager was a young man, not much older than me and perhaps a little shorter. He was thin and looked like a stick onto which had been grafted a uniform and a large head. The Crown Prince was not an imposing figure. I thought this even as I watched him impose a kind of collective fascination on two or three hundred people who moments earlier had been shouting at one another and who now watched in rapt attention as, after Müller had greeted Archibald Auchinleck and Mrs Auchinleck with similarly unctuous courtesy, the royal party moved across the foyer to the stairs that led up to the dress circle.

When the procession had passed beyond the huge maroon curtains that made the stairway resemble the entrance to a Roman amphitheatre, there was a resumption of the earlier cacophony. Voices rose as magically and suddenly as they had subsided; the threads of arguments were seized and tugged; remarks were rescued from the limbo to which they had been consigned; fingers pointed; backs were slapped; and across the room there were expressions of surprise and approval and excitement.

Two young women in long black evening dresses inspected the tickets of the people now queuing to pass through the curtains and begin climbing the stairs. Beside each of the women stood a constable. I glanced at the entrance to the stalls. There were ushers there too, but I didn't see a constable. Just then, flowing through the doors by which I had made my own entrance, came a posse of police. I had no doubt about who they were looking for.

I might have blended into the crowd except that, even before the arrival of my pursuers, a sort of *cordon sanitaire* had developed around me: I was not in evening dress. I was not even respectably dressed for a day in the garden.

The object of the police pursuit, I stood like a lone fox on a treeless plain.

I darted towards the stalls.

'Sir!' One of the startled ushers protested as I passed.

Inside the auditorium, I turned to my right and ran behind the back row of seats and down the side aisle. The incline of a theatre floor can be invigorating when it is encountered at leisure in the minutes before curtain-up. The fact that the floor slopes downward towards the stage is the first intimation of altered reality. When encountered in full flight, however, the gentle slope is precipitate. I swerved around a small boy, who stepped to one side, making it easier for me to fly past, and a rather large lady. The lady leaned on a stick on one side and a girl on the other. I caught the young woman by the elbow, pulled her to one side and raced past, calling an apology as I did so.

There was a doorway halfway down the aisle. From our reconnaissance in the morning, I knew that on the other side was a corridor that led back to the foyer, but indirectly. I doubled back along the corridor and found myself on the theatre side of the maroon curtains, at the foot of the stairs leading to the dress circle.

I slowed my pace and caught my breath and turned abruptly so that I faced away from the constables standing next to the young ushers. I was abreast of two couples who had begun to climb. I could hear the commotion generated by the constables running along the corridor from the stalls. I moved in step with the couple beside me. Two or three rows of people had started to climb by the time the constables arrived at the first step. I had to apply every ounce of self-control not to barge past the people in front. The constables did not labour under any comparable need to observe decorum. I heard them begin to climb the stairs faster than the general pace.

'Hey!' one man objected. 'What on earth?' There were

expressions of surprise and complaint.

The heavy footfall of the leading officer advanced behind me, past the first row of patrons and then the next and then the next. I felt him push me to one side, and I fought back the impulse to turn and face him. Instead, I turned to the lady on my right and said, 'I believe they may think someone has entered the theatre without authorisation. They are worried that the Crown Prince may be at risk.' These were the first words that came into my head. The substance was less important than the tone of voice: I might just as easily have said something about the weather. What mattered was that I turned my head in the direction of the lady and away from the policeman who barrelled past and onward to the top of the stairs. He was followed by three of his comrades. In the compact area of the crowded stairs, my dishevelled appearance did not attract notice.

In this way, I was able to ascend the stairs. The challenge at the top, however, was of a different order. Two of the officers who had passed me on the first flight had continued climbing, up to the cheaper seats above the dress circle. The other two remained at the top of the first flight. They scanned the faces of those who moved into the dress circle.

I resolved to continue climbing. The couple who ascended next to me began to move towards the dress circle when we reached the top step. I felt one of the policemen begin to take an interest in my appearance.

And yet, I had acquired a certain confidence in the cloak that behaviour drapes over reality. It is what mesmerists like

Baron von Herzog depend upon when they enter the minds of their subjects. They play with the mechanisms we use in order to interpret the world, not as it is, but as we would like it to be, or as we *think* it is.

So, I made a parting comment to the lady with whom I had climbed the stairs. 'It would be nice to speak again at the interval.' I nodded to her baffled husband. 'Lovely to see you again.'

I passed so close to the policeman that the cloth on the elbow of my jacket touched one of the brass buttons at the front of his tunic, yet the greeting with which I took my leave of the couple I had never met made me invisible. The constable continued diligently to scrutinise the ascending theatregoers.

I had only the briefest opportunity to glance at the foyer outside the dress circle. It was where Jane and I had stayed behind to speak to one another three nights before.

And, to my astonishment, Jane was standing there again.

She was resplendent in an evening dress. Her hair looked extremely elegant now. Her tresses and curls were topped with a tiara. She was in conversation with a distinguished-looking lady I had never seen before.

It was incomprehensible.

I continued to climb. On this flight, the density of bodies was less acute. I was unable to hide myself within a cocoon of supposed association with other theatregoers. But the theatregoers here were different, too. None of the men were in white tie and tails. A small number were dressed more or less like me, although few, I suppose, had been rowing, fighting, climbing or paddling earlier in the day. I still stood out but not as much. So, when I got to the top of the stairs, without giving the matter very much consideration, I moved directly in front of the policeman who was studying the crowd, and asked, 'Is this the right level for the student seats?'

The man sniggered. 'A cannae help ye wi' that,' he said, mixing incredulity with indignation at the idea of asking a policeman about theatre seating. 'Awa' and ask wan o thon wee lassies.' He nodded towards the ushers at the entrance to the upper circle.

'Baron von Herzog is going to pick me out of the audience,' I told the nearest girl. 'I have to go down the back stairs when the time comes. Can you show me where they are, please?'

The girl looked at me in the appraising way of someone for whom the theatre has not yet ceased to exert an all-encompassing magic.

'The back stairs aren't to be used tonight.'

'Last minute,' I said. 'The Baron has changed his programme . . . because of the Crown Prince. That's why I need to know where the entrance is. I used the stairs this morning, but I didn't have a chance to come up here.'

She looked around and then, having failed to find someone in authority, she said, 'I'll show you then.'

'Are you studying drama?' I asked. She had begun to walk to the other side of the foyer. I followed her through shifting thickets of people chatting and smoking before taking their places in the cheap seats.

The girl beamed. 'Oh, I would *love* to study drama, but my

father won't allow it. The best I can do is music. I'm going to be a piano teacher.'

'I bet you'll be a wonderful piano teacher.'

'Are you an actor?'

'I wish! No, I'm a photographer, but I agreed to help the Baron out. His usual man is off this evening.'

She gave me a strange look. I should not have said I was a photographer. I cursed my indiscretion.

'It's there,' the girl said, pointing to an alcove, but still looking at me. 'Why do you need to use the back stairs now? Baron von Herzog isn't on until the second act.'

'I know,' I said, 'but I have to be in the wings from the beginning of the show.'

'Why?'

I didn't answer but said, instead, 'Well, thank you!'

I moved into the alcove. If you knew what you were looking for, it was easy to make out the fine lines of the door in the wood panelling – but if I couldn't open it, the girl would go at once and speak to the policeman at the top of the stairs. She might do that anyway.

I pressed the top right-hand corner, as Natalia had done that morning.

Nothing happened.

I turned to see the back of the girl's skirt. She was hurrying away.

I tried a little further down.

Nothing.

I cursed and tried pressing at the height where a handle

would have been if there had been a handle.

A click. The door opened.

I stepped inside and quickly pulled it shut behind me. I felt a click as the lock moved into place.

I was completely in the dark.

There must be moments in any difficult undertaking when we experience something close to despair, a kind of fatigue, a sense that success may be within our grasp, but the effort to achieve it has undermined its value. I thought about Jane standing in the foyer downstairs and any such notion vanished. She had shown courage and ingenuity. The dress she was wearing was striking, but it wasn't like the dress she had worn three nights before. Of course, it wasn't. It was a *stage* dress. It must have been. I resolved to emulate Jane's resourcefulness, her presence of mind.

The spiral staircase had no handrail. I struck a match and began to climb down, my right hand moving lightly over the rough surface of the brick wall. The match burned my fingers so I blew it out and lit another. It took three matches to reach the floor below, and as I lit the final match it became redundant, because the door above was opened, sending enough light into the stairway for me to find the door into the dress circle and push it open.

I entered the alcove, closed the door behind me and peeped through the curtain. Jane was no longer in the foyer, which was empty except for a handful of stragglers and four policemen who stood guard at the door to the Royal Box. I slipped into the first box next to the alcove.

There were two rows of four seats, with space to enter and leave along the sides. All eight seats were occupied – four couples. The two men in the back row looked up when I entered. It would have been a matter of seconds before one or both stood up to challenge me, so I didn't hesitate. I stepped nimbly down the passageway, climbed up onto the balustrade and jumped over to the next box. There was a gasp from behind, followed by expressions of indignation that rose quickly to become shouts of alarm.

I did not stop at the next box but ran along the balustrade as though it were the sort of bar that is used by acrobats when they are rehearsing their leaps and somersaults.

My principal emotion was embarrassment. It would have been hard to imagine a venue where antics of this sort would be subject to more detailed collective scrutiny. I knew that I might be incurring a host of charges, most of them criminal, yet I also knew that even if I was mistaken, even if the plot I sought to confound was a figment of my own misjudgement, the greatest casualty would be my pride. If I did nothing, on the other hand, and the plot unfolded as the conspirators must surely intend, then the life of another human being would be forfeit.

And I knew that if I had not acted in that instant, the policeman who followed me down from the floor above would have collared me.

So, I ran across the balustrade and jumped into the Royal Box.

Jane was already sitting there.

She was in the back row next to the lady she had been

speaking to in the foyer. In the same row was a man whom I presumed was the lady's husband and a youth of about fourteen, impeccably dressed and with an instantly recognisable air of entitlement, who might have been their grandson.

In front were Crown Prince Danilo, with Archibald Auchinleck on one side and Mrs Auchinleck on the other.

'What the devil—?' Auchinleck began.

I stared at the Crown Prince. He stared back.

There was a moment of odd clarity; it was as though the Crown Prince and I were alone in the crowded theatre. His eyes, it seemed to me, betrayed an element of resignation in the face of death and – this strangest of all – an element of camaraderie.

Auchinleck had begun to stand up. I placed my hand on his shoulder and he obliged me by sitting down again.

'What the devil do you want?' he asked.

Jane was getting to her feet. The noise from the other boxes and from the stalls below had reached a pitch of collective terror. Every eye in the house was on the Royal Box.

'Your Royal Highness,' I shouted, 'I believe you are in great danger!'

He could barely hear me because of the noise from the audience. He sat forward and began to look round. I gathered he expected help to come from the door at the back of the box, but the door remained closed.

We might have stayed in this position, creating a peculiar tableau, with Jane standing at the back and me standing at the front, the Crown Prince and his guests still sitting, as though awaiting the outcome of events.

The tableau was shattered, however.

As I made out the sound of violent battering on the door of the box, I caught sight of a movement in the corner of my eye and turned to see a man execute the same manoeuvre I had performed moments before. He was coming from the opposite direction. Not only did I recognise the manoeuvre, I recognised the man.

Ratković wore a dark suit and a starched white shirt – when I had last seen him, rowing across the loch, he had been in country clothes, his head covered with a cloth cap, but it was the same man.

The starched white shirt moved towards me like a spectre. I watched its progress across the banister of the adjoining box, as though it were dissociated from any human form. Perhaps this is the way in which the brain processes a great tide of information when it comes upon it at the same time.

I heard the sound of the door being broken down and the sound of the theatre audience screaming. Auchinleck tried to rise again and I pushed him back into his chair. I took a step forward to face Ratković, who leapt into the box. We were on either side of the Crown Prince.

Ratković shouted something in a language I did not understand.

The Prince replied. He spoke in an ordinary tone of voice. I was struck, as I had been earlier, by his apparent serenity.

And then Ratković drew a gun. It rose from his jacket pocket and moved in an arc, as though he were presenting this weapon to the Crown Prince and the audience. The amorphous mayhem of the theatre coalesced into a single gasp.

Ratković pointed his weapon at the prince and there was a shot.

Ratković staggered backward and seemed to sit on the edge of the balustrade; blood spurted from his chest and landed on the Crown Prince's shoes.

I watched this happen from no more than four feet away. It was as though it all happened twice; once when I saw it and once when I understood what it was that I saw.

I looked at the Crown Prince. He remained seated. Auchinleck tried to stand up again, but I think it was a half-hearted attempt, because when I raised my hand mechanically to make him sit, my fingers did not even touch his shoulder before he complied. My head moved – it seemed to me with inexplicable slowness – from the figure of Ratković, clutching his chest and sitting on the balustrade, to the figure of Jane, who was standing in the same place, her arm outstretched, holding her father's revolver.

That was the point at which the door to the box was broken down, and first Captain Smith and then Captain Barkov broke in. Smith began to move towards me. I watched him do this, but for only the smallest fragment of time, because some sort of primordial instinct assumed control of my faculties and, from executing everything with a slowness that would have done justice to one of those glaciers that the polar explorers describe in the newspapers, the ones that move an inch every century, I became more like a panther or a puma, the animals that the other explorers describe when they return from their adventures in Africa.

I bent down and scooped up the revolver that Ratković had dropped.

Smith had reached the point where I stood, and Barkov had reached the point where Ratković sat on the balustrade. I felt Smith's hand on my shoulder and I did what I had very much wanted to do several times by now: I applied the skills I learned when a student in Madrid and, using the judo technique that was taught to me by my Jesuit professor, I swivelled to avoid the oncoming force and extended a foot with which to arrest Smith's right leg, in this way causing him to tumble into the corner of the box.

As I did this, Barkov took up his position next to Ratković, but instead of offering succour to the wounded man, he pushed him with sudden and decisive force so that Ratković tumbled backward over the balustrade and fell into the stalls below. There was a new wave of horror from the entire theatre, that was not diminished when Barkov pointed his pistol not at me but at the Crown Prince.

This time, the sequence of events and my reaction to them was reversed, because, even as I felt Smith recover in the shadowy corner of the box and I knew he was about to renew his attack, I had a clear and compelling premonition of what Barkov was about to do, and I raised my arm and aimed the pistol at Barkov microseconds before he raised his own pistol and aimed at the Crown Prince.

I fired first.

I knew I had killed him. I was conscious of knowing. I knew *I* had killed him and I knew I had *killed* him. There are two kinds of violence. One is physical. The other is of a different order. I knew that Barkov's spirit had been torn from his body even before he fell backward and into the stalls.

The elderly couple who had been sitting with their grandson got to their feet, along with the boy and they filed out of the box just as though they were stepping into the foyer for refreshments during the first intermission. Auchinleck, who had three times tried to stand up, remained seated. I don't think he looked at me or at the Crown Prince. He seemed to be looking into the void between the great chandelier and the stalls. Mrs Auchinleck, on the other side of the Crown Prince, gazed down at the silver and black evening bag that lay on her lap. I believe she was trying to operate the little clasp by which the bag was opened and closed, but she was unable to do so. She struggled with the clip as though it were the most important thing in the world. She muttered to herself. Violence does harm, even after it is over. Mrs Auchinleck, I knew, would never be the same.

Jane had rushed along the back of the box and come down to take my arm, but not before Smith was on his feet. He too was altered. I held the pistol loosely pointed downward, and when he asked me to give it to him, I acquiesced.

'Are you unharmed, Your Royal Highness?' Smith asked, taking the revolver and stepping in front of the Crown Prince.

The Crown Prince shrugged. 'The evening is spoiled,' he said.

CHAPTER TWENTY-FOUR

Long after the events at the Theatre Royal, Alan was inclined at the least opportunity to launch into a tirade against the Glasgow police for the indignity that was done to him. He had been taken from the stage door in a police van and held for several hours. I too have travelled in a police van, and I know that the indignity is as nothing to the discomfort: such vehicles are ill-smelling and verminous. But I think what really galled was that Alan had been abducted and had escaped, both of which involved considerable peril, and had then been prevented from witnessing the most dramatic incident to take place in a Glasgow theatre within living memory.

Something else happened too. Mary, after she had

welcomed her husband home with characteristic indulgence, changed the terms of their relationship. Jane told me that the events of that period in some strange way delivered Mary from the resignation and acceptance with which she had until then responded to Alan's unchivalrous behaviour. 'He will carry on with his nonsense, no doubt,' Jane said, 'but she will exact a higher price.' Mary had made it clear that she would like to spend time away from Scotland, perhaps in the south of Spain. 'I will support this,' Jane said.

At the end of the concert run, Jane and I attended a reception given by Madame Orlova at the Queen's Hotel in Charing Cross. We were still getting back onto what Alan might have called 'an even keel'. Yet, something was not right.

Tristan MacKenzie, the solicitor whose presence was required in order to complete my ownership of property on the Isle of Bute, had at last returned to Glasgow from an extended visit to his brother in Cape Town. Until I assumed ownership of the property, which I intended to sell, I felt that Jane and I were in a kind of limbo. My affairs remained unsettled, and *my* affairs were now *our* affairs.

And there was the matter of Señora LaGuardia, who had made a claim on my father's photographs, and had charged me personally in a manner that Benjamin Jackson described simply as 'libellous'. The violent demise of my father's cousin and his wife must surely be the source of her case against me. The deaths of Paco and Eleanora cleared the way for my inheritance.

When we look back and see how we have behaved in a time of crisis, we may confront a version of ourselves we barely recognise. I viewed the final days in Santiago with confusing hindsight. I knew I had done no wrong and yet, I reviewed the facts compulsively, as though I must persuade myself that I was innocent.

I had written again to Henry Farquhar at Croft & Croft, who had promised to arrange a new interview. I wanted the matter resolved.

The Pushkin Room on the first floor of the Queen's Hotel was a place of generous proportion and considerable elegance. Sandwiches, pastries and cakes had been laid out on a long table that stretched the length of one side of the room. There were sofas along the opposite wall. Armchairs were scattered between the table and the sofas.

Temple and Hall stood on the edge of a balcony at one end of the room looking out onto Sauchiehall Street. Baron von Herzog was nearby, speaking to a woman whom I did not at first recognise, as she had her back to us. I saw others whom I did recognise and many more who were unknown to me. The room was already full when we arrived.

'Miss Macgregor!' The Baron took Jane's hand and kissed it.

Natalia turned and smiled at me, then she kissed Jane. 'It is so good to see you,' she told us both.

I had by now formed a different view of the Baron – necessarily, in light of the single contribution he had made to saving the life of the Crown Prince. When Jane broke away from Alan and me at the stage door, she followed the path we had taken when we explored the theatre in the morning, running directly to the area where the sets were stored. That was when she met the Baron.

'The police are following me,' she said. 'They believe I murdered someone.'

'Did you?' the Baron asked.

'I didn't . . . and the Crown Prince will be murdered here tonight if I cannot speak to him.'

The Baron considered this and then he asked, 'How quickly can you change into something more presentable?'

With von Herzog to vouch for her, Jane was able to acquire an evening gown in the wardrobe department and make her way up to the dress circle, where she was spirited into the seat reserved for Captain Barkov, spirited being the appropriate word: using his power as a mesmerist, the Baron introduced Jane to the heavily guarded Royal Box simply by looking steadily at the constables there and telling them that Captain Barkov wanted Jane to be given his seat.

'Why did they believe you?' I asked.

The Baron deployed one of his irritatingly affected 'aristocratic' mannerisms, an infinitesimal lifting of his open palms to indicate that there was no mystery, on the contrary the answer was simple. 'We say more with the tone of our voice than we say with the words we use. If the tone is correct – the pitch, the *timbre* – then the message is received.'

'And they just let Jane walk through?'

The Baron nodded. 'We know that things are not always what they seem, and yet, when we see things, we believe they are what we see.'

'But we know when people are telling lies!'

'Lies?' he said. 'Think instead of *reality* and how we grasp it, how we try to hold it in our thoughts. Our capacity to understand is limited, flawed. We can present reality in different ways and we can perceive it in different ways, too.'

The Baron was looking at me very earnestly.

'Why,' I asked, changing the subject, 'did you believe Jane?'

He smiled. 'Because I *didn't* believe what we had been told about Jane and about you.'

'When Captain Barkov came to the theatre in the evening, when he encouraged the rumour that Jane, Alan and I were the conspirators?' I asked.

He nodded. 'Since I have delved into the business of reality and illusion, I have a certain advantage over others . . .'

Just as his mannerisms were affected, so too the quality of his voice shifted easily – the *timbre*, as he might have put it. There was a warmth about it now.

He stopped. We waited.

'What's that?' I asked.

'I can recognise when other people are not telling the truth, and I recognised this Captain Barkov as a man who was very deeply mired in a falsehood. There was an urgency in his manner when he explained to us that we must be on the lookout for three fugitives. At first, I thought this urgency was a logical consequence of the danger to his prince, but then I discerned that what was a matter of urgency to him was that *we believed* what he was telling us. He didn't want us to catch the killers but rather he wanted us to think that *you* were the killers. So, I believed Miss Macgregor when she told me she was not the murderer, because I didn't believe Captain Barkov when he told me that she *was*.'

'You were very clever,' Natalia said.

To my complete surprise, the Baron took Natalia's hand and squeezed it, and then, when he had released her hand, Natalia took his arm, and they stood before us as a man and a woman who were more than temporary employees of the same theatre.

Perhaps my expression conveyed my surprise. 'I have an engagement in Berlin,' the Baron said, 'and Natalia has very kindly agreed to accompany me.' He added quickly, 'After we are married.'

Jane and the Baron spoke about Berlin. Her uncle, she said, had been disappointed in his hopes of showing his photographs there. I gathered that Alan's affairs continued to be shaky, and I gathered, too, that Jane had not abandoned her role as his commercial representative.

Natalia drew me to one side. 'What will you do with the portraits you have made, the portraits of Baron von Herzog and the others?'

In the days after the dramatic events at the theatre I had set about completing the portfolio that had been our original premise for being there. I held my palms outward, realising as I did so that this was almost the same gesture the

Baron had used moments earlier. 'Perhaps we can present them to the company?'

Natalia gave me a bright smile and I felt as though the two of us had been wafted onto a different plane, away from considerations of mortality and truth, of action and reaction.

'There was one portrait that you promised to make,' she said. She glanced at the Baron and at Jane and then at the other end of the room, where Herr Müller stood near the door, speaking to Mrs Fellini of the acrobatic troupe. 'It is a small thing, Señor Camarón, and yet, for some people, a portrait would be a kind of . . . *affirmation*.'

I had imagined that Natalia was Müller's mistress as well as his protégée. Now I saw that their relationship was based on generosity – hers towards her mentor.

'I will propose a portrait again to Herr Müller,' I said.

Her hand rested affectionately on my wrist.

'When you opened the stage door,' I said, 'you thought we were from Simpson-Burley?'

She removed her hand and her face clouded over.

'It was an odd time to deliver paint,' I said.

She sighed. There was a long moment in which we both stood quite still, watching the people in the room.

'And Barkov knew that we had identified him, when we were with you at the theatre,' I said. Natalia looked at me as though I had snatched away a key. It would have opened a door to infinite possibility, perhaps to happiness. I spoke quickly and earnestly. 'Perhaps there is another way out of the building,' I said.

She nodded, at first almost imperceptibly but then, as if some interior restraint had been broken, more decisively. 'I had imagined my role in this . . . business might be . . .'

'There were enquiries, of course, about everyone,' I said. 'About me too. We are foreigners. We are always the first to be suspected.'

She looked up at me.

'Your associations,' I said. 'In Vienna . . . and further south.'

Again she nodded. 'The Crown Prince wants an army and a navy. Do you imagine this will feed his people?'

I could think of no reply.

'I would have justice,' she said. Then she jerked her head towards the door. 'You are gallant, Señor Camarón, but if they have come for me, then I must go with them.'

'I will speak to Herr Müller,' I said, 'about the portrait.'

Natalia laid her hand on my wrist again, just for a moment, and then she let me go.

Signora Fellini was a large woman, and one of the more remarkable things about the family's performance was her astonishing agility, notwithstanding her size. She was exceptionally friendly too. When I approached Herr Müller and the signora, she beamed, and when I quickly asked Herr Müller if he would sit for a portrait, Signora Fellini put her hands together and said, 'Bravo, Señor Camarón! Un'idea meravigliosa!'

The Fellinis' daughter, Joanna, joined us. Joanna was twenty-one. She had long chestnut hair and deep brown eyes and her face was bronzed and almond-shaped. Joanna was a tremendous beauty. I asked her about how it was to be the rising star in a family troupe and which were her favourite theatres and whether or not she would like to go back to Italy, and so on. It was the polite conversation that is expected at events such as this.

Jane was still speaking to Baron von Herzog. Natalia had joined them, and so had Madame Orlova.

'Do you really think I would be a suitable subject?' Müller asked, returning to the matter of the portrait.

'Of course you would, Herr Müller!' Signora Fellini said, thus saving me from responding, as etiquette demanded, that while there was a natural reluctance on the part of the house manager to push himself into the spotlight, a portrait would do some justice to his indispensable contribution to the arts.

Signor Fellini struck me as being a little more inclined than his wife to confront the hard edges of everyday life. He was not a dour man, but compared to Signora Fellini, he seemed almost professorial.

He drew me aside. 'Juan,' he said, 'I have been very troubled.'

'Oh?'

'You were extremely brave, and of course, your Miss Macgregor was extremely brave.' He looked at me and his eyes crinkled in an expression that suggested the thought had just occurred to him. 'Your children will also be brave.'

For the second time that evening I could not think of a suitable response.

Fellini carried on speaking. 'How was this Captain Barkov able to come so close to the Crown Prince?'

'He was supposed to be *protecting* him,' I said, 'but he allowed himself to be bribed – there were gambling debts. He arranged for the assassin to enter the theatre and to sit in the dress circle next to the Royal Box. If Jane had not locked the door to the Royal Box and shot the assassin *before* he could kill the Prince, Barkov would have entered the box and shot the assassin *after* he had killed the Prince, in this way eliminating his accomplice. That, we surmise, was the plan.'

'And you smelled a rat?'

'There was a photograph,' I said. 'It showed Captain Barkov and the assassin. They were speaking to one another.'

'Ah,' Fellini said, nodding his head.

I did not see that the information I had given him was sufficient to elucidate what had happened, so I added, 'They were standing by the loch near the house—'

'Where Sir Arthur wrote the Buttercup aria?'

'Yes.' I was rather surprised.

'I heard about the photographs the unfortunate doctor from Vienna was taking.'

He thought for a moment and then he added, 'I will tell this to Sir Arthur!'

'You know . . . Sir Arthur Sullivan?'

'Oh,' he said, 'for a very long time, since I was a boy. It was my father, Vicenzo, who proposed to him the idea for the Venetian opera.'

'The Venetian . . .'

'The Gondoliers.'

'Ah.'

'But what of the policeman?' he said, returning suddenly to the events that had brought us all together. 'The one who tried to knock you out?'

'He thought I was a conspirator. He did not know of Barkov's treachery. He thought that by assisting Captain Barkov he was helping to keep the Crown Prince safe.'

Fellini nodded, and then, looking over my shoulder, he said, somewhat ironically, 'Look out.'

'Juan!' Madame Orlova said, advancing across the room. 'You have not yet photographed the Family Fellini. It is something you *must* do.'

'How exciting,' Joanna said.

'You know,' Signor Fellini said, 'I will see Sir Arthur. Do you still have the photographs, from the villa?'

'I'm afraid they've been confiscated, for the enquiry.'

'Well, perhaps we could have our own photographs – the Family Fellini at the house where Buttercup came into being.'

'Inspired!' Madame Orlova said. 'Juan, you must do this.'

'We are leaving the day after tomorrow.' Signor Fellini became suddenly business-like.

'I am sure it could be arranged,' I said.

Madame Orlova took me aside, suddenly solicitous. 'Juan, you are neglecting your fiancée.'

Jane had stepped away. I had not noticed.

Madame Orlova pointed towards the balcony.

Jane was alone at the balustrade, looking out at the trees

that were just beginning to turn. A breeze caused a fine drift of green and gold to flutter across the cobblestones. A cart made its way from Charing Cross; the driver smoked a cigarette and lolled back on his seat as though he were sitting in an armchair.

I leaned against the balustrade and looked at Jane. I could not imagine a beauty more delicate, more alluring. I would have held her in my arms if such a thing had been within the bounds of propriety.

Jane turned and we experienced a moment of stillness. When she spoke, her voice was very gentle. 'Juan,' she said, 'we cannot be married.'

I did not understand the words.

She repeated them. 'We cannot be married.'

I stared.

'We have rushed into things,' she said.

'But . . .' I cast around for a sentence that would convey what was going on inside my head, but what was going on inside my head could not be conveyed in a sentence.

'Juan, we are not the same.'

'But we *are* the same!' I sounded like a schoolboy. I might as well have stamped my foot and started to cry.

Jane's tone became not cold, but firm. 'I have thought about this, Juan, especially these last few days. I have made my decision. For anything in the world, I would not hurt you, and yet I believe we would both be hurt if we proceeded with our plans. I will not marry you, Juan.'

'But—'

At this point Joanna Fellini came out onto the balcony. 'It

is all arranged!' she said in her bright, innocent voice. 'We will come to the villa in the afternoon, after we have finished our practice, about five o'clock. Will this be acceptable, Johnny?'

Joanna had taken to calling me Johnny.

'Yes,' I said. 'This will be acceptable.'

I was by Jane's side as she said goodbye to the members of the company. I walked down to the front of the hotel with her. She looked straight ahead as the cab drew away from the pavement and moved quickly along Sauchiehall Street. A photograph might have shown a phaeton swept up in a carpet of leaves, borne from the viewer as though on the wings of fate.

Back inside, I crossed the lobby to the area on the other side of the reception desk.

Two constables stood in the corner, where a giant aspidistra occupied the space between an armchair and a sofa.

I was greeted by a familiar voice. 'Señor Camarón.'

Captain Smith walked towards me. He was carrying an envelope.

'I have something for you,' he said. 'Or rather, I have something that you may be able to pass along to the appropriate address.'

He held out the envelope, the same envelope I had noticed under the bed when we went to take photographs in Michael Martin's room.

I held it for several seconds as though it might explode.

'It has the details . . . the propellers?'

Smith shook his head and looked at me with something

like his usual disdain. 'Of course not. That would be a scandal for the government.' Then he smiled. The effect of this was not quite a transformation, but it was striking. When he spoke, there was an uncharacteristic and collegial warmth in his intonation. 'This is Mr Martin's report on Prince Leopold's contract,' he said, 'and that will be a scandal for the ship owner.'

I folded the envelope and put it into my pocket. Martin – and Lawrence Stolz, Alexander Napier and Arthur Knox – would make good use of it. Auchinleck was not to be prosecuted as a public trial had been deemed counterproductive. His lucrative dealings with the Kaiser, however, had been brought to an end, and even in his particular business habitat, his association with slavery would destroy his reputation when it was made public. He was in any case already compromised by the confession of one of his employees, a man called William MacLean, whom I had known only in terms of his gorilla-like physical attributes. Taken into custody after being released from the steel trap in the grounds of Auchinleck House, MacLean had confessed to the murder of Smith's associate in Martin's shed, during his abortive attempt to lay hold of the report. He had also confessed to the attempted murder of Martin and myself, in the back court where he had followed me on the night of Breitling's murder.

I walked to the window and looked out at the street, devoid of sunlight now, but bathed in the melancholy gleam of early twilight.

Presently, we heard voices from above. Several people descended the stairs before Natalia and Baron von Herzog. I watched from the window. Natalia was holding on to the Baron's arm and the Baron was smiling. It was not, I thought, one of his ersatz aristocratic smiles, forbearing and indulgent. His face revealed the genuine happiness of a man in love with the woman on his arm.

The reception clerk, as he had been instructed, approached the Baron and pointed to where Captain Smith sat.

The Baron and Natalia came towards us. Natalia looked first at Captain Smith, then at the two constables, before turning to me. I thought I detected a momentary hesitation, but the Baron proceeded calmly to where the captain, who had got to his feet, waited.

'Miss Aleksandrova,' Captain Smith said.

Natalia nodded.

'I think you know why I am here.'

Natalia glanced at me.

'I do,' she said.

'What?' the Baron asked. It was the point, I thought, at which Baron von Herzog might have revealed himself to be a fraud. He might have broken into a Cockney accent.

But he didn't. He remained the Baron, even when Smith recited a series of 'incriminating' biographical details about Miss Aleksandrova – that she had been associated with an anarchist network, first in Sofia and then in Vienna, and while there she had formed a particular alliance with a 'notorious' agitator, now established in Edinburgh at the head of the Land and Labour League. It was through this connection that she had been introduced to Ratković. The charge sheet concluded with specifics including that Natalia had arranged for Ratković to enter the theatre on the night of the attempted assassination. He was admitted by her at the stage door, hence her surprise when she opened the door the first time and found Alan, Jane and myself instead of Ratković, and she escorted him to his seat in the box next to the Royal Box.

The constables advanced. The Baron remonstrated. Captain Smith spoke in a steady voice. Natalia said nothing.

I watched from just a few feet away, yet I might have been on the moon.

I stood by the window after the little party with its police escort had left the hotel. I do not know why I made my rather diffident attempt to warn Natalia. She had played an active role in a plot that, had it succeeded, would have resulted in murder.

She was right to ask, though: how many people would the Crown Prince's warship feed?

Barkov was a traitor, but Natalia was an innocent soul, and a generous one. Or, at least, a woman of principle.

Breitling – who had nothing to do with anything but the art of photography – was right in a way: heaven protect us from men and women of principle.

I was jolted into consciousness by the approach of a familiar figure.

'They would not let me accompany her,' the Baron said.

He spoke almost matter-of-factly. His tone was unchanged when he asked, 'Did you know this would happen?'

It would have been implausible, not to mention cowardly, to deny it.

'Yes,' I said.

He nodded, and then he sat down heavily on one of the armchairs and stared at the coffee table.

We sat for some time in silence after the reception clerk was prevailed upon to bring two whiskies. Then the Baron said, 'It was from a sense of injustice, you know. It was to right a wrong.'

'I know.'

He took a sip of whisky and looked at me with an expression that was quite different from any I had seen before. 'I *didn't* know,' he said.

I wondered what had transpired between the mesmerist and the young scene painter. Was it a connection so true and good that a man who made his living from the gullibility of others had been thoroughly gullible?

Or perhaps they had simply found in each other a refuge from the hard edges of the world.

CHAPTER TWENTY-FIVE

I was still pondering this when I waited the following afternoon for the Fellinis in the garden of Larch View. I had collected the key from Mrs Anderson, who was distraught at the news that Doctor Ratković had turned out to be a villain – a source of considerable surprise and indignation. She was distraught, too, that he had met such a public and violent end – a source of pity and great compassion. 'He was quite a gentleman,' Mrs Anderson concluded, 'but very foreign.' She looked at me benignly as she said this and I gathered that my own foreignness was for the moment overlooked. I promised to return the key first thing in the morning and she urged me to do this, so that she wouldn't get into trouble for lending it to me.

The Fellinis were such a voluble group that I had no doubt I would hear them when they walked up the drive on the other side of the house. The sound of voices would carry through the trees that separated the north gable of the villa from the road. I had noticed this the first time, when Jane and Doctor Breitling and I stood here to arrange the photographs that saved the life of the Crown Prince but cost Breitling his own. I remembered Breitling's very distinctive way of going about his work and how he was so decisive behind the camera. His politics were radical, in the manner of any decent human being who had recorded poverty and deprivation and asked why such things should be tolerated by a civilised society.

I wondered if art had any power at all to deliver justice or even modest change.

When I met Jane for the first time, in the Fletchers' gallery, it was as though some distant note, some ethereal chord, had sounded at the heart of my being. It began a melody that I had never heard but had always known.

Now, looking across the water towards Auchinleck House I felt that a part of me had been torn away.

The loch seemed smaller now. We first saw it on a warm afternoon when the light shimmered across the surface with the bright light serving to obscure the presence of two figures on the other side and then to reveal them, in sharp and incriminating detail.

Ratković had rowed across regularly to take his instructions from Barkov, who was able in this way discreetly to manage the plot against the Crown Prince while remaining at the very heart of the Prince's circle. While Larch View and Auchinleck House were a mile apart if the distance was covered by road, they were next to one another on either side of the little loch. Breitling's photograph would hang the two conspirators if it ever came to light. Barkov had panicked, hence the bungled abduction, bringing Alan and Breitling to Auchinleck House, and then the murder of Breitling. Though he tried to cover his tracks, Barkov was lost the moment Breitling pressed the button above the viewfinder and photographed the view from Sir Arthur's bedroom.

I heard the sound of Italian voices.

The Fellinis really did have a capacity to spread joy. There was something profound about their energy, something elemental in the way this energy seemed always to be moving forward. The capacity of each family member to execute complicated somersaults and overhead leaps changed continuously. Signora Fellini confided in me that as a girl in Sicily, she had leapt from the tower of Queen Isabella's loggia at the Castel Sant'Angelo, to be caught by fourteen men holding a blanket, before jumping from the blanket onto the back of a white horse that rode in front of the royal party. It was quite clear to both of us that forty men could not now have been relied upon to break the fall, and even the stoutest Clydesdale would no longer serve as an adequate landing place for Signora Fellini. She told me too that when Joanna was little, she used to ascend the human pyramid, at the top of which were Signor Fellini's mother and father, then part of the troupe, now deceased, 'and she was like a little ball of satin and sequins rolling upward with no more than a soft summer breeze to carry her.'

It was Joanna who led the Fellinis into the house. Her mother's reference to a soft summer breeze struck me as still very much valid, though she was no longer a little ball of satin and sequins. She moved with prowess, a vision of loveliness.

The Fellinis had brought their costumes – naturally – and they posed in a variety of remarkable configurations, in which at least two members of the family were off the ground, either resting on other family members, or leaning out at quite impossibly dramatic angles from windowsills or, in one case, dangling from a steel bracket high up on the wall, which had been used at one time to hold a heavy curtain frame. To reach the bracket, the family made a human stepladder for the youngest member, seven-year-old Emilia, to ascend. Then they dissolved the stepladder, leaving Emilia, like an angel in her natural habitat, smiling down from the corner beneath the ceiling. She made a face after I had taken the picture and said, 'There are cobwebs here and many creeping things!'

In what had been Sir Arthur's study, the room where he had composed the Buttercup aria while looking out onto the loch, Signor Fellini proposed that we make a formal family portrait. 'I would like to present it,' he said. 'Sir Arthur has been poorly.' He tapped his lower back to indicate the sort of inflammation of the kidney that is apt to result in acute discomfort; he made a grim face and then, as though a happy thought had just occurred to him, 'I think when he sees the room where such a beautiful *motivo* came to him, he will smile!'

After the Fellinis had left, I noticed a piece of ribbon hanging from the bracket where Emilia had performed her aerial acrobatics. I went upstairs, took a chair from the front room and carried it back down. Halfway down I stopped. It is strange to move furniture in an empty house. You feel like a thief. It is strange too to stop on the stairs in a house that you do not own. I glanced back and saw the carpet in the corridor, at eye level now, slightly puckered at the edge but not so much that anyone would trip over it. Where it was puckered, it made a black shadow on the dark wood, otherwise gleaming faintly in the dusk. Below me, the polished beams in the hall spread out towards the front door and the windows on either side. I could see just a crescent of the circular carpet in the hall.

I lifted the chair and continued down. In the corner of the room I climbed onto the chair. I was just able to touch the tip of the ribbon. From here, the parquet looked like a giant jigsaw. The room seemed bare and bleak, especially as the noise and happiness with which the Fellinis had briefly filled it were now gone.

I flicked the ribbon several times and could not at first cause it to move upward and over the little ridge that had attached it to the bracket.

But after a dozen attempts. I was successful.

I put the ribbon in my pocket and stepped down. The room righted itself; the parquet looked like parquet again and not like a giant jigsaw. I carried the chair upstairs and put it back in the room, in the corner by the window, where I had found it.

Placing the chair on the parquet, I heard a sound at the front door.

Perhaps walking up and down the stairs had changed my perspective; perhaps my thoughts had been prised open, allowing new and brighter possibilities to enter. I heard the sound of the front door opening and I ran out of the room and down the stairs.

I believed that Jane had come back to me.

But there was no one in the hall. I opened the door and looked out. No one. I thought I heard a noise at the other end of the ground floor. I walked along the corridor. This part of the house was already in that phase of twilight where the world outside is blue but the interior has descended into grey. I looked inside the room. Empty.

Then I heard, clearly and without any possibility of misinterpretation, a door being opened and closed on the floor above.

I hurried back along the corridor to the hall. The front door was slightly ajar, though I had certainly closed it after I looked out. I had already packed the Eclipse in its case. It stood next to the tripod in a corner of what had been Sir Arthur's bedroom. I reached down and, trying not to make a sound, unclipped the top of the case and carefully extracted the elevation rod that held up the magnesium ribbon for the flash. It was a tin pole that collapsed into three equal lengths fastened together with a leather strap and buckle. It made a serviceable cosh.

Clutching my makeshift weapon, I began to climb the stairs.

I felt as though the phantom that had haunted me since I first heard Señora LaGuardia's name had at last assumed a physical presence. It was a spectre that had followed me all the way from that burning building in Santiago. I *wanted* to confront it.

I reached the top of the stairs. The door to the room in front of me was open, as I had left it. I could see the chair sitting in the corner next to the window. I turned and faced the corridor. There was a doorway halfway along, to the right, and a doorway a little further on, to the left. I began to move forward, stepping slowly and silently.

There is a point when a frightened person will begin to compound his own fear. I had reached this point. By stepping slowly and silently I fostered a sense of terror that was forming, like a pool of blood from a mutilated corpse, beneath my thoughts.

But in addition to fear there was anger.

The door on my right was open. I looked into the room: nothing. The door on my left was open. I looked in: gathering darkness, a bed and a wardrobe and a dresser, but there was no one there.

The door at the end of the corridor, the door to what had been Ratković's study, was closed.

I reached down, turned the handle and swung the door open.

A figure sat behind the desk.

'Juan,' he said.

I recognised the speaker, yet his presence in this room was

a subject of absolute bafflement to me.

I walked towards him. Everything changed when he addressed me. His was a voice I had once thought rather mild, almost gentle. It was the voice of a man accustomed to soothing the temper of his malicious wife.

In front of me was the concierge from the Marchmont boarding house in Leith. I had seen him there but I had not understood. The mind plays tricks. The lamp in the cubicle spread only a dim light. It wasn't because of the semi-darkness that I had not recognised him, though. It was because I was not looking for him. I thought he was dead.

Now, he removed the glasses, and the beret too. His right eye was nearly closed, the socket severely disfigured where a piece of artillery shrapnel had pierced the skull. I saw, as I had not seen in the dim light of the porter's cubicle, that on the edge of his beard there were scars that ran beneath the hair to the bottom of his chin.

'Paco,' I said. I may not have enunciated the name properly. I may have opened my mouth and made the shape required to speak these two syllables, but I cannot be certain that any sound came out.

He told me to sit down.

To my own astonishment, I did as I was told. This sealed the nature of what followed. Having caused me to sit in a room where he had no right to be, Paco conducted the interview on his own terms.

'You are surprised?'

I was more than surprised.

'Señora LaGuardia . . .' I began.

He shook his head. 'There is a Señora LaGuardia. She has stayed for some time at the place you visited in Leith, but she has gone now. She and her son, whom she visited often in Le Havre, have completed their affairs in Scotland and France. They are travelling to Madrid, where, I believe Señora LaGuardia has a brother.'

'Her husband . . .'

'Her husband was killed at San Juan Heights.'

'With the rebels?'

'With the Spanish army, a major.'

'I thought . . .'

'Things are so often not what they seem, Juan. They are twisted in the telling.'

'Señora LaGuardia . . .'

'Knows nothing of you. Your business is with me.'

'But you lay on the floor. You were . . .' I was speaking to a corpse.

'Eleanora died, Juan.'

I shook my head. 'I tried to help her.'

'You left us both for dead.'

'The house was burning.'

'I was alive.'

'I saw a woman, in the station when I came back from Edinburgh . . .'

I was simply casting through my own confusion, yet this had a useful result – because Paco now looked confused.

'. . . there was a woman who looked a little like Eleanora . . .' I said.

'Why would Eleanora come and look for you?'

'I did nothing! It was you! It was you who killed my father!' I stood up.

Paco looked at me very calmly.

'Sit, Juan,' he said. 'Your father was killed in the square in front of the cathedral where he stood alone in the open. He invited his own death. He walked in front of the cathedral as certainly as he would have walked in front of a firing squad. I do not know why he acted that way. I did not understand your father, but I didn't kill him.'

I collapsed onto the seat.

'Why did you deceive me? Why did you lie to me? Why did you lie to William Collins? They have stopped the publication of my father's work, his life's work!'

'And *my* life's work, Juan? What did you think about that? What did you think about *my* father's life's work? *My* father gave his life to the plantation you inherited. It was nothing when he took it on and he made it prosper. *Your* father couldn't make even his own business prosper so why should he have benefitted from his brother's effort? Why should *you* benefit?'

'It was his by law,' I said. 'My father *owned* that plantation.'

'And you sold it, after you thought that I was dead.'

'Paco, I am glad you are alive. But you did not inherit the plantation. My father inherited it and when he died, when he was murdered, it came to me.'

'You invoke the law when it suits you.'

'Paco, why are you here? You cannot think that I will give you what is rightfully mine.'

'I do not think that you will give me anything, Juan. I know the lie of your heart.'

'You know nothing about me.'

'But because you will not give does not mean that I cannot take.'

'What in heaven's name . . . ?'

Paco laid a document on the table in front of him. It consisted of two pieces of paper joined together in one corner by a ribbon. He pushed this across the otherwise empty desk.

'Read it.'

I read.

'The proceeds from the sale of the plantation.' I looked up from the document. 'I'm not sure I even have that money. I have had expenses since leaving Cuba.'

'You are going to receive the remainder of the money promised to your father by William Collins, Sons & Co.'

'You have prevented that from happening.'

'I will remove my objection.'

I had been drawn into a negotiation – not about money but about love and hate, life and death.

'It can be done easily,' he said. 'I have the plates. They will be returned to you. Señora LaGuardia will withdraw her objection.' He removed a piece of notepaper from the inside pocket of his jacket and passed it across to me. It was a letter from Henry Farquhar to William Collins stating the very terms that Paco had just described. 'That is a copy,' he said.

'A formal communication, duly signed will be sent tomorrow morning, but first you must sign the paper that is in front of you.' He pushed a pen across the table and a small travelling ink pot with the brass top opened so that all I had to do was pick up the pen, dip it in the ink and make my mark.

'But it states here that the value of *two* properties have to pass to you,' I said.

He nodded.

'You have no claim on my Scottish property.'

'What claim do I have to anything that belongs to you?' Paco said. 'If I have no claim, then I have no claim. If I have any claim then I have every claim.'

I sat back. 'I won't do this.'

'Juan,' Paco said, 'when you came to stay with us in Santiago you struck me as a self-absorbed young man. You see the world as it relates to you but not as it relates to others. I am your father's cousin; one could say that you and I know each other pretty well, we have shared the same dangers together; we have cowered fearfully beneath the same furniture seeking shelter from the same shells. Yet when you came to Leith and we spoke, you didn't recognise me. You didn't *see* me. You saw only your own interest. But you are not alone in the world, Juan. You depend on others and others depend on you, and now you must consider carefully how you will proceed because the interests of someone I assume is dear to you will be affected by what you decide.'

'What the devil—?'

I stood up and glared at Paco. Still, he was calm. The

serenity on his face may have been amplified by the gathering dark, which softened and distorted everything. We would have to finish quickly or we would be in the absurd position of sitting on either side of the table in a strange house after night had properly fallen.

'Sit, down, Juan. I am here to offer you a fresh beginning. It won't simply be for you, it will be for the woman you propose to marry and for her family too.'

'I will—'

He raised a hand and said quickly, 'Before you threaten to murder me with your bare hands – and I am alive despite whatever you may have imagined you were able to do to me in Santiago—'

'I did not—'

'—let me finish! Alan Fletcher has a child, a daughter, by the French girl who was sent to stay in the care of Fletcher and his family. Of course, the girl has been paid off and her family in France are not the sort of people who would know how to obtain justice. Fletcher has committed a great crime. I am well acquainted with the details of this and other things that he has done – and this is a man who pretends to be an apostle of progress, an artist who has shown society a picture of itself with all its injustices. He has photographed the injuries that the rich do to the poor, and yet he has inflicted an injury as ancient and unanswerable as man himself. I will destroy him, Juan. I will destroy him . . . unless you sign that document.'

I had sat down while he spoke, because I felt foolish standing, and because this and everything that had happened had produced in me a kind of physical and mental exhaustion. In the deepening dark I simply wanted to be rid of this man.

'I cannot trust you,' I said.

'You can trust your own interest. If you do this, I will withdraw the obstacle to the publication of *The Architecture of Cuba*' – for some entirely unfathomable reason I was profoundly affected by the fact that he used the proper title of my father's book – 'and I will transfer to you the documents I have that show that Alan Fletcher is the father of Agnès Chennier's daughter.' He leaned across the table. 'You will be rid of me, Juan. This will be the new beginning that was withheld from you when you came to Cuba . . . and withheld again when you left. Sign this document and be free.'

I saw two people in my mind's eye. I saw my father gazing up at a building, absorbing shapes and textures to be celebrated in a photograph, a thing of beauty. And I saw Jane, even as we parted, my fleeting vision of what life and love can be, the woman who had touched me and changed me. I believed that with a handful of letters on a page I could banish the long shadow of failure and unhappiness.

I dipped the pen into the inkpot and formed the letters of my name.

Paco drew the document across the table. I do not know how long he waited for the ink to dry. I didn't see him fold the paper and put it in his pocket. I do not believe I can say for certain when he stood up or if he bade me goodnight or goodbye as he left the room.

I sat in a dream, a waking dream, so that at one point I was conscious of the fact that the room was perfectly dark though there was a glimmer of light still in the garden. I got up and walked along the corridor. Faint sunlight still drifted through the window overlooking the stairs and when I went into the room that had once been Sir Arthur's bedroom I was able to see clearly enough to pull the wooden bulb that released the lock on the French windows. I stepped out onto the veranda and walked across the lawn to the water's edge.

The sky had become a particular shade of blue that reflected on the water, creating a twilight of luminescent delicacy. I watched ripples play across the surface of the loch and felt a cool breeze begin to envelop me as in a welcoming embrace, and for the first time in a very long time I felt completely free.

AUTHOR'S NOTE

Sir Arthur Sullivan conducted concert seasons with the Glasgow Choral Union in 1875 and 1876. These were hugely successful, and the musicians that Sullivan brought together formed the core of what later became the Royal Scottish National Orchestra. Sullivan's first night in the city, on 21st July 1875, was so uncomfortable that he left the apartment he had rented and moved to a hotel. The villa described in the novel is fictional but reflects the sort of accommodation a visiting conductor of the period might have expected to occupy.

Frédéric Chopin spent several weeks in Scotland in the Autumn of 1848, giving a recital at the Merchants' Hall in

Glasgow on 27th September. A concert in Edinburgh on 4th October was, effectively, Chopin's final public performance before his death in Paris the following year.

The Scottish Land and Labour League was co-founded in the mid 1880s by the Austrian socialist Andreas Scheu. It was one of several organisations that eventually coalesced around the Independent Labour Party, though splinter groups remained active outside the ILP.

In the novel, Madame Orlova remembers singing as a child in the Marijnsky rooms of the Winter Palace in St Petersburg. However, the diva's recollection may have been flawed as there is no reference to Imperial apartments with this title in the second half of the nineteenth century.